CAPTAIN PICARD WAS SITTING IN THE ALIEN COUNCIL CHAMBER . . .

. . . when Commander Riker's urgent call came in.

"Captain!" Riker said. "We're tracking two large unmanned chemically powered craft heading right for your location!"

"It's the Krann!" Kerajem, head of the council, said sadly. "They mean to kill us all."

"Not if I can stop them," Picard replied grimly.

"Captain," Riker reported, "the hostiles' present distance from you is 49.3 kilometers. Estimated time of impact at your location: two minutes, fifty seconds. . . ."

Look for STAR TREK Fiction from Pocket Books

Star Trek: The Original Series

Star Trek: The Next Generation

Star Trek: Deep Space Nine

Star Trek: Voyager

STAR TREK
THE NEXT GENERATION®

THE LAST STAND

BRAD FERGUSON

POCKET BOOKS
New York   London   Toronto   Sydney   Tokyo   Singapore

An *Original* Publication of POCKET BOOKS

POCKET BOOKS, a division of Simon & Schuster Inc.
1230 Avenue of the Americas, New York, NY 10020

Copyright © 1995 by Paramount Pictures. All Rights Reserved.

A VIACOM COMPANY

STAR TREK is a Registered Trademark of
Paramount Pictures.

This book is published by Pocket Books, a division of
Simon & Schuster Inc., under exclusive license from
Paramount Pictures.

ISBN: 0-671-50105-4

First Pocket Books printing October 1995

10 9 8 7 6 5 4 3 2 1

POCKET and colophon are registered trademarks of
Simon & Schuster Inc.

Printed in the U.S.A.

For Sammie,
most faithful and furry
of collaborators

THE LAST STAND

Prologue

IT WAS A BRIGHT, BEAUTIFUL MORNING, the sun blazing hot and white in a cloudless green sky. His hands clasped behind him, Kerajem zan Trikotta stood at the east window of his elaborately appointed office atop Government Tower. The seven members of the Council of Ministers sat silently in comfortable chairs around the room, each alone with his thoughts.

The ministers had been there all the previous day and through the night. They had talked endlessly of peace and war, of good and evil, of life and death. They had argued with each other until their voices had gone, along with their patience. The room air was stale with the sweat of their effort.

Now it was midmorning of the next day, and time was nearly up. The First Among Equals had a decision to make, and so Kerajem was being left to himself for the few moments left.

Kerajem looked down forty-one flights to the busy streets below. It seemed that everyone in the world must be outdoors today, enjoying the suddenly fine weather. Kerajem knew that most of the people down there were government bureaucrats who should have been at their desks on this workday. He smiled slightly. If the smaller wheels who drove the massive machinery of government wanted to take an hour or so off to enjoy the sunshine, then why not? It had been a long, hard winter, and this was the first truly pleasant day the capital had seen in months.

The facts were what they were, and they would not change. That had not stopped several of the ministers from arguing, bargaining for time, hoping against hope that things would work out nevertheless, and that a way out of the crisis would be found.

Kerajem looked up toward the eastern horizon. It was so clear today that he could see all the way to the mountains, which were still white with snow and ice. The mountains were the foothills of the great Kajja Kojja, the range that divided the eastern coast of this continent from the interior plains.

Kerajem knew those mountains well. He had been born among them, in one of the old mining towns. It had been a hard life back then. Kerajem had been drafted to work in the mines at the age of six, as the laws had then required. Children of both sexes were sent into the mines because, being small, they could scramble and wiggle and force themselves into dark, narrow places where grown men could not go. It had been highly dangerous work that provided only the most meager reward to the children's families.

"You came from there, too, Rikkadar," Kerajem said over his shoulder. "The mountains. You remember how it was."

"Yes, First," the finance minister replied from his chair. He was the only other man in the room above the age of sixty, and he was the only one there who Kerajem thought of as a friend. "That was a long time ago."

"Not very. A mere matter of decades." Still facing the mountains, Kerajem looked at his hands. He could not remember a time when he had possessed all ten of his fingers. He might be who he was now, but the mines always found him again whenever he tried to hold a cup or sign his name.

It had been Kerajem's generation which, when it had come to maturity and power, had at last eased the relentless preparations for war instituted and maintained for millennia by their forefathers. Kerajem himself had helped to form the more liberal policies of modern times when he was younger. There had been great opposition, mostly by the old, the self-interested, and the superstitious, but reform had finally come. As a result, living conditions for the people were generally much better than they had been when Kerajem was a boy.

Social reform had finally come in the conviction that the old stories of doom and destruction had been merely the exaggerated stuff of hoary legend, tales of horror believed only by the stupid, the gullible, and the obsessed. However, the world had discovered the terrible truth just thirty-three years before, when the first signals from space had been detected and the first probes intercepted. Those who would destroy the world were real, and they were coming. Now they were almost here, and they promised that everything Kerajem knew and loved would soon end in fire and blood and death.

That promise did not leave the First Among Equals much choice.

There was a transmitter on Kerajem's desk, a direct line to the War Room. It suddenly beeped politely for his attention. Kerajem crossed the room and, thumbing a button on the side of the unit, spoke into the pickup. The eyes of everyone were on him.

"General, this is the First," Kerajem said, seating

himself at the desk, impossibly trying to make himself comfortable. "You are speaking to the entire Cabinet."

"Yes, sir. I have a report."

"Go ahead."

"The test schedule has been completed. Results are nominal."

"Very well," Kerajem said quietly. "Please stand by."

The First took a last moment for himself and then made his decision. Rikkadar saw the promise of doom in his friend's haunted eyes. "Plan Blue doesn't even represent a real defense," the finance minister said, his voice cracking. "Bring them back, Kerajem. Recall them before it's too late."

"Blue sets a high price for our demise," said Hattajek, the minister for defense. He rubbed his eyes wearily. "We've been all over this, First."

"Indeed we have, Hatta," Kerajem said gently, "but I would be disappointed if this order were to be given without objection."

There were several small, neatly framed photographs set in a group near a far corner of Kerajem's cluttered desktop. The foremost photo was a nice portrait of Kerajem's only granddaughter—raven-haired, freckled, unscarred by life and fate. Little Kara and her contemporaries had never known the inside of the mines and the factories. Kerajem and his fellow reformers had at least accomplished that much.

Of course, it was not nearly enough.

The First gazed at Kara's picture for another moment and then he gave the order. "General, execute Plan Blue Ultimate according to schedule."

"Yes, sir."

"I'll be there shortly with Minister Hattajek." Kerajem broke the connection. "Thank you all," he

4

said to the ministers, dismissing them. "Hatta, you go on ahead. I'll be along presently."

"Yes, First." Hattajek left and, one by one, the others began to drift out of the room after him.

Rikkadar was the last to leave. "Are you sure about this, Kerajem?" he asked softly, when they were alone. "Are you really sure?"

"Of course not, Rikky," the First answered kindly, "but it's all we've got."

Rikkadar sighed. "I suppose so. I wish it were otherwise."

"So do I. Go home. Get some sleep."

"So should you, Kerajem."

The First Among Equals shook his head. "I have to go to the War Room now," he said quietly. "We're at Blue Ultimate. I . . . won't be home again for a while."

"All right," Rikkadar said, "but I'll be back here later today. Sooner if you need me, of course."

"Of course."

"Be well, my friend." Rikkadar closed the door gently behind him.

Kerajem was alone now. Closing his eyes, he reached far back into his childhood and muttered what little he remembered of the prayer his mother had taught him to keep him safe in the mines. Only a miracle could save the world. Though he did not believe, Kerajem bowed his head and prayed to his mother's god for a miracle.

Chapter One

Captain's log, stardate 45523.6. Our survey of this previously unexplored sector is now well into its second week. We have departed the star system we have temporarily designated 30452 Federation Astrophysical Survey and are on course for the next system on our list.

I am about to begin going over the various summaries of preliminary findings that have been filed by our department heads concerning 30452 FAS. Given the results of this survey so far, we are certain to make a rather hefty deposit in the bank of cosmological knowledge.

The work of our Science Division people is providing not only revelation, but respite. Many of those aboard who are not directly involved in survey work are taking advantage of this admittedly welcome lull in our usually hectic routine to relax a bit—oh.

THE DOOR SIGNAL *SQUEEPLED*, and Jean-Luc Picard put his log entry on hold. "Come," he called, and the door to the ready room slid aside. "Ah, Number One.

What brings you here?" Picard greeted him. "Isn't this your off time?"

"I've been keeping busy, Captain," Will Riker said, handing Picard a padd. "Here's the correlated environmental data on the third and fourth planets of '452. Thought you might want to see this sooner rather than later."

Picard smiled, took the padd, and leaned back in his chair. "Thank you, Will," the captain said as he began to scan the display. "With the ton of work we've yet to get through, I didn't feel right in making this a priority item. It was thoughtful of you to run this on your own." He tapped the padd with a finger. "Ah, *here's* what I was hoping to see."

"Let me guess. The ambient radiation spike on Planet Three?"

Picard nodded slowly. "Precisely. As we thought, it's coincident with the date of the formation of the ruins, within the margin of error—that is, the spike agrees closely with the date we've established through other evidence. Whoever wiped out this civilization came quickly, struck hard, and didn't leave much behind."

"Everything suggests that Planet Three suffered a massive thermonuclear bombardment from space," Riker agreed. "Whoever it was used weapons designed to scatter as much killing radiation as possible. Everything on Planet Three was intended to die, and the planet *is* dead for all practical purposes. All that's left are bacteria and insects, a few hardy plants, and not much else."

Picard read further. "We estimate that it has been six thousand years since the bombardment," he said, "yet the planet is still badly contaminated. What remains of the ecosphere is extremely fragile." The captain picked up one of the padds on his desk and

handed it to Riker. "The geological survey has identified several areas that could have been the sites of
ground-based launching facilities on Planet Three,"
the captain told him. "Spaceports, more or less. Large
ones."

Riker read the display. "I agree," he said. "They
had to have been launching facilities, given their size
and proximity to the sites we've established for Planet
Three's major cities. Think the natives could have
escaped?"

Picard shook his head. "The ruins suggest a native
population of more than two billion humanoids at the
time of the bombardment. The launching facilities—
if that's what they are—would be inadequate to
handle that number in anything like a reasonable
time, and I doubt the natives had time. What do we
have on Planet Four, Will?"

"Our analysis of the ruins there confirms that
Planet Four was not as technically advanced as Planet
Three," Riker said. "However, the natives of Planet
Four seem to have had space travel of some sort. As
for the plague virus we found during our orbital
bioscans, Dr. Crusher's still working up the schemat-
ics," Riker replied. "To quote the doctor, 'I'll have it
soon. It's complicated. Please go away.'" He grinned
and then grew serious. "Beverly's theory is that the
virus might have been tailored to kill off all higher
animal forms on Planet Four."

"Tailored, you say? It was purposefully designed?"

"She says it might have been, sir," the first officer
said. "The virus is still present in Planet Four's
ecosystem, and its effects remain potentially devastating. Beverly says, from what she's already seen, that
the odds against a virus like this one evolving naturally and then remaining relatively stable for six
millennia are prohibitively high. Viri just don't work
like that."

"But Planet Four is ecologically stable at present," Picard pointed out. "It actually seemed quite lovely."

"Yes, sir. Higher forms of animal life are not present on land, but lower forms are prospering, and plant and marine life seem to have been completely unaffected."

Picard read quickly through the report from the exobiology section. "What about that life-form Bergeron located just before we left?" the captain asked. "That brightly colored slithering thing that looked a bit like a Centaurian *bhobb?* It seemed to be the most highly evolved land-based life-form left on the planet. Any worthwhile findings?"

"Nothing much, Captain," Riker replied. "Hibberd replicated the thing before we left, returned the original to its habitat, and dissected the duplicate. There was some initial hope that the creature might be sentient, but Bergeron says, quote, 'If you give it ten million years, it might amount to something, emphasis on *might.'* Unquote."

Picard nodded. "I see. Too bad."

Riker continued. "All in all, Planet Four seems the next best thing to a paradise, in some ways—except, of course, that the natives are all gone, their cities and other artifacts have been crumbling into dust for six millennia, and we would die within fifteen minutes if we beamed down to the surface unprotected."

Picard shook his head. "I wonder who came through here and did all this, Will. Two planets devastated, one apparently irredeemably. It seems incredible—"

"Worf to Captain," came a distinctively deep voice.

"What is it, Lieutenant?"

"Sir, sensors have detected a warp-field generation pulse, eighty-seven point three light-years off, bearing

four hundred ninety-five mark twenty-three. Duration was zero point one seven seconds."

"Any sign of a ship in that area?"

"No, sir. Wait—there it is again. Same range and bearing. The duration was zero point five eight seconds."

"Commander Riker and I will be right there," the captain said. "Picard out."

"Now *that's* odd," Riker said, climbing out of his chair.

"Indeed." The captain rose and, adjusting his jacket for the umpteenth time that day, glanced at the survey summaries that still lay, unread, on his desk. *They say there is no such thing as a useless fact,* Picard thought, *but sometimes I wonder.*

The captain and first officer left the ready room and stepped directly onto the bridge. Ensign Ro Laren was in the captain's chair. "Captain, Commander," she greeted them as she rose. Her tone was as formal and correct as ever. Without another word, Ro moved away from the conn and relieved her replacement at the flight control console.

"Any indication of warp-field strength, Mr. Worf?" Picard asked as he took his seat. Riker plopped down to his right.

Worf shook his head and frowned at his Tactical panel. "Neither pulse lasted long enough to be able to tell, Captain."

Riker spoke up. "A bit over eighty-seven light-years from here at that bearing—isn't there a system near those coordinates, Mr. Data?"

"Yes, Commander," Data replied, nodding. "There is a system with a G_0-type star at that location." The android paused for a moment, awaiting the results of a long-range sensor scan. "Sensor readings coming in now. The system in question has eleven planets. The third and fourth may be class-M. The system lies well off our course through this sector, and so it was not included on our survey list."

"That may change," Picard said dryly. "Anything else, Mr. Data?"

"I am not sure, sir. The star seems to be generating more interference in midrange space-normal EM frequencies than might be expected."

"Oh?" Picard thought about that for a moment. "Is there anything about the nature of the interference that might be considered unusual?"

"No, sir," replied Data, shaking his head. "There is simply more of it than I would expect to see from this type of star."

"Captain," Worf called. "There has been a third pulse. Same bearing, same range, duration zero point eight three seconds. This pulse lasted long enough for us to derive a reading of field strength, sir. It was sufficient for warp factor one."

That was more than enough for Picard. "Ensign, set course for that system, warp factor three."

"Laid in, sir."

"Engage."

Chapter Two

Captain's log, supplemental. The Enterprise has just crossed the orbit of the outermost planet of the star system we have designated as 30453 FAS. As we have drawn closer, we have determined that the extra electromagnetic interference that we thought was somehow being emitted naturally by the star is actually coming from the third planet of that system. Therefore, the interference cannot be natural. Someone must be transmitting it on purpose, but who—and to what end? And who is responsible for generating the warp-field pulses we detected?

I intend to find out before we leave here.

We will drop out of warp just inside the orbit of Planet Five, a Jupiter-class gas giant that is very nearly in opposition to Planet Three at this time. This will place us some six hundred fifty million kilometers from Planet Three. We'll then head in for a look about. I do not intend to attempt contact with the natives of Planet Three—if any—at this time.

THE *ENTERPRISE* DROPPED OUT OF WARP precisely on schedule, and Data studied the readouts on his Ops panel. "Captain," he reported, "short-range sensors have detected meta-cetacean life-forms inhabiting the upper atmosphere of Planet Five, as is typical for gas giants of this class. The planet possesses fifteen major natural satellites and a class-two ring system. Diameter is approximately one hundred forty-five thousand kilometers. Typical, sir."

"Any signs of habitation on the satellites?" Picard asked. "Colonies or mining operations, perhaps?"

"No, sir. However—"

"Yes?"

"I am reading an object at three hundred forty-four mark twenty-three, range eighteen thousand seven hundred kilometers."

"Mr. Worf?" Riker called.

"It is an artificial construct of unknown configuration in orbit around the local star," Worf said. "It is not under power, but I am getting low-level internal power readings. There appear to be no life-forms aboard."

Picard glanced at Troi, who nodded.

"Let's take a look at it, Mr. Worf," the captain ordered. "On screen."

The majestic image of Planet Five on the main viewscreen swam for a moment and was then replaced by an unremarkable starfield. In the center of the screen there was a very small something.

"Increase magnification," Riker directed, and the object grew.

"Not a ship, I think," Picard said softly.

"It looks like it might be a surveillance satellite," Riker said. "I think I see what might be sensor arrays—many of them."

Picard nodded. "If that is indeed what they are, Number One, then this is a surveillance probe of almost monstrous complexity. Those arrays appear formidable. Are there weapons aboard it, Mr. Worf?"

"None, sir. It is harmless."

Picard nodded. "Mr. Data, are there any other objects out there like this one?"

The android briefly consulted his readouts and nodded. "Sir, I am reading a second object of similar size and configuration at one hundred ninety-eight mark forty, range eighty-three thousand six hundred kilometers. There is a third, bearing oh twenty-three mark twelve, range three hundred fifty-three thousand one hundred kilometers. A fourth——"

"Never mind, Mr. Data," Picard interrupted. "Thank you."

"Whatever these things are, they appear to be pretty closely set," Riker observed.

"Indeed they do, Number One," Picard agreed. "Someone has gone to a great deal of trouble to post a line of sentries. Clearly, those probes are on the lookout for someone, and I very much doubt that we are it. Mr. Worf, long-range sensors ahead. I want to know everything there is to know about Planet Three before we get there. Ensign, lay in a direct course for Planet Three, one-quarter impulse."

"One-quarter impulse," Ro repeated. "Aye, sir."

"Engage. Arrival time at Planet Three, Mr. Data?"

"Standard orbit in two hours, twenty-one minutes, thirty-five seconds, sir."

"Captain," Worf reported, "we are being scanned. There is a radar signal coming from the probe."

Picard blinked. "Radar?"

"Radar, sir," Data said, nodding. "It is an acronym that stands for 'radio detecting and ranging'——"

"Not now, Mr. Data," Riker cautioned.

"That can't be possible," Picard continued, puzzled. "Radar is much too primitive to see us. They couldn't bounce a radio wave off us, not with our shields up."

Riker frowned. "Perhaps they're using radar as a carrier wave for something we can't detect. We may have been spotted, Captain."

"Sir," Worf suddenly said. "The object has just transmitted a tightly beamed signal on space-normal radio wavelengths. It appears to be a coded burst transmission."

Picard sighed. "To whom?"

"The transmission was beamed in the direction of the third planet, sir."

"Of course. Can you decipher it?"

Worf looked at his console. "Doubtful, sir. The transmission appears to have been enciphered and compressed using several random number sequences. It could take us years to decompress and decipher the message."

"The signal must have been about us," Riker said. "The burst occurred just after we dropped into normal space near the probe."

"Perhaps it was only a coincidence," Troi said. "The probe may issue regular status reports on a set schedule, and we just happened to be there for its latest. After all, we're shielded. We should be undetectable."

Riker shook his head. "I'm afraid I don't believe in coincidences. Whoever put that probe here knows we've arrived—or they will, once they receive that signal. Captain, may I suggest yellow alert?"

Picard thought about it for half a second, and then nodded firmly. "Make it so."

The heavy, bombproof doors of a shaftcar rolled open slowly, and Kerajem and several of his assistants stepped onto a narrow gangway that lay far below the surface of the capital city. They walked down the passage a few meters to the VIP entry gate of the Shrine, their footsteps echoing oddly off the polished metal walls. The soldiers on guard duty at the gate came to attention and saluted as the First and his party passed through. Kerajem's assistants followed the leader through the gate one by one, like ducklings following their mother.

They all headed quickly to the War Room, which was located at the center of the Shrine. The Planetary Defense Complex, as it was more formally known, was located in a series of caverns three hundred meters below a nondescript building located across the city from Government House.

This was the second Shrine. The original had been built on the same spot more than a millennium before, shortly after the caverns had been discovered by explorers. There had been an actual shrine here then. The Shrine had served as the Holy See of a totalitarian theocracy that controlled the planet at that time and for centuries thereafter. The many generations of monks who had lived, worked, and died at the first Shrine had spent their entire lives praying to ward off the day when the enemy might find their world and destroy it.

When the revolution came, the Shrine had been abandoned in the belief that it was no longer needed and never had been, that the threat it was designed to counter had never been more than the fever dreams of deranged prophets. The monks who had lived and worked here had been secularized and sent away, never to return.

Not quite a generation ago, when the world had discovered the terrible truth about its impending doom, there was suddenly a need for a planetary defense headquarters immune to any imaginable form of attack. Strategy had demanded an invulnerable location, and tradition and convenience had suggested the Shrine.

The facility no longer looked anything like a monastery. All traces of that sort of thing were gone. Years of effort and billions of work units had been expended to build a fully modern facility. The new Shrine was staffed not by monks but by military personnel, skilled civilian technicians, and a gaggle of bureaucrats.

The Shrine was now a fit fighting machine. It would do the job, if anything could.

Kerajem's people would not run.

Not this time, and never again.

Defense Minister Hattajek was standing in the command well, talking quietly with several top officers. All of them straightened a bit as Kerajem approached. The First nodded to them in greeting. "Status report?"

The chief of staff, General Blakendet, stepped forward. "Sir, Blue Ultimate is in force. Force Red continues to decelerate, course unchanged." He gestured at the wide display screen at the front of the War Room. "As you can see, sir, there they are."

"Well done, General," Kerajem said quietly. "All we can do now, I suppose, is wait—"

Suddenly there was the low, insistent sound of an intrusion alarm. Heads turned to study the main screen.

There was a glowing red disk there that had not been visible a moment before.

"Now what in the name of darkness is that?" Kerajem wondered. "Malfunction, General?"

Blakendet shot a look across the room to his watch officer, who shook his head vigorously: *No.* His face told the rest of the story.

Blakendet turned to address Kerajem. "Sir, we have a confirmed intruder just inside the orbit of Ma'ak Unselbe." He read the displays before him. "Speed—dear gods! Excuse me, sir. Speed of the unknown is one quarter that of light. The unknown is on a direct course for us. We have a visual from the probe now, sir."

"Let's see it."

Part of the War Room tactical display was replaced by a blurred photograph of—something. "It looks like a flying dustpan," Kerajem said. "I don't recognize it. What *is* that thing, General?"

"It appears as if Force Red might have come up with something new, First—something we didn't expect," the general replied. "Traffic, try to raise the unknown. See if it answers." The old soldier paused as he studied the most recent data from the early-warning probe. "Sir," he told the First after a moment, "energy readings from the unknown are off the scale. Given the situation, we must assume hostile intent. I recommend we go to alert condition one."

Kerajem felt all hope die within him as he gave the necessary orders.

"Captain," came Worf's strong voice. "I am showing indications of military movements on Planet Three. There have been a large number of aircraft and ground-to-space rocket launches in the past minute. The pseudostellar interference we have been reading has also increased greatly." He paused. "It appears that the interference is being generated on purpose in order to mask communications traffic."

"They don't appreciate eavesdroppers," Riker said.

"Apparently not," Picard said. "Can you penetrate the interference, Mr. Worf? If Planet Three is making offensive moves against us, I'd like to know what's going on down there."

"Aye, sir."

"Should we hail them, Captain?" Riker asked.

"I wish I could, Number One, but I won't until I am

certain they know we are here. The Prime Directive is still in force. They could be in a panic for some other reason, although I admit that seems unlikely to me."

"Captain," Data said, "if I might—"

"Yes?"

"The military moves on Planet Three detected by Lieutenant Worf began within one minute of the time the light-speed radio signal would have reached the planet from the probe we encountered near Planet Five."

Riker looked at Picard. "Data's right, sir. The timing fits. It's a clear indication that they're reacting to our presence."

"I see," Picard said. "Any success, Mr. Worf?"

"Some, Captain. As we draw closer to Planet Three, it is becoming easier to detect the coherent broadcast signals behind the interference."

Picard nodded. "Very well. Number One, I want those broadcast signals thoroughly analyzed. If those people are talking to each other, I want to know what they're talking about." He looked at the main screen.

They continued to rush sunward, leaning into the dark and listening carefully.

Chapter Three

WORF SPOKE UP. "Captain, we are being scanned again."

"Damn," Picard breathed. "From where?"

"Several points on the surface of Planet Three, as well as from a number of probes in high orbit around that planet."

"Well," Riker said, "that answers *that* question."

"Indeed," Picard muttered.

Worf looked up. "Captain," he said with an air of resignation, "we are being hailed."

"On screen," Picard said automatically. Standing, he straightened his jacket and positioned himself.

"Sir, it is a standard radio message sent over the space-normal spectrum."

"Oh." He sat down again and relaxed. "On audio, then."

The incoming radio signal was weak and almost lost in a sea of whistling static. "Can't you clean that up a bit, Mr. Worf?" Picard asked with a trace of annoyance.

"I *am* trying, sir." Cutting the speaker out of the bridge audio system, the Klingon quickly set up a real-time digital filter that would separate and dismiss most of the static from the transmission while boosting the volume level of what remained. "There," he said after a moment. "That should be better, Captain. I am now putting the transmission back on audio."

"Central Control of Nem Ma'ak Bratuna to spacecraft. Identify yourself immediately."

Picard paused for a moment, collecting his thoughts, and then he addressed the air. "This is Captain Jean-Luc Picard of the Federation starship *Enterprise*. We are here on a peaceful mission of exploration. To whom have I the honor of speaking?"

There was silence. "Where are they, Mr. Worf?" Picard asked after a moment. "Did we lose them?"

"This is a standard radio signal, sir. It is traveling at light-speed. We will not receive an answer for some time."

Data spoke up. "Twenty-nine minutes and fifty-three seconds, sir, at this distance and given our own velocity—that is, if they transmit a reply immediately."

Picard frowned. "Half an hour," he complained. "Ridiculous! How can one do any meaningful business under these conditions?"

Riker considered it. "We could get to Planet Three fairly quickly at warp three, sir. The light-speed delay to standard orbit is on the order of a quarter of a second each way. It would make talking to them a lot easier."

"Mr. Data?" Picard prompted.

"Estimated travel time to Planet Three at warp factor three is two minutes and twenty-nine seconds, Captain."

"Thank you." Picard thought about it and then shook his head. "No. We've frightened these people more than enough already. No doubt we're under close observation by whoever is running things on Planet Three—on Nem Ma'ak Bratuna, that is. It's bad enough that we were detected; being seen going into warp under these conditions might be profoundly disturbing to this culture. We'll maintain our present course and speed." He paused. "It's not all bad, you know," he said, smiling a little. "The light-speed delay will give everyone time to think a bit."

"*—Captain Jean-Luc Picard of the Federation starship* Enterprise. *We are here on a peaceful mission of exploration. To whom have I the honor of speaking?*"

"This is Nem Ma'ak Bratuna Central Control," the War Room communications officer sputtered into his microphone. "You are *who?* Of the *what?*"

General Blakendet whirled. "No unauthorized transmissions!" he barked. "Order the unknown to stand by, and then *be quiet.*"

"Yes, sir!"

"A starship?" Kerajem asked. "I wonder what that might be?"

Klerran fes Dresnai, the minister for science and education, cleared his throat to speak. "First Among Equals, if I might—"

Kerajem turned. "Yes, Klerran?"

"First, the term 'starship' is frequently used in, uh, fantastic literature—fiction, I mean to say. Starships are said to be able to travel fast enough, much faster than light, to make an interstellar trip possible within a practical period of time. We use the term ourselves when we talk of future design possibilities."

Major Hassandit snorted. "Excuse me, First, but do we have to listen to this nonsense? Faster-than-light travel is impossible. This is a waste of time."

Klerran turned red. "With all due respect, Major, this may be important. Fantasy is fantasy, but this is

23

reality—and the truth is out there." He pointed to the screen, where the big crimson disk representing the unknown glowed brightly to denote the speed of its approach.

"Let the minister talk, Major," Blakendet said brusquely. "The unknown *did* report itself to be a 'starship,' whatever *that* is, and I know as much about that as you do. I'm much more concerned about how the unknown managed to get as far in-system as Ma'ak Unselbe without our detecting it first."

Hassandit persisted. "General, the unknown may be nothing more than a ploy to distract us at this most critical moment. If so, it's working."

"If the Krann could build *that,* they'd have been here long since," Klerran said bitingly. "This isn't a trick, Kerajem. This is real. Those are *aliens* out there."

Kerajem scratched his chin in thought. After a moment, he asked, "Do you think we could have been able to detect the unknown during its approach if it had been traveling through the outer system at a speed faster than light?"

"The major is right," General Blakendet said. "It's not possible to go that fast."

"Assume it is somehow possible," the First said coldly. He was growing impatient. "What then?"

General Blakendet shrugged. "I simply don't know, sir. Under those circumstances, we probably could not detect it." He paused. "The fact that the unknown has gotten this far indicates that no one else spotted it on the way in, either."

"A ship from somewhere else," Kerajem said, almost to himself. "A *starship.* I wonder . . ."

The First Among Equals turned to General Blakendet. "General, we are going to assume that the unknown is what it says it is. Send them our greetings

first contact, yet we have to make as little contact as possible. I feel as if I'm tap dancing on unusually thin ice."

"If I might ask a possibly stupid question, sir," Troi began, "why don't we just *leave?* We would be an unexplained mystery."

"We can't leave now, Counselor," Picard replied. "There are things going on here that we need to know about. We particularly need to know if this civilization has indeed cracked the secret of warp drive. Aside from those brief warp-field generation bursts that initially attracted our attention to this system, we haven't detected any further evidence of warp technology. That's fairly odd."

"These people seem to have *no* idea that faster-than-light transportation or communication is anything but theoretical," Riker observed. "If they're able to equip ships with warp drive, they're doing a good job of hiding the fact."

"They hide a great deal," Picard said. "They've made an absolute fetish of secrecy. Why are these people camouflaging their broadcast signals? Are they hiding from someone? Who did they think we were when they first detected us? And what do they think we can do for them now? Picard sighed, suddenly tired. He rubbed his eyes. "Number One, get the away team ready. We've got less than an hour."

"*—will take up orbit around your world in about fifty minutes. I look forward to meeting you shortly after that, sir. Picard out.*"

"Less than an hour," Kerajem said. "Good."

"The *Enterprise,* as it is called, will actually assume orbit in thirty-seven minutes, nineteen seconds," the traffic controller reported. "That corrects for the speed-of-light delay between the time Captain Picard sent us his message and our reception of it."

27

"Even better." Kerajem silently studied the main status viewer. It was designed to dominate the room, and it did so easily. It was presently set to show the sky as seen from this longitude and latitude. Kerajem looked at the glowing red disk that represented the *Enterprise* as it hastened toward his world. There were also thousands upon thousands of more distant, bright white lights on the screen. None of them were stars.

Kerajem wearily rubbed his eyes.

"Is there something wrong, sir?" General Blakendet asked.

"Nothing more than usual," Kerajem replied, blinking. "I'm going to the spaceport. The other ministers will meet us there to greet Captain Picard and his people. General, clear the *Enterprise* through our inner and outer defense blankets. Hattajek, you're to remain here with the general. If anything happens and I'm out of touch, command will pass to you. You'll know what to do."

"Yes, Kerajem."

Chapter Four

SHUTTLECRAFT *JUSTMAN* DROPPED ELEGANTLY through the atmosphere of Nem Ma'ak Bratuna, Worf taking care in his piloting not to let the speed of their passage create a corona around the little ship. The Klingon security chief wanted the shuttlecraft's sensors unobstructed by any interference, because the sky around him was full of weapons. *Justman* had been granted clearance by Nem Ma'ak Bratunan authorities, and a safe approach path had been charted for the shuttle, but Worf was not one to take chances . . . especially with his captain on board.

The *Enterprise,* traveling far faster than the decelerating shuttlecraft, lay far ahead of and above them at standard orbit altitude. It was no longer visible to even the sharpest warrior's eye.

"It's a beautiful world down there," Deanna Troi said softly, looking at Nem Ma'ak Bratuna on a small viewscreen. "Much of it looks untouched, despite the pollution along the coasts."

"There are large, arable areas that have apparently

never been settled," Picard said. "I must admit I find that rather strange. The population here is over two billion—a rather hefty number—and these people certainly have the technological ability to go anywhere they wish on the planet."

Data spoke up. "The southern continents, in particular, are largely unoccupied by the natives. The concentration of population in the northern hemisphere *is* highly unusual, sir. The Nem Ma'ak Bratunans have congregated in mineral-rich areas along the coastal mountain ranges of the three northern continents."

"But not in the south," Troi said. "The population there is small and scattered. There are no big cities and very few towns."

"The south seems perfectly habitable," Data pointed out. "Indeed, it may be more habitable than the north. The industrial pollution index in the northern hemisphere is an average eight point one. They are doing little to prevent or mitigate the poisoning of their environment."

"Perhaps the problem is cultural," Troi hazarded. "The Nem Ma'ak Bratunans remain in the north because they choose to."

"That seems an unlikely matter of choice," Picard said. "No, Counselor, there is something going on here that I simply do not trust." He smiled ruefully. "This is hardly a normal first-contact situation."

Data nodded in agreement.

"Data—"

"Yes, Captain?"

"Data, please don't take this the wrong way, but you have been nodding and shaking your head a great deal of late. Is there something wrong?"

"Ah," Data said, nodding. "No, sir, there is nothing wrong with me. I am practicing my incidental capital motions. I have noted that humans tend to confirm whatever it is they are saying by nodding or shaking their heads, as if they are agreeing with themselves. Since I always agree with myself, I feel I must nod and shake my head more than, say, you or Counselor Troi might."

Picard nodded. "You nod and shake very well indeed, Mr. Data," he said agreeably. "You may stop now."

The android blinked. "Yes, Captain. Thank you for your concern, sir."

Worf spoke up. "Captain, the *Enterprise* is relaying a digest of telemetry analyses during the last hour. One moment, please." The Klingon extracted an isolinear optical chip from a reader and handed it to Troi, who was sitting just behind him.

"Thank you both," Picard said, taking the chip from Troi. Seating himself at the shuttlecraft's compact science station, he inserted the chip into the reader there and watched silently as text and graphics began to flow across the screen.

"Now this is very interesting," Picard said, almost to himself. "Come here and have a look." The captain returned the display to the beginning of the bioscan telemetry analysis as Troi and Data crouched behind him, reading over his shoulders.

Data took in the contents of the display at once. "Remarkable, sir," he said.

"Wait a minute," Troi complained. "I'm still reading—oh! I see now. Well, this may explain something, but I'm not sure what." She sighed.

"You know that every indigenous life-form on a given planet can be shown to be related to every other on that planet through analysis of its DNA. There are basic patterns that repeat from species to species all the way up and down the evolutionary tree. The principle is well established. We have found that the DNA of a Nem Ma'ak Bratunan humanoid is not related to that of the majority of life-forms here. In other words, the people of Nem Ma'ak Bratuna are not native to this planet. Their species could not have evolved here."

"It could also mean that most forms of life on this world *except* for the humanoid population and its related parasites and symbiotes did not evolve here," Data added, "but that is not very likely."

"Thank you, Mr. Data," the captain said distractedly as he read further into the summary. He was looking for something, and he found it quickly. "Now here," he said to the others, pointing at the display. "That's what linguistics got from their local broadcasts."

Troi read aloud from the screen. "The star we are calling 30453 FAS is called Ma'ak Indawe by the people here. The name translates roughly as 'Stronghold.'"

"'Stronghold,' Captain?" Worf added from his station. "They must expect a battle."

Picard nodded. "A culture at this apparent sociological level most commonly calls its star 'the Sun,' if it doesn't go and name it after a mythic figure of some sort—a favorite god or goddess, perhaps. 'Stronghold' does not fit that pattern at all. And look here: The name of the planet, Nem Ma'ak Bratuna, is derived from the name of the star and carries a more refined meaning—'The Last Stand.'"

"'The Last Stand'?" Troi wondered. "What does that mean?"

"The name denotes a refuge of last resort," Data said. "The name strongly suggests not only that the people here are alien to this world but that they are fully aware of the fact. This also may be significant: The name is of recent vintage."

"They've recently renamed their planet?" Troi

asked. "How strange. But if they're not from here, then where *are* they from?"

"I've been giving that some thought," Picard told her. "Mr. Data, I want you to contact the *Enterprise* and have LCARS send you the bioscan reports we collected from the third and fourth planets of 30452 FAS. Compare the DNA profiles we found among the remaining species on those planets to the one we have found in the humanoid population here. See if they correlate."

"Yes, Captain. It will take me a moment to contact the ship and complete the download."

Picard nodded.

"Captain," Troi asked, "did you finish reading the linguistics summary?"

"Not quite, Counselor. What else did you find?"

"We don't need to call them the Nem Ma'ak Bratunans any longer, sir. Their name for themselves is 'the Lethanta.'"

Picard read the summary. "I wonder how they came by that," he said. "It seems to be untranslatable."

"Estimating landing at spaceport in ten minutes," Worf reported. Suddenly, his tone changed. "Captain," he said quickly, "three unidentified craft are approaching from the west."

"Range and speed?"

"One hundred fifteen kilometers, sir. Speed eleven hundred seventy kilometers per hour."

"Any sign of weapons activation?"

"I have scanned them already, sir. The craft are only lightly armed. I am reading air-to-air tactical nuclear missiles, four to each craft, twelve in all. They have not been activated. No energy weapons of any sort, sir."

"They won't take us by surprise with ordnance such

as that," Picard said, frowning. "Can they follow us into space, Mr. Worf?"

"No, sir. The craft are powered by turbines that burn a fuel-air mixture for thrust. These kinds of systems can work only in atmosphere. The missiles contain their own fuel, but their range and speed are not troublesome to us."

Picard nodded. "Understood. Mr. Worf, at the first sign of weapons activation or missile launch, get us out of here and head us back toward the *Enterprise*. In the meantime, keep her steady as she goes."

"Captain," Worf said suddenly, "the flight leader is hailing us."

"Very well. On audio."

"Shuttlecraft Justman, *this is Captain Fesnerkall of the Defense Forces Air Division. Welcome to Nem Ma'ak Bratuna, Captain Picard. I and the other members of my flight have been given the honor of escorting your spacecraft to the spaceport at our capital city."*

"Open a channel, please, Mr. Worf," Picard ordered. "Captain, this is Captain Picard aboard *Justman*. Thank you. We appreciate the courtesy of your escort, and we will follow you all the way in."

"Very good, Captain. I estimate rendezvous in ninety-three seconds. Eh, Captain, if you would have your pilot slow up a bit after the rendezvous point, we won't have to go to afterburners to keep up with you."

"Will do, Captain Fesnerkall. Thank you again. Picard out." To Worf, he said, "Cut our speed to match theirs once we rendezvous, Lieutenant—but be ready to kick her in the tail if we need to get out of here quickly."

"Aye, sir."

Data rose from his seat at the science station. "Captain," he said, "I have completed the new DNA comparison, as ordered. The Lethanta definitely evolved on 30452 FAS Three. They are from there, sir."

"Ah. Thank you, Mr. Data," Picard said. "So that world was perhaps a 'last stand' as well."

"And someone blasted the Lethanta off it a very long time ago," Troi added. "Six thousand years."

The captain nodded. "We had better find out exactly what occurred," he said. "Fantastic as it seems, whoever did it to them may be around still."

Nemtar Ship Commander, the disgraced captain of the equally disgraced Krann scanner ship *JTO-52D*, was standing in the prisoner dock located in a small chamber that was the traditional venue of Fleet courts-martial. Nemtar was brightly lighted by a spot beam set into the ceiling directly above his head. The rest of the room was in darkness. He could hear but not see his accusers. Once in a while, Nemtar could hear one of his otherwise silent judges cough or stir. That provided him data. It amused Nemtar in what were probably the last moments of his life to analyze what he was perceiving, the way he had been trained to do nearly since birth. From the small aural cues he was getting, Nemtar decided that there were five people sitting about three meters in front of him in a shallow semicircle. As it happened, he was exactly right.

There was a handrail there in front of him, designed to be gripped by the nervous and the afraid. The metal of the rail was polished at those two points where one's hands were most likely to be placed. Nemtar ignored it. He stood easily, outwardly relaxed, his hands clasped behind him as if this proceeding were nothing more significant than a standard lecture on air purification.

Nemtar would probably meet his death today. There was nothing to be done about that, and he accepted the fact.

But he could still try to save his ship.

Presider Hek himself was chairing this board. That

was a sure measure of how angry he was. "It was not hard to extrapolate the incoming course of the alien ship, once it was finally spotted by units stationed near the orbit of Ma'ak Unselbe," he said, continuing his interrogation of Nemtar. "That ship traveled right through your watch area undetected. All six hundred uncloaked meters of it just slipped by you within seventy-two thousand kilometers of your position. Now just how did you and your people manage to miss a thing like that?"

"There was no indication of the presence of the alien ship in our watch sector, Presider," Nemtar Ship Commander replied calmly. "The sudden appearance of the ship near Ma'ak Unselbe registered on our long-range detectors, as my report indicates. The instant it appeared on our sensor boards, I immediately issued a level-one advisory to the flagship—"

Hek interrupted him. "But by then, Nemtar, the alien ship was one hundred million kilometers sunward of the Fleet and heading straight for Nem Ma'ak Bratuna. Your alert was useless."

"You have the full transcript of what occurred during that watch, Presider," Nemtar responded. "Our equipment was operating flawlessly. My people were performing at optimum. As you will see from the transcript, the presence and condition of every single one of our *own* ships then operating in our watch sector was properly logged and updated throughout the watch."

The Presider was growing impatient. "The question begs, Nemtar: Why did you and your fellow wizards of detection fail to detect the presence of the alien ship until it was too late?"

"I have no facts to offer, Presider."

"I see," Hek said from the darkness. There was silence for a long moment, and then he spoke again.

"Return Nemtar Ship Commander to the . . . holding area."

Three guards suddenly appeared out of the darkness, their hand weapons at the ready. Nemtar nodded to them almost pleasantly and followed them out of the light and into the surrounding darkness.

The others in the star chamber heard, briefly, the echo of several sets of footsteps in the dark. Then they listened as Nemtar walked on ahead of his guards with a sure and certain stride. They heard him stop and, a moment later, there came the heavy sound of a pressure-tight door *shuff*ing itself closed. Those in the star chamber did not hear anything as the small room behind the door was opened to the hard vacuum of space.

"He was a brave man," came a new voice. "A pity he had to be remaindered."

"What do we do about his ship?" someone asked. "A Fleet enforcement scout is standing by."

"We have found no evidence of procedural errors or system failures in the transcript," a third voice observed. "Perhaps we need not go the full route this time."

"I still think these spacings are wasteful," one of them complained. "We lose nearly four cubic meters of air every time we remainder someone, not to mention the biological material and so forth."

"Discipline must be maintained," another said sternly.

"The losses don't matter anymore, not when we're so close to our goal," yet another observed. "We'll restock."

"What will we do about Nemtar's ship?" the first one asked again.

"Have a dispatch team from the scout go aboard *JTO-52D* and remainder the top officers," Hek said almost absently. "No need to remainder the ship as well, given these circumstances. Reassign *JTO-52D* to ferry and light cargo work in the rear until we can restaff its officer complement and return the ship to normal duty. That will allow us to put one of the veteran cargo runners on the front line."

The light level in the room was brought up, and the members of the court-martial panel were able to see each other again. The five panelists were sitting behind a trial bench that curved around the prisoner dock in a gentle arc. Hek Portside Hull Patcher, currently the Presider of the Fleet Congress, was in the middle chair. Hek was a burly, middle-aged man, one who looked as if he'd spent most of his life wearing a pressure suit and working outside, which he'd done day in and day out until he entered Fleet politics. Now he was the youngest Presider in six generations.

"I wish that Nemtar had had an answer for us," Hek told his colleagues. "We need to know how that alien ship slipped by our security watch."

"The high-velocity probes will arrive at Nem Ma'ak Bratuna in a matter of hours," someone pointed out. "They have been ordered to examine the alien ship as part of their surveillance routine. We will know more about it then."

Pelaka Theoretician sighed. "We already know enough about it," the old man said. "I almost wish Nemtar Ship Commander and his people *had* made an error. That would have explained everything rather neatly."

"Your considered opinion of what occurred, then, Pelaka," the Presider said. "I think we've all been waiting to hear it."

Pelaka cleared his throat. "As the late ship commander just told us, Presider, I have no facts to offer you."

"The tone of your voice suggests you have more to say, though."

Pelaka nodded. "I do, Hek. I believe I could make a good guess."

"Give it to us, then."

"Very well," Pelaka said. "Our JTO-series scanner ships are equipped and personnel trained to detect everything there is to detect, see everything there is to see, and make note of it all. I believe the alien ship evaded detection because it was never really there to be detected."

"Pardon me?" The Presider rarely needed to fumble for something to say, but this was one of those times. "Of course it was there, Pelaka. It *had* to be."

"No, Hek, it need not have been there at all. The alien ship did not *seem* to appear suddenly near the orbit of Ma'ak Unselbe. It actually *did* do so."

The Presider laughed gently. It was a dangerous sound, and the others stirred. "How do you figure that?" he asked.

The old theoretician would not be intimidated. "We know a great deal now about this ship from our long-range observations of it," Pelaka explained. "This is a spacecraft, a 'starship,' from an obviously technologically advanced organization called the United Federation of Planets. It is a ship of impressive size, but it is *not* large enough for interstellar travel—that is, interstellar travel as we know it. Not even one generation of travelers aboard it could survive a star trip."

"How do you know?" Hek asked.

"Simple, Presider. We have detected the presence of more than a thousand beings aboard the ship, yet they have with them enough consumables to last for only a few months, at best. Further, while the engines of the alien ship are of a type unknown to us, we can easily detect the extent of the ship's energy reserves. They are enormous, capable of generating almost unimaginable motive power."

"Your conclusion, then?"

"There can be only one, Presider," Pelaka said. "The alien ship is able to travel at speeds faster than light."

The others around the bench, including Hek, gasped.

"Since we know translight travel to be impossible in normal space," Pelaka continued, "the aliens must travel in another *kind* of space. Perhaps it is one that is coexistent with ours. If this is true, then the alien ship did not pass through the sector under watch by scanner ship *JTO-52D* at all. Instead, it decelerated and dropped back into space, normal space, near Ma'ak Unselbe. It then proceeded on course for Ma'ak Indawe at a quarter of the speed of light."

"A faster-than-light vessel," Hek breathed. He clenched a fist. Instinctively, he knew the old man was right. "At last."

"A wonderful thing, Presider," Pelaka said, his own eyes shining. "A miracle, to find such a ship at this historic time."

"I want that ship," said the Presider. "I *want* it."

Chapter Five

JUSTMAN MADE ITS FINAL APPROACH to the VIP landing pad at the spaceport that served the Lethantan capital. The shuttlecraft's escort flew on by overhead. Captain Fesnerkall saluted the *Enterprise* landing party with a last waggle of his wings.

"Friendly enough," Picard said approvingly. "Good protocol. Fine sense of fitness on the part of that Fesnerkall."

Deanna Troi nodded. "I sensed nothing inimical from any of them, Captain. They were curious about us, perhaps a bit fearful, but disposed to be friendly. The other thing, the apprehension I told you about earlier, overlays all their thoughts and colors all their actions."

"The other thing is what we need to find out about," Picard observed.

"Yes," Troi replied, touching her forehead in something like weariness. "Their fear hangs over everything they think and do like a thick, dark blanket. It is suffocating them, in a way."

"Captain," Worf called. "There are people waiting for us."

Picard turned to a small viewscreen that was right at hand and dialed for the view below. Casting about, he soon found a group of perhaps thirty people standing not far from their designated landing spot.

"What do you think, Counselor?" Picard asked.

Troi pursed her lips. "There is a great deal going on among them. Their emotions are—are roiling." She paused. "The strongest feeling is coming from this one, Captain—the tall, white-haired man in the middle of the group. To him we represent salvation."

Picard nodded. "Do you have any idea of what the danger might be that these people face?"

Troi winced as she attempted to read closer.

"Are you all right, Deanna?" Picard asked, concerned.

"I'm sorry, Captain. This isn't very easy for me. Everyone here is, is keyed up about whatever this is. Tapping into it, trying to read it, is a bit uncomfortable. It's like trying to grasp the lyric of a song by putting your ear against an output unit set at its highest volume. Whatever the danger is, they view it as both enormous—and quite nearby."

"No one else is around," Data said. "There appears to be a conflict between what Counselor Troi perceives and our appraisal of the tactical situation."

"Appearances can be deceiving," Troi observed.

"Landing now, Captain," Worf called.

"Do a nice job, Mr. Worf. They expect to be impressed."

Jemmagar, the minister for security, was perturbed. Shielding his eyes, he squinted up into the bright sky. "Is *this* the alien ship we've been waiting for?" he asked Kerajem, exasperated. "*This* tiny thing? Hardly seems worth closing off the spaceport for it."

"It's not so very small," Kerajem said patiently. "In any case, this is what the aliens call a shuttlecraft. The mother ship is still in orbit. *That* one should be large enough to impress you. Really, Jemmagar, you ought to try listening to the briefing reports once in a while."

Jemmagar set his lips in a tight line. "There wasn't a great deal of time, First," he said fussily. "I've had about half an hour's sleep in the past three days. I'm afraid I was grabbing a nap in the groundcar while the driver got me here."

"Very well, Jemmagar," Kerajem said, holding up a hand. "Never mind, never mind. We've all been a little short on sleep recently."

The ministers watched as, overhead, the shuttle-craft spun smartly about and settled down slowly onto the landing pad. There was only the smallest sound as the little boat contacted the surface.

The engines died and, after a moment, the hatch opened. Captain Picard and his officers stood in the hatchway. All of them were smiling in as friendly a manner as they could manage.

"One of them is quite nonhuman," Jemmagar whispered. "He appears rather grisly."

"I wish he wouldn't try to smile like that," Kerajem whispered back.

"There's another one who looks, well, rather pale."

"They do seem disposed to be friendly."

Jemmagar snorted. "Well, I hope you're right. These people surely don't seem very concerned, considering what's going on."

"They may not feel any need to be concerned," Kerajem observed. "That might be the most hopeful sign yet."

The force of two dozen security personnel accompanying the Council of Ministers kept a discreet watch on Picard and his people as they left *Justman* and walked across the landing pad to the spot where Kerajem and the other ministers were waiting for them.

"Captain Picard, I presume," Kerajem said, smiling broadly. He put out a hand in the friendly manner common to many humanoid cultures, and Picard shook it.

Kerajem indicated the six men standing immediately behind him. "We of the Council of Ministers of Nem Ma'ak Bratuna extend greetings to you and your people on behalf of all the citizens of our world."

Picard smiled back pleasantly. "And I, sir, and my officers greet all of you in the name of the government and citizens of the United Federation of Planets. Thank you for your most gracious welcome. May this initial meeting be only the beginning of a long and productive relationship between our two cultures."

Kerajem nodded. "Indeed."

"Allow me, please, to introduce my colleagues," Picard continued. "This is Counselor Deanna Troi, my closest and most trusted advisor. To her left is Lieutenant Commander Data, second officer of the *Enterprise,* and to *his* left is Lieutenant Worf, our chief of security."

"I am pleased to meet all of you," Kerajem said. "If you will, Captain, allow me to present some of the other members of the Council of Ministers." Together, Kerajem and Picard walked to the head of a short receiving line formed by the seven waiting men.

The first minister was a burly, determined-looking sort. "Captain, allow me to present Presinget fes Kwaita, our minister for labor."

"Ah. A pleasure, Minister Presinget."

"The pleasure's all mine, Captain," the burly former miner replied, shaking Picard's hand with a bone-crushing grip. "Glad to meet you. Pretty exciting, you know. People don't drop in on us from outer space every damn day."

"Uh, I can imagine," the captain said.

They came to a slight, balding man. "Captain, this is Umbeltag zan Swannet, our social services minister."

"How do you do, Captain?"

"Very well, thank you, Minister. It is an honor to meet you."

The next minister was a short, fussy-seeming man. "Captain Picard," Kerajem said, "this is Jemmagar fes Kah, our minister for security."

Picard put out his hand and smiled. "A pleasure to meet you, Minister Jemmagar."

Jemmagar looked at Picard for a long and impolite moment, letting the silence linger until he saw that Kerajem was gritting his teeth. "As you say, Captain, a pleasure," Jemmagar said lightly, finally giving Captain Picard's hand a quick, limp shake.

Kerajem noted that if Picard had been offended by Jemmagar's studied rudeness, he was giving no sign of it. That was a relief. He and Picard came to the next man, one who seemed younger than the others. "Captain Picard, this is Klerran fes Dresnai, our minister for science and education."

Klerran grinned and extended his hand. "Don't let these others get to you before I do, Captain."

Picard smiled back. "I think that's more or less up to you, Minister Klerran." They shook.

The next minister was an older, slender man with a whiff of the diplomat about him. "Captain, allow me to introduce you to Terrestak zan Pettok, our minister for state."

"Welcome to our world, Captain Picard," Terrestak said politely. He shook Picard's hand with just the proper pressure for exactly the right length of time.

"Thank you for inviting us, Minister," Picard replied.

They came next to a much older man. "Captain, let me present Rikkadar zan Therrka, our finance minister—and my oldest friend."

"Greetings, Captain," Rikkadar said warmly as he shook Picard's hand. "May ours be a long and lasting friendship."

"Let us be sure to make it so, Minister Rikkadar."

Kerajem indicated another landing pad about fifty meters away. There were two large craft standing by. "I thought you might enjoy flying into the city by jethopper," the First said. "They may be a bit old-fashioned, but they travel slowly enough to give one a chance to appreciate the scenery."

"And I would appreciate the chance to see it," Picard said, looking toward the distant Kajja Kojja. "Those mountains to the east are really quite beautiful."

"Thank you, Captain," Kerajem said. "I was born there, as was Minister Rikkadar."

"Then I'll be certain to go see them," Picard said agreeably.

"I'll be happy to take you there myself, Captain, a little later during your visit with us," Kerajem told him. He gestured toward the waiting jethoppers. "Meanwhile, perhaps we'd all best get started for town."

"That suits us very well," Picard said.

Kerajem, Security Minister Jemmagar, and old Rikkadar were sitting with Captain Picard and the rest of the *Enterprise* party in a comfortably appointed lounge in the forward section of the lead jethopper. The other 'hopper, with the remainder of the Council of Ministers aboard, was following theirs into the capital.

Picard was looking out one of the panoramic passenger windows as the countryside rolled past and under them. "I see we're following a highway," he observed, smiling. "More fun than instrument flying any day. I suppose pilots are pilots, wherever they might be found."

Kerajem smiled back. "Highway One is the only road to and from the spaceport," he said. "This is a regular run for me. I take it, then, that you yourself have flown something like this craft we're in, Captain."

"Yes," Picard said agreeably. "Yes, I have—something very much like it, anyway. I think they're great fun." The captain leaned back in his seat and put his fingertips together in the almost prayerful way he had whenever he was about to broach a difficult subject. "Kerajem, I hope we can discuss matters freely, when it comes time. There is a great deal we would like to know."

The First Among Equals nodded. "I think I can promise you that we will be at least as forthcoming as you, Captain. After all, trust begets trust."

"Indeed it does," Picard said, nodding. He looked out the window. "Kerajem, I hope you don't mind my asking you a rather direct question."

"Please do."

"The countryside here seems rather, well, bare," Picard said, gesturing toward the outside. "I see no towns and few structures of any sort. There seems to be no infrastructure—only that one highway below us, for example. That's not typical of the surrounding territory of the planetary capitals with which I am familiar, sir. Usually such areas are quite crowded."

"You find it curious?" Kerajem asked, genuinely puzzled. "I suppose I don't see anything strange about it. It's the way we do things. There are historical reasons for that, of course. There always are."

47

Picard was all attention. "I'd surely like to hear all about those reasons, Kerajem."

"Certainly," the First said. "We'll talk at Government House. I expect that we will find that we have much in common. After all, you've already—"

Jemmagar interrupted. "That's all very well," the minister for security said, "but I dare say that we had better not be the only party to this conversation who will be forthcoming. Kerajem, I tried to warn you—"

"I need no warning, Jemmagar," Kerajem said quietly, holding up a hand. "Captain, you must excuse the . . . enthusiasm of my colleague. As you will surely understand, he is, shall we say, caught up in the moment. These are trying times, as you will surely understand, and the strain on all of us has been enormous."

"Of course," Picard said reassuringly. *Trying times? What the devil is he talking about?* "I would assure Minister Jemmagar, and you, sir, that we are here to further mutual understanding and cooperation between our two peoples." The captain chuckled in his most sincere and diplomatic manner. "I assure you that we are as curious about you as you are about us."

"We need to know about the Krann," Jemmagar said bluntly.

"Come, come, Jemmagar," Rikkadar said wearily. "We haven't even arrived at Government House yet. Surely even you can wait *that* long."

"The Krann?" Picard asked. "Who are the Krann?" He looked at Data, who shook his head from side to side in a perfectly practiced manner.

"As if you didn't know," Jemmagar sneered. "Is *this* the kind of forthrightness we are to expect from the Federation of United Planets?"

"The United Federation of Planets, sir," Data corrected him.

"Whatever," Jemmagar snapped.

Picard cleared his throat. "Kerajem," he said, "I assure you that we have never heard of anyone called the Krann. We are the first Federation vessel ever to enter this region of the galaxy. Everything and everyone here is new to us."

Troi was having trouble pinning down the apprehension behind Jemmagar's studied rudeness. There seemed to be no reason for it, and certainly neither the captain nor anyone else from the *Enterprise* had offered Jemmagar any offense. Suddenly the counselor caught the slimmest glimmer of the root of Jemmagar's fear. It was shared by all the Lethanta. The wellspring of this particular fear lay far down in the dungeons that are built and strengthened in early childhood, where the myths and legends dwell forever even after one has forgotten all about them. They live on without tending. These deepest dungeons represented territory Troi had explored many, many times in psychotherapy, both as therapist and patient. Whatever the fear was, it was big, it had power, and each one of the Lethanta was gripped by it.

The counselor wondered if that fear had a name. *Could it be the Krann, perhaps? But who could they be—?*

Troi had a sudden thought. "Captain," she said, "perhaps Minister Jemmagar is referring to whomever is responsible for the present condition of 30452 FAS Three and Four."

"Why, yes," Picard said, seizing upon the notion. "Kerajem, just before we came here, we visited a star system eighty-seven light-years away. We know your people once lived on the third planet of that system—"

Picard was surprised to see Kerajem's eyes suddenly grow wide. The two ministers sitting with him looked stunned. "You know this thing for a fact?"

Kerajem whispered. He had grown pale. "How? How is it possible?"

Picard looked at Troi. Her face mirrored something of the awe felt by the Lethanta. "Captain," she said very quietly, "they did not know this before now. This is very important to them."

"Of course." Picard took a moment to search for the right words. "Kerajem," he said, "we have means available to thoroughly examine a biological form."

"Please," Kerajem said. "Tell us about the planet in that other system, Captain. Why do you believe we came from there?"

"More to the point, can you prove it?" Jemmagar rasped.

"Are you certain you want him to?" Rikkadar said.

"I want the truth," Jemmagar insisted.

"All I can do is tell you how we happened to go there, and what we found when we arrived," Picard said. "To begin with, we are in this sector on a mission to extend the database of the Federation Astrophysical Survey—that is, we are finding out all we can about this sector of space and everything in it. We visited a nearby star that we have since listed as 30452 FAS on our charts, hence Commander Troi's reference to that designation."

"Captain, didn't you say that this star was eighty-seven light-years from here?" Rikkadar asked.

"Yes, Minister Rikkadar. Yes, I did."

"The concept of 'nearby' has changed since this morning," Kerajem said wryly. "Please continue, Captain Picard."

"We found the third planet of that system in a particularly severe state. Our findings were that, some six thousand years ago, the planet was bombarded from space, possibly from orbit, by someone using high-yield nuclear weapons designed to eradicate all life upon it with hard radiation."

"Doomsday weapons," Klerran hazarded.

"Yes," Worf said. "Some cultures have called them that. Such weapons are specialized nuclear devices that are jacketed with a substance—sometimes cobalt—that pulverizes when exposed to the detonation of the parent device. The substance turns highly radioactive and disperses throughout the ecosystem of the target area. The radioactive agent has a very long half-life. The many such devices dropped on the planet in question were clearly intended to sterilize it."

"But they didn't succeed in ridding that world of all life," Rikkadar guessed.

"Not entirely," Data told him. "Some lower life-forms did survive the bombardment. The planetary biosphere is stabilizing, but extremely slowly."

"There are no people there, however," Rikkadar said.

"No, sir," Data confirmed. "There are no people there."

"So how do you know what you say you know?" Kerajem asked.

"We analyzed those lower life-forms quite thoroughly," Picard told him. "Our studies showed that those life-forms, and you, evolved from the very same source."

"So we are really from the third planet of that star?" Klerran asked in wonder.

Picard paused, then carefully continued. "That is what we believe."

Rikkadar's eyes were wide and shining with tears. "The homeworld," the old man breathed. "That third planet must have been the homeworld."

"I wouldn't want to draw any rash conclusions from this story," Kerajem said.

"It is just as the ancients wrote," Rikkadar continued, not hearing him. "'The homeworld was cleansed by fire and storm in payment for sin, and few escaped.'"

"There must be some other explanation," Jemmagar said uncertainly. "There *must* be."

"Can we have been so wrong?" Rikkadar said, almost to himself. "Can we have been so desperately wrong about everything?"

Picard sneaked a look at Troi, who shrugged just enough for him to see. She looked as puzzled as he.

"We will speak more of this later," Kerajem said distractedly. He looked out the window and saw that they were flying over the capital city. "I see we're approaching Government House," the First Among Equals said. "We hope you and your officers will feel at home, Captain."

"I am quite sure we will, Kerajem," Picard replied, and he tried very hard to sound as if he meant it.

The *Enterprise* bridge routine had settled back into something approaching deadly dull. Will Riker was in the command chair. As per Picard's orders, he was maintaining yellow alert status, but everything that needed to be done about that had long since been done.

Ensign Ro was handling both Ops and Flight Control in Data's absence. Aside from a visual and systems check every ten minutes, Ro was letting the automatics do their job of maintaining standard orbit. She was much busier doing something else. Sector by sector, almost cubic meter by cubic meter, Ro was directing the ship's sensors in an almost unimaginably thorough and dogged sweep of the Ma'ak Indawe system. She was determined to find the source of the warp-field blips that had originally attracted their attention.

There was still no sign of what might have caused them. Instead, she found something else.

"Commander?" Ro called. "I have been going through recent sensor logs. Fifty-three minutes ago, we picked up a brief energy blip of some sort. I'm working on an analysis."

Commander Riker rose from the center seat. "Where away?" he asked as he walked forward.

"Well outsystem from here, sir," Ro said as her fingers flew across the Ops panel. "Somewhere just inside the orbit of planet five. I'm trying to narrow it down. I can already tell you the latest blip had nothing to do with warp-field generation, though. This is something else, something in another spectrum entirely."

Riker stood behind Ro and leaned forward a bit to look over her shoulder at the Ops display. "Nothing out of the ordinary there now," he said. "Let's get a visual of the area in question."

"Yes, sir." Ro rapidly hit a series of controls, and the real-time view of Nem Ma'ak Bratuna from orbit swam dizzily and was quickly replaced by a static starfield. "That's full magnification, Commander."

Riker looked intently at the viewscreen. There was nothing to be seen there.

"Commander," Ro said, "the analysis of the energy blip has just been completed." She paused for a moment and then tapped another rapid series of commands, never taking her eyes off the panel. "The sensors say the phenomenon in question was a tightly contained pocket exposure of class-M environmental conditions for a duration of one point three seconds. I am already running the sensor diagnostics, Commander, because that sounds like nonsense."

"I agree," Riker said, walking back into the command area and reseating himself. "There's nothing out there to support class-M conditions. Maintain yellow alert, Ensign."

"Yes, sir," Ro replied. A moment later, she said,

"Commander, you're not going to like this. The sensor diagnostic programs have completed running. All systems read nominal."

Riker exhaled. "You're right," he said, scratching his chin. "I don't like it. Not a bit. It doesn't make sense."

"Sir?" Ro said, swiveling around to look at Riker. "If I may?"

"Yes, Ensign?"

"There's one profile I can think of that fits these readings."

"And what is that?"

"Temporary breach of a cloaking device, sir, as reported by *U.S.S. Nemesis* during its confrontation with Romulan warbird *Night Raven*. Sometime around stardate 42400, I believe."

"The 'open door' phenomenon," Riker said, remembering. "The Romulan ship briefly lost hull integrity due to a coolant line blowout along its inner hull. *Night Raven*'s cloaking device could not compensate quickly enough for the suddenly changed physical condition of the ship. Sensors aboard *Nemesis* picked up the resulting exposure of class-M environmental conditions inside the warbird."

"As I recall, Commander," Ro said, "the 'open door' lasted for about a second, until the Romulan cloaking device could compensate. We may be seeing something like that here, sir."

The commander looked at the viewscreen for a long moment. There seemed to be absolutely nothing there.

"Keep a close watch on that sector, Ensign," Riker said thoughtfully. "The captain is still in transit to the local government's headquarters. I'll call him."

Chapter Six

THE DOORS TO THE MAIN CONFERENCE ROOM at Government House swung open, and the Council of Ministers entered, closely followed by the party of four from the *Enterprise*. Kerajem and the seven ministers took their places in front of seats that ran along one side of a large, highly polished oblong table. The table looked to Picard to have been made—no, to have been *crafted*—from a rich, reddish brown heartwood, something like mahogany. Such high-quality wood might be as common as charcoal here—Picard doubted that, but it might be so—but the craftsmanship evident in the making of this table bespoke an uncommonly high order of skill. People who were capable of doing this kind of work were to be reckoned with. Technology was gadgets; *this* was civilization.

Picard took his place at the center of the other side of the table, opposite Kerajem's seat, and Data and Troi stood to his left and right, respectively. Worf stood next to Troi.

As Picard stood there, waiting for some sort of signal to be seated, he almost absently ran a finger along the intricately carved filigree that ran all the way around the rounded rim of the table. If the Lethanta were trying to make an impression on him with this thing, they had succeeded.

Kerajem had been watching him. "We're proud of our craftsmanship here, Captain," the First Among Equals said. "This conference table used to belong to the—the previous ruling class here. They used it for banquets, usually. It's several hundred years old."

"It is quite well preserved," Data said.

"Thank you, Commander," Kerajem said, smiling. "It's been restored several times. We try to keep it in good repair." He leaned slightly forward and looked down at the tabletop. "I sometimes find this restful."

Picard looked, too. It was like gazing into a pool, with only his own mirror image guarding the border between the surface of the table and the infinity that began just below it. The gloss of the finish used was unmarred and incredibly reflective. Out of the corner of his eye, Picard spotted Data and the others from the *Enterprise* doing the same.

"It's lovely," Troi said quietly. "So peaceful."

"We have it refinished every so often," Kerajem said. "Each time we repair the table, it comes back to us better and stronger."

Picard looked up. "I sense there's a parallel there to the experience of your entire world, First Among Equals."

Kerajem smiled a secret smile. "I believe there is, Captain. Shall we all be seated? We have a great deal to talk about."

"Certainly." Everyone took their seats.

"If I may, Kerajem," Picard began, "I would like to ask you about these ancient writings that Minister Rikkadar referred to aboard the aircraft on our way here. Perhaps they might offer us further clues about your past—"

Out of the corner of his eye, Picard saw Troi suddenly sit up perfectly straight. Her hands were clasped easily in front of her on the table, but the captain saw that she was holding one forefinger slightly elevated. *Wait.*

Picard saw that, suddenly, several of the faces across the table had grown clouded with something that seemed like anger. With the skill of long practice, the captain smoothly changed the course of his remark. "—but, of course, all that can come later. We feel sure that all of you must have many questions for us." He smiled encouragingly. "Please proceed."

Security Minister Jemmagar had something very much like a sneer on his face. "Captain Picard, there is only one thing we want to know about," he said bitingly. "How did your ship get past the Krann line?"

Picard looked at him. "The Krann line? I told you that we know nothing of these Krann you've been talking about—"

Jemmagar slapped a hand on the flawless surface of the table, leaving a palm print. Worf stiffened. "Come, Captain!" Jemmagar prodded. "You know very well what I am talking about! How did you do it? How did you get past the Krann?"

Picard looked straight at Kerajem. The captain knew that his face was coloring with anger, and he did not bother to hide it. "First Among Equals, this is insulting and completely needless. I have assured you repeatedly that we have come here in peace—"

"Captain, please," Kerajem said, holding up a hand. "I tell you in all candor that no one here greeted the arrival of your ship with more anticipation, more hope, than I—but your lack of response to this vital question is straining even *my* goodwill."

"Please, Captain Picard," Minister Klerran said, pain in his eyes. "Please tell us how you got through the Krann line unmolested. It is so vitally important to us. Surely you must see that. Surely."

Picard shook his head in puzzlement. He did not need Troi to tell him that Klerran was sincere. "We went through no line, sir. We have seen no Krann and have no knowledge of them. The first thing we encountered in this star system was your very own probe."

"The one that first detected you in the region of Ma'ak Unselbe," Jemmagar said. "Yes."

"Captain Picard," Minister Presinget said, "we really don't have much time for this nonsense. Please tell us about the Krann."

"We know of no Krann," Data said.

Jemmagar leaned back in his seat. "Of course you don't," the security minister said in a bored tone as he gazed absently at the ceiling. "You came here out of simple curiosity, is that it? How nice for you."

Picard ignored his tone. "We came here because we detected a certain form of radiation, a pulse, that was of interest to us."

"Do you generally go more than eight hundred trillion kilometers out of your way just to look at interesting forms of radiation pulses, Captain?"

"Frequently," Picard responded calmly. "Our mandate is to explore, to find out what we can, and to send back the information we gather. That is our job. That is what we do."

"I believe him," Minister Umbeltag said suddenly.

"You would," Jemmagar sneered. "Liberals!"

"What kind of radiation pulse was this?" Klerran asked. "It might help if we knew more about it."

"Indeed it might," Picard said, "but we have rules about revealing our technology to those who have not yet reached that stage on their own. Suffice it to say that it was radiation relating to the method by which we travel faster than light. Tell me," Picard asked cautiously, "have you been working on developing such a technology?"

"Don't answer that," Jemmagar said quickly.

Kerajem looked at the security minister with a sour expression. "Oh, come now, Jemmagar," he said. "No, Captain, we don't have any such program under way. We *do* have a presence in space, of course. We have many of the kind of probes you encountered, all of which are unmanned. We have people in orbit aboard weather monitoring stations."

"Sir," Data said, "forgive me, but your people *did* come here from another star system."

"Yes, we did," Minister Terrestak said. "Ages ago—if our legends are to be believed."

"We will see," Captain Picard said quickly. "We will be glad to provide the Council of Ministers with all the data our rules permit."

"The question remains, sirs," Data continued. "How do your legends say you got here, to this planet?"

Kerajem looked at them for a long moment. "I can't answer that adequately," he said. "In fact, I probably can't answer that at all. We have a number of ancient writings that may bear on this matter, however."

"I would like to see those writings," Picard said.

"We can provide them to you," Kerajem said. "They are contained in a religious tract that was used when the old theocracy ruled our world. The old religion was purged after the revolution, but there must be some copies of the scrolls left somewhere."

"I have one," old Rikkadar said quietly. "I've always had one."

Jemmagar sat back forward. "That's not allowed, you know."

The finance minister shrugged. "So? What are you going to do, Jemsy boy? Arrest me?"

Kerajem held up a hand. "It's all right, Rikkadar. My mother kept hers, too. Many people did. Captain, you'll have your own copy shortly."

"What about the Krann?" Jemmagar said, his voice dripping with sarcasm. "Supply these people with all the illegal religious documents you care to, by all means, but first I want to know about the Krann."

Picard calmed himself. "Once again, Minister Jemmagar," he said, "we don't know anything about any Krann."

"Really?" Jemmagar continued. "You sailed through our entire solar system without seeing any Krann? You, who were able to detect three brief radiation blips from nearly a million billion kilometers away?"

"We saw no Krann," Picard said again. "We saw no one."

Jemmagar turned to Kerajem. "First Among Equals, it's time we ended this farce. Show him."

Kerajem paused in thought for a long moment. "Captain Picard," he finally said, "I suspect you might not have been entirely forthcoming with us. I must tell you that I'm disappointed. I'd hoped for much more from you."

"Kerajem, I assure you—"

"Never mind," the First Among Equals said, holding up a hand. He addressed the air. "Raise the cover panel," he called, and the wall behind Picard and the others began to slide smoothly into the ceiling.

"About time," Jemmagar said under his breath.

Every one of Worf's senses was at full alert. The Klingon, unarmed as everyone in the landing party was, had every intention of ordering an emergency beam-up should the Lethanta try anything. The sudden light touch of Troi's hand on his arm startled him.

"We are in no danger from them," she whispered to him. "They are apprehensive and angry, but nothing more."

Worf gave her a small nod. Nevertheless, he held himself in readiness.

The wall slid fully up into the ceiling to reveal a large mirror about three meters tall and five meters wide. "Opaque," Kerajem called, and the mirror went dead black from end to end.

"Project real-time correlated view from all sentinel probes," Kerajem called, and an image swam slowly onto the black surface. It was a starfield, an unusually dense one.

No. It *looked* like a starfield, but there were too many stars. Far too many.

"That is a 360-degree view of the Krann fleet, Captain," Kerajem said. "As you can see, it surrounds us."

Picard's mouth opened. "A *fleet?* Do you mean to say that each one of those lights is—?"

"A Krann ship, of course," Jemmagar said impatiently. "At our last count, the oncoming Krann fleet consisted of one hundred sixty-three thousand, two hundred forty-seven ships of various sizes and configurations. We estimate that there are more than three billion Krann aboard those ships. Don't play the fool for our benefit, Captain Picard. Surely you knew all this already."

"I see one hundred sixty-three thousand, three hundred ninety-six Krann ships indicated on this display panel, Captain," Data said. "Minister Jemmagar is incorrect."

"Some of those blips are false echoes," Jemmagar grated. "A completely accurate count is impossible. Might our friends from space condescend to allow us a certain margin for error?"

"Uh, thank you, Mr. Data," Picard said distractedly. "Kerajem, you say *these* are Krann ships? But we never saw them!"

The First Among Equals studied Picard for several moments. "I could almost believe that," he almost whispered.

Picard was still looking at the display panel. "On our way here to Government House, Kerajem, my first officer reported to me that we had detected a brief indication of class-M conditions—that is, normal environmental factors—in free space near the orbit of the fifth planet in this system. He was monitoring the situation closely, as the phenomenon could be interpreted to indicate the presence in this system of a known adversary of ours. There was no clue that it could have been anything like—*this.*"

"The leading elements of the Krann fleet are just inside the orbit of Ma'ak Unselbe," Klerran pointed out. "Your ship may well have detected a temporary failure of the camouflage system of one of the Krann vessels. They are rare, but they occur. We've noted them in the course of our monitoring the approach of the Krann."

"You are able to track their ships?" Worf asked. "Their camouflage system, as you call it, is of no consequence to you?"

Klerran shook his head. "It was at first, Lieutenant. We knew they were coming, though, and we kept looking for them in all sorts of ways until we finally found them. We have gotten very good at finding things, you know. We found *you* quickly enough, after all—"

"First Among Equals," came a voice from a hidden loudspeaker. *"There is a priority call from Minister Hattajek at the War Room."*

"Put it through immediately," Kerajem ordered. "Yes, Hattajek. What is it?"

"Kerajem, we are presently tracking two large craft

of unknown type approaching the city at high speed. We are assuming that they are hostile. Estimated time to your position is three minutes."

"I wonder whose they are," Jemmagar muttered, staring at Picard.

"Defense condition one," Kerajem snapped. "How come we didn't spot them sooner, Hattajek?"

"Unknown, First. General Blakendet suggests that they used a new type of camouflage that we were not initially prepared to detect. We spotted them only as they entered our atmosphere and left an ionic trail. We are tracking them closely now."

"Launch interceptor missiles," Kerajem ordered.

"Interceptors launched," came the reply.

Picard's communicator buzzed.

"Enterprise to Picard," Riker said. *"We're tracking two unmanned chemically powered spacecraft of unknown origin. They're leaving a significant ionic trail behind them. The unknowns are flying at an altitude of fifteen thousand three hundred meters at a constant speed of two hundred ninety meters per second, bearing seventy-seven degrees grid north and heading straight for your position. Present distance from you, forty-nine point three kilometers. Estimated time to target, two minutes fifty seconds."*

"Are the unknowns dangerous?" Picard asked.

"We're not reading any explosive materials aboard either of the unknowns, Captain. There are power sources aboard that seem independent of engine configuration, however. Those sources may be part of onboard energy weapons systems. But at that speed, the two unknowns would be able to do considerable damage to the building you're in simply by crashing into it. They need not be carrying warheads."

"Understood. Stand by, Number One. Kerajem," Picard said, "if there's anything we can do to assist you, please let us know."

"Thank you, Captain, but I believe we have this situation well in hand." The First Among Equals addressed the air again. "Hattajek, relay your tactical display of these two unknowns and the approach of our interceptors."

The view of the Krann fleet on the display wall was immediately replaced by a schematic map of the immediate region. The coast was shown as a jagged, glowing green line separating a black land mass on the left side of the map from a light blue ocean that dominated the right. The capital city area was a neatly bounded yellow zone between the coast and the Kajja Kojja mountains to the west. A group of six green streaks was moving rapidly from left to right across the map toward two red squares moving more slowly in the opposite direction.

"Those unknowns are not far off the coast," Picard observed.

"They will not get much farther," Kerajem said. "We are about to—"

The six green streaks suddenly disappeared from the map.

"Kerajem," came Hattajek's voice, *"the interceptors are gone. We've lost all telemetry from them."* There was a brief pause. *"General Blakendet has just launched a second flight. We will try an interception over land."*

Kerajem's voice was calm. "Do you have any idea what happened to the first flight?" he asked.

"No, Kerajem. It seems obvious that the unknowns shot down our interceptors somehow."

Picard's communicator buzzed again.

"Captain," Riker's worried voice reported, *"each of the two unknowns emitted a short, high-frequency energy burst that cleared the sky in front of them as the interceptors were making their final approach. The burst shattered all six interceptors. We're tracking the*

debris. It's crashing into the ocean in a three-kilometer-long path approximately thirty-five kilometers east of you."

"Stand by, Will." Picard looked at the schematic map. He and everyone else in the room watched for a minute as a flight of more than a dozen interceptors launched from near the capital headed toward the red squares.

"It looks as if they will meet not far from here," Picard observed.

"Eight point seven kilometers east of here, sir," Data said. "However, my estimate may be off by a minor amount if this schematic is not to consistent scale."

The dozen interceptors drew very close to the unknowns and then disappeared from the map, just as the first flight had.

"Riker to Picard. They've just done it again. All twelve interceptors in the second flight are gone, and we're tracking debris."

"The unknowns will arrive at these coordinates in thirty seconds," Data said.

"We're dead," Jemmagar said simply.

Kerajem turned to Picard as the red squares crossed over the boundary of the yellow zone that represented the capital city area. "Captain, I am most deeply sorry," the First Among Equals said. "We have no way of stopping those—those things—in time. We've involved you in our troubles, and now it seems you're to suffer for it."

Picard said nothing. He kept his face carefully blank.

"Unless—unless you can do something about this. Can you?"

"Yes."

Kerajem seemed a little dazed. "Then please do so."

"Number One," Picard said, "lock on to and destroy those unknowns."

"Aye, sir. Phasers armed and locked. Firing phasers."

The red squares disappeared from the map as a blinding greenish white light burst through the windows.

"Kerajem?" came Hattajek's voice. *"What just happened? We've lost the unknowns. We suddenly had a very high energy reading, and now we're not even reading debris. They're just—gone. Uh, final range from Government House, five point eight kilometers."*

The First Among Equals was still blinking. "The problem has been taken care of," he told the defense minister.

"Eh?"

"We have some friends upstairs," Kerajem said. "Take us down to defense condition two, Hattajek."

"Yes, First. War Room out."

Kerajem turned to address Picard. "Captain, it seems you've saved our lives. On behalf of the Council, I thank you."

There was a murmur of agreement.

"I wonder," Picard asked, "why the unknown craft were not detected before they entered your atmosphere, however."

"I would like an answer to that myself," Klerran said. "I believe I will get on the communication links straight away and ask the people who are paid to know such things."

"It seems likely that these unknown spacecraft were probes launched by the Krann to test your defenses, Kerajem," Data said.

The First Among Equals nodded. "They proved that our defenses are not as good as we thought they were," he said. "We were lucky, thanks to you."

"Captain," Worf said, "obviously the Krann are

using a cloaking device that operates in ways unfamiliar to us. It appears that not even the Lethanta know everything there is to know about the camouflage system developed by the Krann. I suggest we become familiar with the camouflage system as quickly as possible."

Security Minister Jemmagar had a practiced look of disinterest. "I think," he said, "that we have been gulled by these people long enough. Now they want us to give them the greatest secret of our counterintelligence operation." Jemmagar laughed without humor. "I admire the sheer gall of it, Captain. I'm curious. Just which of the Krann ships did you command before the fleet constructed that sham currently in orbit above us?"

"What?" Picard was taken aback.

"You were in charge of the flagship, I'll bet," Jemmagar said. "You have a certain style about you, I'll admit that."

"Jemmagar, mind yourself!" Kerajem barked.

"I'm doing my job!" Jemmagar shot back. "We first detect this *Enterprise* inside the orbit of Ma'ak Unselbe a mere hundred million kilometers ahead of the leading edge of the Krann fleet. It was traveling at a quarter of the speed of light. That's fast, but not impossibly fast, and not hard to achieve if you've got the energy budget. Call it two gravities of acceleration applied for a period of, oh, about six weeks—"

"Ridiculous," Picard said. "You are mistaken."

"—from a distance of about a hundred and thirty billion kilometers. Quite a ways out, Captain, and a fast, uncomfortable ride sunward to boot." He was sneering now. "You and your people must be pretty tired. You *look* a bit tired to me, you know."

"Minister Jemmagar," Kerajem said sharply, "control yourself. These are our guests."

The security minister paid no attention to him.

"You people must have been working on this little fraud for quite some time, constructing that so-called starship of yours," he continued. "It took the Krann fleet quite a while to get from that point to where it is now. Why, you almost didn't make it to our world in time, did you? The vanguard of your fleet almost beat you here."

"I don't know what you're talking about," Picard said icily.

"Certainly you do," the security minister responded. "We've been able to read incredible energy reserves aboard your vessel—more than enough to provide constant boost for an indefinite period. You might even have been able to get here much faster than I think, since you decelerated so quickly once you reached orbit. I'd even venture to guess that you've come up with some way to negate the effects of acceleration and inertia. We'd be very interested in obtaining something like that for ourselves, you know."

"This has gone far enough," Picard said, rising, and the other *Enterprise* officers stood with him. "Perhaps we should recess, let things calm down a bit. My colleagues and I will be leaving immediately."

"Please, Captain—" Kerajem said. "Jemmagar, this is outrageous! These people are not Krann, you idiot!"

"I believe they are," Jemmagar said, "and none of them is leaving just yet. I have the building under a security alert." The doors to the room opened, and a squad of armed guards entered. "Guards, make these four comfortable. They will be staying with us for a while."

"On the contrary," Worf said, tapping his communicator. "Transporter. Emergency beam up."

"We'll pick up the shuttlecraft later," came Picard's voice as he and his officers faded away.

The ministers and guards gaped at the empty space where Picard and the others had been standing.

"You surely can clear a room, Jemmagar," Rikkadar said.

"But—but—" the security minister stammered.

"Jemmagar, you screaming idiot," Kerajem said, suddenly very weary. He rubbed his eyes with thumb and forefinger. "Those people are our only hope. You may have doomed us. I'd fire you, you complete jackass, if there were enough time left to make firing you worthwhile."

Presider Hek was sitting at the small desk in his working quarters, waiting for the results of the initial probe by the high-speed attack drones. He had finished his lunch, a pretty good one, and shoved the plates and utensils into the reclaimer. Now he was just sitting there, waiting. For once, he was leaving his military people to themselves.

Fleet tacticians were fairly sure that at least one of the probes would get through, and Hek would be content with that. While the object of the exercise was to see what ground defenses the Lethanta might be able to bring to bear to destroy a determined attacking spacecraft, the destruction of their political headquarters would be a strategic bonus.

And he had thousands of drones. Thousands of them.

Hek had waited his entire life for the coming struggle. Every one of his ancestors had lived their lives and died their deaths to bring Hek and the Krann to this point. His people had missed a chance thousands of years before to eradicate the Lethanta from the universe, but Hek would not permit that to happen again.

His ancestors cried out in their deaths for the completion of vengeance. Hek would not fail them.

The door signal rang. "Enter," Hek called.

It was Graff Starboard Water Line Tester, his military attaché. The look on Graff's face fairly shouted that the news he had to tell Hek was not good.

"You look troubled, Graff," Hek said, carefully keeping the disappointment out of his voice. "I take it that things went poorly."

"Presider, I regret to report that both of our drones were destroyed just short of their target."

"Both? What happened?"

"The drones became detectable by the enemy upon their entry into the atmosphere of Nem Ma'ak Bratuna, and the Lethanta went to full military alert immediately upon seeing them."

"We'll have to have a little talk with the research and development people about that," Hek said. "We knew that the secret of our present concealment apparatus was probably compromised. I was told the new version of the apparatus would render a concealed craft completely undetectable."

"Yes, Presider," Graff said, nodding quickly. "It was an unexpected result, perhaps due to our inability to properly test the new apparatus in an atmosphere—"

"Never mind that now," the Presider said, waving a hand impatiently. "What about the destruction of the drones? What did the enemy use to do it?"

"As nearly as we can tell, a phased energy weapon of some sort was used to cause the constituent molecules of the drones to dissociate. In other words, they were vaporized."

"And we didn't realize they had anything like that," Hek said.

"No, Presider," Graff said. "They do not have such weapons at all. The phased energy weapon that was used was not fired by the Lethanta—"

"—but by the alien ship in orbit around their

world," Hek finished for him. "Of course. The aliens have become involved on the side of the Lethanta." Hek chuckled, a sound that sent a shiver up his attaché's spine. "We'll have to delay further action until we can sort this matter out." He smiled a dangerous smile. "This gets more interesting by the minute, doesn't it, Graff?"

"Perhaps, Presider, the aliens were operating out of self-interest," Graff pointed out. "We already know from our monitoring of their communications that alien representatives were to meet with the leaders of the planetary government at about the time the drones were due to arrive. The aliens may have destroyed the drones simply to save themselves."

The Presider looked at him in that intimidating manner he so often used on his subordinates. Graff stood his ground, trying to appear more calm than he felt. The Presider's last two attachés had disappeared after short terms of service, never to be seen again. Everyone in the officer corps believed the attachés had gone through that special door in the star chamber, the recently installed air lock to nowhere that the officers called Hek's Closet.

"All right," Hek finally said, frowning harshly. "I'll admit the timing fits, Graff. You could be right. Damn, what a dismal turn of events. We would have had the Lethantan leadership cold if only we'd launched the drones a bit earlier. Whose fault do you think it was?"

"There is no blame to be assigned here, Presider," Graff said. "The alien ship had not even entered this star system when we launched the drones several weeks ago. The transit time to target was considerable at this distance, even for a high-velocity drone. The timing of the launch was based on the position of the fleet relative to Nem Ma'ak Bratuna and the tactical need for the drones to arrive during the workday, to enhance our chances of catching the members of the leadership inside the building."

"I didn't ask you that, Graff," Hek said coldly. "I asked you whose fault you thought this disaster was."

"I, uh, I will begin investigating the matter immediately, Presider."

"Do that," Hek said abruptly. "The High Council will want to know. I'll expect your report on this desk by the dinner hour." He pointed at the door. "Go."

As Graff left the room, he wondered which of his friends in the officer corps he would sell out this time. The list of Graff's sacrificial offerings to the need of Presider Hek to punish simple bad luck was becoming a rather long one.

Chapter Seven

THE BRIDGE WAS QUIET, as it usually was before everything was about to happen. Picard thought of the bridge as being in "calm before storm" mode.

The contact team had been back for about an hour. Upon their return to the *Enterprise*, Picard had ordered a shuttle pilot beamed directly into *Justman*, which had then been flown back to the *Enterprise* without incident. The captain had spent the time since then sitting comfortably in his chair on the bridge, sipping at a cup of tea, and waiting for the Lethanta to call him. If they did not, he would have no choice but to leave them to themselves.

"I believe it will be all right, Captain," Troi said. As usual, she was sitting to his left, a quiet presence that steadied him. "They need us, and they know it."

"I'm not worried about that, Counselor," Picard said, "but we're losing time. I wonder how Geordi and Data are doing—"

"La Forge to Captain Picard," came Geordi's voice.

"Ah. Yes, Mr. La Forge?"

"If you'll take a look at the main viewscreen, Captain, I think you'll see that we've defeated the Krann cloaking device."

Picard nodded to himself as thousands of bright specks began to appear on screen. "Thank you, Mr. La Forge."

"Incredible," Riker breathed. "You told me about this, Captain, but seeing it is something else entirely. There seems to be a million of them."

Ro glanced over at the Ops panel. "Only a little over a hundred and sixty-three thousand, sir," she reported.

"I stand corrected, Ensign," said Riker. "That's *much* better."

"Data and I have refined the tachyon sweep routine of the main sensor array to defeat whatever it is the Krann are doing to hide themselves," La Forge continued. *"This should work for any expectable cloaking configuration the Krann manage to come up with for their probes, their manned ships, whatever. We figured that since the Krann don't have faster-than-light drive or communications, they wouldn't know enough about tachyons to be able to hide theirs from us."*

"Well done, both of you," Picard said. "Mr. Data, when you're finished down there, please return to the bridge."

"Aye, sir."

Picard turned to Troi. "Now all we do is wait for a call," he said. "I don't believe Kerajem will wait much longer, if he's going to call us at all."

"Captain," Worf said, "I am now able to display a visual of the lead Krann ships. They have come close enough now to be visible under full magnification."

"Excellent," Picard said. "Let's see them."

The view of the Krann armada disappeared and

was replaced by a visual of a single ship. "This is full magnification, sir," Worf said.

The ship was a vast, spindly looking cage, inside of which were contained a large number of spinning spheres of various sizes. Each sphere was rotating on an axis attached to the cage. There was an array of conical shapes on the sunward side of the cage.

"It looks like a bunch of big balloons caught in a net," Riker said.

"A clockwork starship," Picard said. "Incredible. Each sphere must represent an independent environment."

"Why are they spinning?" Troi wondered.

"Artificial gravity, I should think," said the captain. "It's an old idea. The acceleration of spin on the inside surface of each sphere would substitute nicely for a gravity field."

"This ship is fifteen to twenty times larger than we are," Worf reported, "and it is the largest ship I can detect. Those conelike objects to sunward appear to be engine outlets. They are putting out large streams of hot ions. That must be how they decelerate, Captain."

"The outlets are up front?" Troi asked.

"That's where you'd expect to see them on a ship of this type during deceleration, Counselor," Picard said. "The outlets would be opposite the direction of flight."

"I can see what must be radiative fins here and there," Riker commented. "There are a good many of them. They must carry internal heat away from the core of the ship and allow it to leak very slowly into vacuum. All the heat is wasted to space. This suggests that the Krann can't do anything about entropy except to succumb to it. I've seen designs like this— ancient ones that were drawn up before the development of warp drive. It was back when the old Earth nations were contemplating sending colony ships to the star systems nearest Sol. They came up with kludges like this one."

"The hull seems to be festooned with gadgets," Troi said. "Those over there look very much like sensor dishes."

"I'll bet that's just what they are," Riker said. "The sensor dish is about as basic a design as you can get. Related designs go all the way back to the nineteenth century on Earth. Mr. Worf, let's see some other ships."

"Aye, sir," the Klingon replied. The view shifted, and three smaller Krann vessels appeared on screen.

"The same thing," Troi observed, "only smaller. Fewer spheres inside the cages."

"There are much smaller ships as well," Worf told them. He worked the Tactical panel for a moment, and the scene changed yet again. Now framed in the center of the screen was a small, boxy spacecraft that looked not unlike a Starfleet shuttlecraft of the previous century. "This one appears to be a personnel transport vessel, Captain—small, chemically powered, not much in the way of energy reserves, and no detectable weaponry. I'm reading a complement of seven aboard, and all bear the same life signs. With your permission, Captain, I will provisionally log these readings as representative of the Krann race, and I will add them to our database."

"Make it so," Picard said, "and put the long-range view back on screen. Ro, how far are the lead Krann vessels from Nem Ma'ak Bratuna?"

"I'm sorting the forward vessels out, sir—ah. The lead wave of the Krann fleet is presently located eight hundred million kilometers from standard orbit at Nem Ma'ak Bratuna. That's just outside the orbit of the fifth planet in this system, sir. These leading elements of the Krann fleet are presently traveling at a speed of just under four thousand kilometers per second and are decelerating under power at a constant one gravity of boost. They will arrive at Nem Ma'ak Bratuna in four days, sixteen hours. Elements of the fleet toward the rear seem to be changing course and speed, however."

"Where are they going?" Picard asked. "Worf?"

"They are forming an attack pattern, sir, to center on Nem Ma'ak Bratuna," the Klingon replied. "It is similar to the classic Brunckhorst pincer movement, but the Krann are going about forming the pincer very slowly."

"Well, that makes their motives clear," Picard observed. "That pattern is in no way defensive."

"What we're seeing strongly suggests that the Krann are constrained by classical Newtonian physics," Riker said. "The Krann can't just wheel around, change course, and accelerate any which way. Their technology just isn't up to it. They're slaves to the laws of motion and thermodynamics. That gives us a decided advantage."

"I wonder, really, how much of an advantage our technology *does* give us," Picard mused. "It seems to me—"

"Captain," Worf interrupted, "the head of the Lethantan government is hailing us."

Picard winked at Troi. "On audio, Mr. Worf," he said. "Yes, First Among Equals?" Picard's tone was purposefully cold.

The speed-of-light delay from ground to orbit was negligible. *"Captain Picard,"* Kerajem began, *"on behalf of my entire government, please let me apologize for the conduct of our security minister. He has been severely reprimanded by myself and the council for his precipitous actions and accusations, none of which were authorized by us or even known to us before he made them. We beg your forgiveness for this serious breach of diplomacy, Captain. Let me assure you that this is not the way we usually treat our friends."*

Picard signaled to Worf to cut the audio. "What do you think, Counselor?" the captain asked Troi.

"He's sincere," the counselor allowed. "He's also very worried. I think he's telling the truth. The altercation with the security minister was not planned."

"I knew he was telling the truth," Picard said. "Nevertheless, the incident with Jemmagar shows that Kerajem has a certain lack of control over his subordinates. I'm reluctant to send a contact team again if I don't have to. The situation is still unstable."

"Sir?" Riker interrupted. "We could meet with them here aboard the ship."

"Exactly what I was thinking," Picard said. "Put the First Among Equals back on, Mr. Worf."

"On audio, sir."

"Ah, there you are, Captain," came Kerajem's voice. He sounded relieved. *"I was afraid we'd lost you."*

"Not at all, Kerajem. I accept your apology. I'd like nothing better than to put this unpleasantness behind us."

"Most generous of you and your people, Captain. I and the council thank you most sincerely. So, what next?"

"I would like to propose that our second meeting take place here, aboard the *Enterprise.* We will furnish transportation and facilities. You may, of course, bring along as many ministers of the council and their staff people and assistants as you require. My first officer, Commander William Riker, will personally handle the arrangements with your people."

The First Among Equals hardly hesitated. *"Excellent, Captain Picard. We're pleased to accept your invitation. I look forward to meeting Commander Riker. I and a subcommittee of the council will be there at your earliest convenience."*

"Very well," Picard said. "Commander Riker will be calling you shortly. I look forward to seeing you again, Kerajem. Picard out." The captain turned to the first officer. "I want the Lethanta up here as soon as courtesy permits, Will. We still don't have answers to our questions. There's a great deal we need to know before—"

"Before what, sir?" Riker asked.

With a nod of his head, Picard indicated the thousands and thousands of lights that dotted the main screen. "Before we have to deal with *them.*"

Picard, Riker, Troi, and Worf were waiting as Kerajem and four members of the Council of Ministers materialized on the chamber platform in transporter room two.

"Welcome aboard the *Enterprise,*" Picard said.

"Thank you, Captain," Kerajem said, looking around him. "An amazing experience, to say the least." The ministers with him were working hard to maintain their sang-froid, but they were not doing very well. They had seen the Federation officers beam away, but that was a far cry from experiencing it themselves.

"Is this how you managed to get your shuttlecraft back from the spaceport, Captain?" Klerran asked. "Did you perhaps place a pilot directly inside it? We'd assumed you'd flown it back by some sort of remote control."

"That's not really important," Picard said smoothly. "Commander William Riker, allow me to introduce you to Kerajem zan Trikotta, First Among Equals of the Council of Ministers of Nem Ma'ak Bratuna; Presinget fes Kwaita, the minister for labor;

Klerran fes Dresnai, the minister for science and education; and Rikkadar zan Therrka, the finance minister. Gentlemen, Commander Riker is the first officer of this vessel and my second-in-command. He'll get you settled."

How does *he remember all those names?* Riker wondered as he extended his hand. "I am very pleased to meet you all," the first officer said in his best company manner. "We have guest quarters ready for each of you. We thought you might want to refresh yourselves after your trip."

"Trip?" Klerran said, a bit bewildered. "That was a trip? I still don't believe we went anywhere."

"Did our staff people get here all right?" Rikkadar asked.

"The other members of your party beamed aboard several minutes ago and have already been escorted to their guest quarters," Picard told them.

Presinget looked around him. "I'd like to see those quarters you mentioned, Commander," he said gruffly. "If this transporter gadget is how you people get around, then the bathrooms around here must be something terrific."

"We're rather proud of everything aboard," Picard said agreeably. "I thought we might begin our next meeting in, say, half an hour, if that's all right with you."

"That will be fine, Captain," Kerajem answered for all of them.

"Excellent. We'll send someone to escort you to our observation lounge at that time. I think you'll appreciate the view."

"If you'll follow me, gentlemen?" Riker called as the door to the transporter room slid aside. He gestured them through the doorway and onto the gangway of Deck 6. Kerajem and the ministers moved out slowly, looking from left to right and all around as they moved through the exit, even though there was not yet much for them to see. With a last, resigned glance at Picard, Riker followed the Lethantans out of the transporter room, and the doors slid closed behind him.

"This is always Will's favorite part," Troi said.

"Don't I know it," Picard replied, not without humor. "One of the better things about being captain is that you can assign these kinds of jobs to others."

"Sir," Worf said, "with your permission, I will return to the observation lounge and complete preparations for our meeting with the Council of Ministers."

"How is the hospitality team doing?" Troi asked.

Worf frowned. "The team is having trouble resetting the replicators to duplicate the food and refreshment items Kerajem's assistants sent us in preparation for the council's arrival. They have not had much time to do so."

"Perhaps they'll like chocolate," the counselor ventured half seriously.

"I will suggest it to them, Counselor," Worf said tightly. "They may have to live on it while they are here. Captain, if you will excuse me—?"

"Of course, Lieutenant." The door opened for the Klingon and slid closed again after he passed quickly through the entrance.

"We'd better get going ourselves," Picard said to Troi. "That meeting starts in less than thirty minutes—and this time we shan't be interrupted. I mean to find out exactly what's been going on around here, and without any further delay."

"—and it took me about five minutes to figure out the damn thing, but I finally did," a slightly out-of-breath Presinget whispered to Klerran. They, along with Rikkadar, were sitting on one side of the conference table in the observation lounge, waiting for Kerajem and Picard to appear. "I'm just glad I managed to get here before the First did."

"So what did you do?" Klerran asked him.

"All I did was say the world *flush* out loud, as though it could hear me and do what I wanted it to, and it worked. Uh, what's the matter, Klerran? You look as if something's bothering you."

"Oh, nothing," the science minister replied. "I was just thinking that the sooner I got back to my quarters, the better."

"I'd just as soon get home to plumbing I can trust," the labor minister groused. He turned in his chair to look out the lounge windows. Nem Ma'ak Bratuna shone green, its clouds glaring white. A thin, hazy envelope of atmosphere softened the curvature of the planet.

"Sure is pretty," Presinget said. "The pictures don't do it justice. I never thought I'd get to see it for myself. Only pretty-boy Space Force types ever got to go into space, when I was younger."

"It's absolutely beautiful," Klerran agreed. "I hope we can keep it that way."

"We'll try real hard, old friend. Right, Rik?"

"Eh? What's that, Presinget?" Rikkadar asked, startled. "I'm afraid I was wool-gathering. Happens a lot at my age."

"You were dreaming about that cute lady sitting over there, that's what you were doing," Presinget leered. He indicated Deanna Troi with a twitch of his tangled brow. The counselor was sitting on the other side of the table with Riker, Worf, and Data.

Old Rikkadar smiled. "No, actually I was thinking about how lucky I am."

"Lucky?" Klerran asked. "Even now?"

"Even now," Rikkadar replied, nodding. "I began

my life as a boy working down in the mines, and here I am—nearly at the end of it, no matter what happens—an old man flying among the stars. I suppose I was waxing philosophical about it all, and feeling myself a very fortunate person indeed, despite everything." He suddenly grinned. "Sorry. Won't happen again, I promise. Oh—I think someone's coming."

The door to the observation lounge slid open as Captain Picard and Kerajem entered the room together. Everyone stood.

"Please be seated, all of you," Picard said, taking the center seat on the *Enterprise* side of the table. "Let's begin."

"Yes, let us make a fresh start," Kerajem said, taking the chair opposite Picard's. "The first order of business, Captain, is this." The First Among Equals handed Picard a Lethantan data cube, a bright, shiny box about ten centimeters on a side. One face bore some simple controls. "It is a copy of the ancient writings you were curious about, along with a self-contained apparatus with which to read them," Kerajem continued. "We chose this form instead of providing you with a printed copy, as the actual scrolls run the equivalent of several hundred modern volumes."

"I'll look at the contents of this cube later today," Picard said as he set the device on the table. "Many thanks for your courtesy in providing this to us, Kerajem. I know it will be very helpful. Please, now, let's discuss your situation with the Krann."

"Certainly," Kerajem said. "What would you like to know?"

"Everything you would care to tell us about your people, and about your conflict with the Krann."

Kerajem folded his hands together in front of him

and looked at them. "I'm afraid our history is not a proud one in some respects," he began after a moment. "At times, it has been rather dark. One of the most terrible periods in our history concerns the Krann."

"We were once an empire, Captain," Klerran said. "We were limited to one star system and two planets, but we were an empire nonetheless. It was our native star, Ma'ak Terrella, the sun under which our race evolved—the star that you visited before you came here."

"There were two habitable planets circling that star, the third and fourth out from the sun," Kerajem continued. "We lived on the third planet, Eul Ma'ak Lethantana. The fourth, Ma'ak Krannag, was inhabited by the Krann."

"Some think we and the Krann are of the same race," Klerran said, "and that we were separated from one another in antiquity."

"We know very little about the Krann, actually," said Rikkadar. "We don't even know exactly what they look like."

"You don't?" Riker asked, surprised.

"That is not unreasonable, Commander," Data said. "The Lethanta need never have met or even seen any of the Krann to be on the brink of war with them. Recall the conflict between the Romulan Empire and the Federation approximately two hundred years ago."

Kerajem continued. "As I was saying, we don't know much about the Krann—except that the ancient writings say they are not unlike us."

"Humanoid, you mean?" Riker asked.

"If that's the term for it, then, yes, Commander," Kerajem said with a small smile. "Many of us do think the Krann are humanoid. Before today, I would have said something like 'They probably look a lot like people.' I have trouble thinking of myself as a 'humanoid.'"

"Kerajem, you mentioned that the Krann represented a terrible period in your history," Picard asked. "What did you mean by that, and does it have anything to do with what's going on out there now?"

"I'm afraid it does," Kerajem said heavily. "Our people went into space in the normal course of things, and one of our first objectives was to explore and colonize the fourth planet in our home system. That was Ma'ak Krannag. We planned to exploit its resources as fully as possible, as our own were rapidly becoming depleted. When we got to Ma'ak Krannag, we discovered the Krann, who lived in tribes scattered all over the surface of their world. The most advanced of these tribes had just developed agriculture. They were no match for us."

The First Among Equals paused, clearly uncomfortable with what he was about to say. "We enslaved the Krann, Captain," Kerajem said, staring at the tabletop, unwilling to meet Picard's eyes. "We took everything they had. We stripped their resources from them. Over the following centuries, we poisoned their air and water and food with the runoff from the industries we had relocated to Ma'ak Krannag to keep our own world pristine. We even gave the Krann a religion and forced them to worship us as gods. We worked them to death and made them sing our praises for it. We slaughtered the ones who were of no use to us—the sick, the old, the ones who could not or would not work."

"It went on for centuries," Rikkadar said softly, his eyes watering. "Centuries."

"When did all this occur?" Worf asked.

"As nearly as we can tell, we first landed on Ma'ak Krannag about seven thousand years ago," replied the First Among Equals.

"How long did your occupation of Ma'ak Krannag go on?" Riker asked, tight-lipped.

"We think it lasted for just under a thousand years," Presinget said. "It could not have been much longer than that."

"What happened to end it?" Troi asked.

"There was a revolt," Rikkadar answered. "The Krann rose up almost as one and drove us out. They'd had a millennium to learn our weapons, our ways, our tactics, our weaknesses, and they'd learned them well. They'd had a thousand years to educate themselves in our ways and come up with effective means to fight and defeat us."

"How did the rebellion occur?" asked Picard.

"There were many more of them than there were of us on Ma'ak Krannag, of course," Kerajem said, "since ours was only an occupying force bent on control and exploitation. We were only tens of thousands to their billions. They rose up one night, each with a knife, and slaughtered every Lethanta they found—men, women, children, it made no difference. Obedient housemaids slaughtered families. Dedicated nurses killed their patients. Faithful workers murdered their overlords. It came to be called the Night of Blood."

"What did the government on Eul Ma'ak Lethantana do in response?" Picard asked.

"There was not much to be done," Presinget answered. "By the time the government found out what was going on, our occupation forces had been effectively destroyed, and our facilities and industries on Ma'ak Krannag had been taken over. The Krann were in control of their own world for the first time in some ten centuries."

"The revolt wound up costing many more Krann lives than Lethanta," Kerajem added, "but in the end, the Krann won, and they kept their victory. During the following few years, we sent police forces and then entire armies to Ma'ak Krannag in repeated attempts to reestablish our control over the planet, but it was all for naught. The Krann fought us off and, using our own captured ships, carried the war to Eul Ma'ak Lethantana."

"Did you seek peace?" Troi asked. "Did you finally come to terms?"

"We did," Kerajem said. "Our economy was in ruins following our loss of the labor and facilities on Ma'ak Krannag, and the ensuing war drained us even further. Peace was in our best interests, even if the settlement did not especially favor us. We agreed to recognize the Krann as sovereign on Ma'ak Krannag and pay heavy reparations for our past exploitation of their world and their people. They smiled and signed the treaty, and we got along well enough for a century or two, at the end of which time they attacked us in force."

"The Krann could not get over their hatred of you," Riker observed. "Revenge is a powerful motive."

"Your continued presence threatened them," Worf guessed. "Your star system was not big enough for both peoples."

"We think it was a little bit of both," Kerajem replied. "Revenge and fear make a deadly mix. Whatever the motive behind it, the final attack devastated our world. The Krann had developed weapons designed to eradicate all life on our planet by sterilizing it with radiation. All of Eul Ma'ak Lethantana must have been dead within a week of the Krann bombardment."

Picard held up a hand. "Yet you are here. You and your people live."

"We do indeed," Kerajem said, not without pride.

"At the time of the attack, our people were mounting our first deep-space colonizing mission. The only other habitable world in the Ma'ak Terrella system was Ma'ak Krannag, and we surely weren't welcome *there*. We needed to go to the stars."

"Without warp drive?" Riker asked.

Kerajem nodded. "We lacked the ability to travel faster than light as you people do, but our population was increasing while our resources were diminishing. We had to do something to relieve the population pressure on our world. One plan involved building independent space-faring colonies inside hollowed-out asteroids. These asteroid ships were designed to sustain succeeding generations of colonists bound for the stars."

"Hollow asteroids?" Troi wondered. "Wait a moment. I think I've heard of this."

"So have I," Picard said, nodding. "Many civilizations have briefly considered using such asteroid ships for one-way interstellar journeys, but by the time these cultures go about actually planning such ships, they either stumble across the secret of faster-than-light travel, or they become decadent and lose interest in interstellar travel altogether."

"There is at least one exception, sir," Data pointed out. "Consider the asteroid ship *Yonada*—"

"Thank you again, Mr. Data," Picard interrupted. "What happened, Kerajem?"

"All we know is that the colony ships were launched some months before the ultimate crisis came for Eul Ma'ak Lethantana and Ma'ak Krannag," the First Among Equals replied. "Perhaps someone in power saw the attack coming and tried to make sure that some of our people would survive. A story is told about the captain of one of the colony ships who looked back not very long after the launch, from many millions of miles away, to see Eul Ma'ak Lethantana suddenly glow with a fierce light of its own. Our homeworld is supposed to have died at that moment." Kerajem paused. "Now we know what that captain might have been seeing. In any case, the story of the death of our homeworld and how it happened was brought to the asteroid ships by a handful of survivors who had managed to escape Eul Ma'ak Lethantana in high-boost conventional ships."

"Didn't the Krann chase the asteroid ships?" Riker asked.

"We think they would have if they could," Presinget said. "Either they didn't have ships with sufficient range to pursue our people, or they couldn't find the asteroid ships to destroy them." The labor minister laughed without humor. "The ships looked like asteroids, after all. Hard to sort them out from real ones."

"How long did it take you to arrive in this star system?" Picard asked.

"The religious scrolls say only that we were in transit for 'years upon years,'" said Klerran. "We think our people were on their way here for something like two thousand years."

"My word," Troi said.

"A flight time of approximately two thousand years for an eighty-seven light-year trip, given the level of technology one would assume for the culture on Eul Ma'ak Lethantana at the time of departure, is not unreasonable," Data said.

"And you were there just a day or two ago," Klerran said, shaking his head in disbelief.

"Another question, Kerajem," Picard said. "I believe you mentioned something about a theocracy having been overthrown by a revolution—a rather recent one, if I understood correctly."

Kerajem looked at his hands again. "Yes, Captain," he replied. "When our people finally arrived on Nem Ma'ak Bratuna after their long journey, they fell almost immediately into barbarism. The rigid civilization that had preserved us and our ways inside the asteroid ships could not be sustained after we made landfall. We had lived with great discipline and self-control for two millennia. That was more than long enough."

"It was a bloody, brutal time," Klerran said. "The historical records of our people before their escape from Eul Ma'ak Lethantana are sketchy to nonexistent, but the record of our life *here* is fairly complete. We entered a long, dark age, losing our technology along with our civilization."

"We spent centuries conquering each other, killing each other, and losing whatever it was that made us Lethanta, a united people," Rikkadar said. "Then came the monks. That was about twelve hundred years ago."

"Monks?" Troi asked, a little puzzled.

"The monks," Rikkadar said. "They were few at first, but they went about preaching peace, love, and tolerance to the warring tribes. Many of them were killed for their pains, but enough lived to spread what they called the Word of Reconciliation to most of the world. Over the course of time, things began to calm down, and real societies began to form. The monks gradually came into power because, once we had a civilization again, someone had to run it. The monks were the only people that everyone would listen to."

"They eventually formed the theocracy you mentioned," Picard observed. "What went wrong?"

"The theocracy lasted a very long time," Kerajem said, his mouth a tight line. "It wound up making slaves of us. About six centuries ago, the leadership of the monks was taken with the notion that our new world must prepare for an eventual assault by our old enemy, the Krann."

"But is that not what has happened?" Worf asked.

"This was not a rational plan, Lieutenant. This was theology gone awry, religious ritual run amok. The monks had no more idea who the Krann were, or what they could do, than we did."

"Like building tanks to fight the Devil," Riker said.

"Eh?" Kerajem was puzzled. "Well, if you say so, Commander. We 'built tanks to fight the Devil' for some five and a half centuries. The entire effort of all our people was bent toward preparing for an assault by unknown forces from no one knew where. Generations of our children were raised with the notion that they could be killed by invading Krann at any time, any place. All of our people, young and old alike, were put to work in war-related industries—and *all* industries were war-related, in one way or another. Six hundred years ago that meant making candles and gunpowder and digging in the mines. More recently it meant building fighter aerocraft—and the mines were *still* there. I was down in the mines myself, as a boy."

Kerajem held up his hands for the *Enterprise* party to see, spreading his fingers and the stumps of his fingers. "I've caught all of you glancing at my hands from time to time," he said. "My guess is that you don't often encounter people with these kinds of injuries."

"Kerajem," Picard said, "we apologize deeply if we have given you any offense."

"There is no need for that, Captain," Kerajem said kindly. "I only wanted to make the point that age was no bar to dangerous work when I was young. By the time I was twelve, I'd lost four fingers and a dozen of my friends in the mines. I swore to do all I could to end that, to make it impossible to work children to death."

"He became a subversive," Rikkadar said, smiling. "I knew him then. I was a subversive, too. The monks tried very hard to catch us at it, let me tell you."

"But they never did," Picard hazarded. "There was a revolution, you said."

"Yes, there was," Kerajem said, "and Rikkadar and I helped lead it. So did Presinget. Klerran was one of our lieutenants. The theocracy tumbled very quickly, with little loss of life—on our side."

"We killed a lot of monks," Presinget said unsympathetically. "Too bad."

"We established a free government and set about instituting social reforms," Kerajem continued. "One of the first reforms we carried out was to end the constant, ceaseless preparations for the invasion of the Krann—an event we did not believe would ever happen." The First Among Equals paused. "That was all a little over forty years ago. Thirty-three years ago, we heard the first signals from space. They were from the Krann."

"They'd found us," Klerran said in low tones. "They said they had been pursuing us for six thousand years, and they promised our complete destruction. They swore that none of us would escape this time. In response, we initiated a rapid defense buildup—not the superstitious preparations against bogeymen carried on by the monks as a matter of ritual, but a carefully planned program to meet a very real threat from the actual Krann."

"Shortly after the Krann announced their presence," Kerajem said, "we found a way to disguise our broadcast signals so that they could not be studied by the Krann. We've maintained that security for a generation. We don't believe the Krann know much about us, or how we intend to resist them."

"You say that the Krann race has been on its way here for fully six thousand years?" Picard asked.

"Yes," Kerajem replied.

"It seems incredible," said Troi. "How could an entire race of people stay so angry for so long? And why?"

"It does not seem to me that your enslavement of the Krann so many millennia ago would explain this . . . this jihad of theirs," Worf observed. "There is something missing from your story."

"Well, why didn't you ask the Krann on Ma'ak Krannag about it yourself?" Presinget sputtered. "I mean, you were just *there*, you said."

"Captain, perhaps we should now discuss our findings concerning Ma'ak Krannag with the Lethanta," Data suggested. "In my opinion, it will not adversely impact their culture."

Picard nodded. "I agree, Mr. Data," he said. "Kerajem, ministers, I must tell you that we found no Krann living on Ma'ak Krannag. They were all gone. They and their culture are dead."

Kerajem blinked. "No one was there? No one at all? Was their world destroyed like ours?"

"No," Picard replied. "Ma'ak Krannag is intact. A specially bred virus killed all the land-based higher life-forms on the planet, including the Krann."

"This virus you speak of was used as a weapon?" Klerran asked.

"It is possible," Data answered. "Your own people may have used the virus on the Krann in retaliation for the destruction of Eul Ma'ak Lethantana. Alternatively, the Krann may have destroyed your homeworld in retaliation for a sneak attack by *you* on *them.*"

"There is one other matter," Picard said, "and that is the matter that originally attracted our attention. We need to know, Kerajem, if your people are working on obtaining the secret of faster-than-light drive."

"No, Captain, we are not."

Klerran leaned forward. "Before you came here, Captain," the science minister said, "we had thought that traveling faster than light was an impossibility. Our entire physics was based on the notion that the speed of light represents an absolute limit."

Picard glanced at Troi, who nodded slightly.

"Kerajem," Picard began after a moment, "we operate under strict rules of conduct that forbid us to interfere with the affairs of others. But if you would wish it, we can initiate negotiations between you and the Krann. The Federation would be glad to act as mediator, should you both agree."

Kerajem closed his eyes for a moment. Picard did not need Deanna to tell him that the First Among Equals was relieved. "Yes, Captain," he said in a soft voice. "Please go ahead and do whatever you need to do to open talks with the Krann. The hopes and good wishes of everyone on our world go with you."

"Amen to that," Rikkadar breathed.

That was good enough for Picard. "I think we should recess these talks for now," Picard said, smiling amiably. "I suggest that our next meeting be held at Government House at a time to be announced. Mr. Worf will have someone escort you back to your quarters before you leave the ship, if you like, or you may go with him directly to the transporter room."

"Can you send me directly to my home, Captain?"

"Surely, Minister Klerran. We can send you wherever you like."

"I've got quite a story to tell my wife." Klerran glanced out the window for a moment. *"Quite* a story."

After they left, Troi turned to the captain. "You're worried," she said to him.

"You're right," Picard told her candidly. "After all, we *did* detect those warp-field traces. They were generated within this star system, and they were real

94

enough. If it isn't the Lethanta who are developing warp drive, then it's the Krann."

"Now *that's* an intimidating prospect." Riker frowned. "One hundred and sixty thousand starships armed for planetary conflict suddenly take up station right on the edge of Federation space. The Krann would become an instant superpower—and a potential threat."

"Yes," Picard said, nodding, "We are going to have to talk with those people as soon as possible—not only to try to avert their attack on the Lethanta, but quite possibly to protect the Federation as well." He handed the Lethantan cube to Data. "It seems you've got a great deal of reading to do, Mr. Data," he said. "Please get through these religious scrolls as quickly as you can. I'll expect your précis by twenty-one hundred hours."

"Certainly, Captain."

"Excellent," Picard said, nodding. "Thank you for your good work today, everyone. Dismissed."

Chapter Eight

TEN-FORWARD WAS EMPTY when Picard entered—empty, of course, except for her. She was polishing a glass that didn't need it, killing time. As usual, everything was neat as a pin, waiting for him.

"Uncanny," the captain said, standing at the entrance and shaking his head. "How did you know?"

"How did I know what?" Guinan asked, putting down the glass she was polishing and picking up another. She was smiling a sly, close-lipped smile that told him quite clearly that she already knew.

Picard said it anyway. "How do you know to be here, waiting for me, whenever I feel a real need to talk?"

"It's a gift," she said, shrugging. "You find it uncanny?"

"I find it utterly necessary and most convenient." He took a seat and accepted the drink proffered by Guinan. "Ah," he said, holding it to the light and studying the contents. "Just what I was in the mood for."

Guinan kept her eyes on the glass she was polishing. "Uncanny, isn't it?"

Picard saluted her with the glass. "Thank you for getting up in the middle of the night," he said, and sipped.

"Who says I wasn't up already," she said, smiling. "Well, I figure we've got about ten minutes to ourselves before someone decides to come in here. What's bothering you, Jean-Luc?"

"We're to leave orbit later this morning to make rendezvous with the craft we have identified as the flagship of the Krann fleet."

"'Have identified'?" Guinan asked, taking a third glass from the rack. "That implies you haven't talked to them yet."

"No. They haven't responded to our hails."

Guinan looked up. "And you're going to go talk to them anyway?"

"Yes. I must."

She nodded and turned her attention back to the glass. "What's kept you up tonight, Jean-Luc?"

"Data supplied me with a report on the religious writings of the Lethanta, the inhabitants of the planet below. I've been going over it."

"And?"

"And they're about what I expected," the captain replied. "The writings represent the usual mixture of historical record and basic moral principles that one usually finds in the ancient literature of humanoid cultures, but at least the writings are internally consistent. I was gratified that they bore out what the Lethanta leadership had told me about their past."

"The writings may have been lies themselves when they were written, you know."

"I know that, but they do tell me that the present-day Lethanta are being as honest as they know how to be. The writings record that the Lethanta enslaved the

Krann, that there was a revolt, and that the Lethanta eventually had to flee. There is also an account of their long voyage to this star system. Not incidentally, the enslavement and exploitation of the Krann is described repeatedly by the Lethanta themselves in the writings as a great evil."

"I see." Guinan kept on polishing the glass.

"I think the Lethanta are sincere about wanting to open meaningful talks with the Krann," Picard said.

Guinan said nothing. She picked up a fourth glass and began polishing it.

"You're going to wear that thing out," Picard finally said.

Guinan looked Picard in the eye. "I think I could wear this glass out with this rag before you could get the Krann to see sense."

"Ah. So you've heard of these people?"

"Traveler's tales," she replied, shrugging again. "Legends. You know. Things get passed around."

"What have you heard?"

"Nothing I'd base policy on, Jean-Luc. Rumors. Word is that they're nomads, of course. They go from place to place, and they take a very, very long time to do it, which makes everybody happy. Some say they're looking for somebody. Oh, and you don't want them dropping in on you."

"Why is that?" Picard asked.

"If they come calling, they'll stay a long time, and they'll pick you clean before they go." She thought for a moment. "I recall a friend of a friend who knew somebody who'd talked to a trader who'd been through a system visited by the Krann not too long after they'd gone."

"And?"

"He didn't stay there very long," Guinan said. "There wasn't anything for him there. I mean *any-thing*. They'd been cleaned out." She put down the glass she'd been working on, dropped the bar rag behind the counter, and gave Picard her full attention. "That's what I hear, anyway," she finished. "Never met the folks living on those ships myself, and I don't know anyone who has. All I've got is a feeling, a bad one."

Picard pressed her. "But what do you think?"

"What do I think? I think anybody who's mad enough to go on a six-thousand-year-long joyride to find the people who once did them dirt is sociopathic in the extreme, and I think they are likely to behave poorly in any number of ways. Avoid them, Jean-Luc, or be prepared for the consequences." She indicated his empty glass. "Want another?"

"No," he said, and there was a bit of a sigh in it. "No, thank you, Guinan. I think I'll turn in. I've got about three hours before alpha shift begins."

"Sleep well, then, Captain," Guinan said. "Come on down some night when there's not a crisis brewing. We'll raise a glass to a few old friends."

"I look forward to it," Picard said. "Good night, Guinan." The captain turned to leave just as the doors slid open to admit several couples who had come to unwind a bit following beta shift. He nodded pleasantly to them as he passed.

Guinan watched her friend go with eyes that seemed as old as space itself. Then she greeted her newest guests.

The *Enterprise* was under way again three hours and two minutes later.

There was the usual quiet buzz of practiced activity on the bridge as the starship rapidly pulled away from Nem Ma'ak Bratuna. "Half impulse, sir," Ensign Ro confirmed. "Distance to craft identified as Krann flagship is presently five hundred eighty-six million kilometers at bearing one hundred eighty-seven mark twenty-one. We'll be standing right off the bow of the flagship in just over one hour."

"They are still ignoring our hails, Captain," a frowning Worf reported, "as they have been since we initiated them yesterday."

"Keep on knocking, Mr. Worf," Riker said, "and they may let us in yet."

Picard frowned at the viewscreen. "I guarantee it. Mr. Worf, are there any signs of unusual activity among the Krann fleet?"

"None, sir. The elements of the fleet are proceeding as before. Most ships are decelerating to arrive at Nem Ma'ak Bratuna in four days, while thousands have diverted to take up a Brunckhorst-style attack position against the planet sooner than that." The Klingon frowned. "Use of the Brunckhorst maneuver makes it impossible to establish a likely ETA."

"I'm curious about one thing, sir," Riker began. "The Lethanta know the Krann are coming and that they plan to attack. We've already seen that the Lethanta are armed to the teeth. So why aren't they doing anything about the Krann?"

"That's been bothering me as well, Number One," replied Picard. "There's been no response by the Lethanta whatsoever, not even to yesterday's attack on their government headquarters. I must admit that I admire their restraint, but it is not logical."

"Perhaps the Lethanta are waiting for the Krann to draw closer before doing anything," Data said.

"Why would that be, Mr. Data?" Riker asked.

"I do not know, sir," the android replied. "Perhaps the Lethanta prefer to make a stand closer to their own world."

"That's odd," Riker said. "If you're going to make a stand, leave yourself some room in which to fall back—even if it's to be a 'last stand.'"

"If you're going to make a stand at all," Troi said, almost to herself.

"Eh?" Picard said, turning in his seat. "What's that, Counselor?"

"I'm not sure, Captain," Troi said, slowly shaking her head. "What Commander Riker just said made me realize something. Nothing I've been picking up throughout our meetings with the Lethanta leadership suggests to me that they intend to fight an all-out battle with the Krann."

"Do you actually believe that the Lethanta are *not* going to resist the Krann with everything they have?" Worf asked, clearly shocked. "Aside from the disgrace involved, there is the fact that the Lethanta are quite adequately prepared for battle. They have weapons and the people to use them. They apparently have the need *and* justification to defend themselves against attack. Why would the Lethanta *not* fight?"

"I don't know, Worf," Troi replied. "All I know is what I feel."

"Is that really what you're getting from them, Counselor?" Picard asked.

"Yes, Captain. The Lethanta seem—well, it's almost as if they're resigned to their fate somehow."

"Another damned mystery," Picard groused. "Well, I hope we'll get some answers from the Krann, forthcoming as they've been so far."

A few hundred million kilometers farther out from Ma'ak Indawe, thousands of delegates to the Fleet Congress watched the main monitor in the Great Hall located at the center of the Krann flagship. The vast monitor occupied the entire wall behind the congressional rostrum. It showed a real-time computer reconstruction of the *Enterprise* heading straight for the flagship, her white hull aglow with the golden light of the sun astern. The greenish orb of Nem Ma'ak Bratuna was shrinking rapidly behind the ship.

A lone, dark figure walked up to the lectern located at the center of the rostrum, just in front of the monitor screen. A spotlight slammed on, outlining the form of Presider Hek.

"They are coming," Hek told the delegates in a booming voice that hardly needed amplification, even in that enormous hall. "The alien ship is on a course that will intercept the flight line of this vessel. The aliens will make rendezvous with us in less than an hour."

"Are they going to attack us?" came a worried voice.

"Probably," the Presider said.

Hek knew better, of course. He had heard every single hail from the *Enterprise* over the past day and more, and he had ignored them. Hek knew that this captain, this Jean-Luc, wanted to negotiate, to talk peace—but there was no point in informing the Fleet Congress of that fact. Hek wanted the members of the Congress excited, scared, and apprehensive. Indeed, spurred by this manufactured crisis, the Congress was about to cede to Hek what power remained to it "for the duration"—a duration that Hek and his inner circle knew would be effectively unlimited.

"What can we do to stop them?" asked a delegate. "My ship will fight valiantly, of course, but we've all seen the energy readings on this alien craft. Even our entire squadron would be hopelessly outmatched."

"We've also seen this ship wheel about and accelerate without regard for physical law," said another. "There's no ship in the Fleet that can match the maneuverability and speed of this alien craft."

Hek watched and listened, hiding his pleasure.

"Why does this have to happen just at the moment

of our triumph?" a third delegate cried. "Our people have a right to deliver Retribution!"

It was all going according to script.

"Perhaps it is fate," another delegate called. "Perhaps we are not intended to deliver it at all."

Hek frowned.

"Traitor!" someone spat, and the Presider brightened. There was a sudden flurry of fists around the dissenting delegate. When it ended, the delegate had disappeared.

"I've spent my whole life preparing for this," a burly delegate snarled. "My forefathers lived and died to bring me here. Are seven thousand years of suffering, sacrifice, and privation to be wasted just as we are about to achieve Retribution?" The delegate suddenly stood on his seat and waved a fist above his head, howling the rest of his speech.

"No!" he cried, just as he had rehearsed it with Hek's closest advisors a few hours before. "My ship will *never* surrender! We will *not* disappoint our ancestors! We will *not* squander their sacred devotion to duty! Let our forebears continue to drift easy in their orbits! I don't *care* about these alien friends of the Lethanta! Let them come! We'll send them and their Lethanta friends to the Black Drifts together! *Death to the Lethanta! Death to the aliens! Death! Death! Death!"*

Instantly there came a giant, unreserved roar of approval, an instinctive cry from the guts of nearly every delegate in the Great Hall. Soon there came a chant: "Guide us, Hek! Guide us! Give us Retribution!" The incantation was quickly taken up by others. The few who dared say anything in opposition, even those delegates who appeared merely unenthusiastic, were mobbed and brought down as the mad demonstration went on uninterrupted.

The Krann were in full cry.

The Presider looked out over the thousands of delegates in the Great Hall, left and right and center, and then he held out his arms to them, as if to embrace them all. It was the gesture of a savior, and the delegates responded to it with yells and cries for his intercession. They beseeched Hek to secure for them a vengeance that had been so long denied.

Hek let them go on for several minutes, knowing that they were his now. With just the proper amount of solemnity, the expression on his face utterly commanding, Presider Hek made the motion himself and called for the vote.

Chapter Nine

Captain's log, stardate 45527.9. We have been standing five kilometers off the bow of the flagship of the Krann fleet for nearly twenty hours. The Krann have ignored every one of our hails, but neither have they made any aggressive moves toward us. Meanwhile, the front line of their fleet continues to draw ever nearer to Nem Ma'ak Bratuna, and the Lethanta have become more and more apprehensive.

We know the Krann are receiving our signals. Every time we hail them, several of the Krann step up to the windows on the bridge of their flagship to stare out at us for a while in curiosity and, it seems, a bit of fear. It turns out that the Krann are indeed humanoid. They are built rather like the Lethanta, but they seem pallid—just as you might expect, I suppose, from a race that has remained confined within walls of steel for much of its recent existence.

Whatever the reason for their reluctance to speak with us, I must overcome it. We must try to avert the coming

*war between the two races. With some five billion
sentient lives at stake, I am game to try something new—
a gambit that I think the Krann might respect.*

TEN-FORWARD WAS AGAIN CLOSED, but this time
Guinan was not present. Picard, Riker, and Troi
stood just before the frontmost window in the lounge.
They could see the huge Krann flagship quite clearly.
According to the sensors on the *Enterprise,* the flagship was by far the largest spacecraft in the Krann
fleet, the next largest being just over half its size. The
spidery little constructs keeping station near the
flagship—its tenders, Picard thought—were quite a
bit smaller, only about a twentieth of the flagship's
size. That made the tenders merely gigantic, about the
size of the *Enterprise* herself.

"I always did think the view from here was rather
remarkable," Picard said. "I never seem to have
enough time to enjoy it." He looked down that part of
the Krann line that was starboard of the flagship, his
eyes drifting to the point far away where the ships
grew too small to the naked eye to appear to be
anything more than points of light. "This is a rather
remarkable formation, don't you think?" Picard
asked Riker. "They're holding a line that's several
hundred million kilometers across."

"Given their technological limitations, sir, I would
have thought it impossible," Riker replied. "It shows
they have enormous control over their vessels."

"And they possess enormous skill in flying them,"
Picard added. "Lord knows they've had enough time
out here to learn how to handle a spacecraft. Well,
we've had a bit of experience to that end, as well—as
the Krann are about to find out." The captain paused.
"Picard to Commander Data. Execute the pending
program."

"Aye, sir."

The line of the Krann fleet tilted and disappeared from the lounge windows as the *Enterprise* began a roll to port.

The part of the Krann line that lay to port of the flagship came into view as the *Enterprise* completed half its end-over-end roll. The Krann were much closer now.

"They're scared, Captain," Riker reported. "Running-around scared."

"They probably think we're going to hit them," Troi said.

"Not if Mr. Data is as capable of handling the ship as I know he is," Picard said. "Let the Krann *be* a little scared, Number One. So long as they don't go to their weapons, everything will be fine."

"Completing maneuver, Captain," Data reported.

"We're ready, Mr. Data," Picard replied. The three of them stood straight in front of the frontmost, centermost window in Ten-Forward as the bridge of the Krann flagship suddenly swung up into view not three meters away. The *Enterprise* and the Krann flagship were flying nose to nose, precisely as Picard and Data had planned it.

Data killed all ship motion at that instant, and Picard found himself looking straight through the Krann ship's large forward viewport and at—someone. While all the other Krann standing around him on the bridge appeared nervous and fearful, this particular individual stood there, his arms crossed. He appeared supremely confident. He was even grinning, perhaps in admiration of the *Enterprise*'s deft maneuver.

"That one's the leader of this bunch, or I'll eat that chair over there," Picard said.

Troi frowned. *Emptiness.* "I'm afraid that I can't read them, sir."

"I was afraid of that, Counselor. Picard to Worf. Hail the Krann flagship one more time."

"Channel open, Captain."

Picard stared across three meters of space and straight into the eyes of the one he took to be the Krann leader. "Krann flagship, this is Captain Jean-Luc Picard of the Federation starship *Enterprise*. I wish to discuss with your leaders the increasingly dire situation between yourself and the residents of the third planet of this star system. We wish to offer our services as mediator. We have no interest here other than to avert needless bloodshed between your two races. We are fully prepared to listen to your side of the story and, if necessary, seek redress for you from the native population of this system. We await your prompt reply."

The three *Enterprise* officers stood by silently, doing their best to appear patient. After a moment, Picard saw the Krann leader gesture.

"Incoming message, Captain," Worf said. *"Coming through now."*

"Captain Jean-Luc, this is Hek Portside Hull Patcher, Presider of the Fleet Congress. I'm the one you want to talk to."

"A pleasure, Presider Hek Portside—"

" 'Presider' or 'Presider Hek' will do, Jean-Luc Captain. We need not be formal with each other."

"Very well, then, Presider. Please do call me Captain Picard, then."

"I am honored, Captain. Well, then, what can we do for you, Captain Picard?" His tone was amused. *"Let me assure you that you have our full attention."*

"As we said, Presider Hek, we would like to offer our services as mediator between your people and the people of the third planet in this system—"

"Oh, Captain," Hek said, and Picard and the others

108

could see him smile. *"I appreciate that you are trying to show some regard for our sensibilities without really knowing what they are, but you really can say the word 'Lethanta' if you want to. We won't be offended."*

"All right, then, Presider Hek," Picard said. "We are offering our services as mediator between your people and the Lethanta. May I suggest a meeting between my top officers and your people, to be held at a location of your choice? We would, of course, welcome you aboard our ship if you should choose to come here—"

Hek held up a hand. *"As I am sure you'll understand, I can't leave my post at this critical time, Captain Picard. You and your people are, however, welcome over here at any time. I presume you can dock somehow with this ship?"* He grinned again. *"Or run a gangplank between here and there, perhaps?"*

"We can come over there by shuttlecraft, Presider Hek," Picard said. "We can be there soon, if you like."

"Time does seem to be of the essence," Hek said, and they saw him grin again. *"Shall we say, eh, thirty minutes? Our intrafleet docking facility is located amidships, and it should be adequate to handle a shuttlecraft the size of the ones you use—the very one you used to visit our friends on Nem Ma'ak Bratuna, for example. We'll set indicator lights for you to guide you in."*

"That should be fine, Presider. We will see you in thirty minutes, then."

"I look forward to our meeting," Hek said. *"Out."* He waved at them and, turning, walked away from the bridge window. Several Krann followed him, but most of the others moved closer to the windows to stare at Picard, Riker, and Troi.

"They are off the air, Captain."

"Thank you, Mr. Worf. Computer, opaque these

windows in front of me." The windows instantly went dead black.

"Well, what do you think?" Picard asked his two officers.

"Interesting how he let you know that *he* knew about your visit to the Lethanta," Riker mused. "He even mentioned the use of the shuttlecraft on Nem Ma'ak Bratuna."

"He's just trying to spook us, Number One," Picard said dismissively. "I'd expect anyone with a halfway decent sensor array to be able to detect gross phenomena such as a shuttlecraft launch from a starship I'd been keeping a close eye on since I first spotted it." He sighed. "Do either of you think we might be able to deal with this Hek person?"

"He only seems approachable, Captain," Riker said. "I think it's an act."

"That's certainly a possibility, Will, but the question is, *will he do a deal with us?* Can we still avert this attack by the Krann on Nem Ma'ak Bratuna?"

"Yes," Riker said, nodding. "Yes, Captain, I think we can—if not by convincing Hek, then perhaps by persuading his associates."

"One way or the other," Picard said. "Picard to Worf. Get yourself to *Justman* as quickly as possible, Lieutenant. We're leaving for the Krann flagship—you, the counselor, and I. You'll serve as shuttle pilot. Given the circumstances, I want Mr. Data to remain here with Commander Riker."

"Aye, Captain."

"Picard out. Number One, you have the conn. Take the ship back out to five kilometers and maintain station there."

"Aye, sir," Riker acknowledged. "Good luck."

Picard nodded grimly as he and Troi left Ten-Forward together.

* * *

"It is a huge spacecraft," Worf observed as he flew *Justman* slowly along a heading designed to allow the three of them to eyeball the huge Krann flagship while still pretending to follow the indicator lights along the length of its hull. "However, it does not impress me very much."

"Why not, Mr. Worf?" Picard asked.

"I mean, sir, that this design is haphazard. There is no elegance to it at all, not even the elegance of form following function. The other ships of the Krann fleet appear to be the same, only smaller. They appear to be constructed of a bunch of dissociated parts put together almost in random order. In addition, many of the ships seem to have suffered moderate to severe hull damage, which has gone unrepaired."

"Your conclusion?"

"I am not moved by seeing ships such as these, sir. The only impressive element to them is their number. I am merely vaguely alarmed by the Krann, Captain. I am *not* intimidated."

"The flagship looks about as elegant as a bologna sandwich," Troi observed.

"Eh?" Picard looked puzzled.

"Something my father used to say," the counselor told him. "There are very few things that are less elegant than a bologna sandwich, but it gets the job done. It may be that the Krann have a culture that breeds no love for grace and beauty."

"Or has no need for them," Picard said. "A civilization that exists entirely on spaceships in transit may seem very strange to us in many ways, Counselor." He looked out the window as they passed over a series of what appeared to be tightly arrayed sensory receptors mounted on the flagship's battered hull. "Now look at those," he said, pointing. "They seem rather slapdash to me, but I'll bet you they 'get the job done.' Mr. Worf?"

Worf glanced briefly at the Tactical panel. "We are not detecting any scanning activity from those units, Captain," the Klingon reported.

"Interesting," Picard said thoughtfully. He watched as the receptors swung their pickups to follow the progress of the shuttlecraft as it neared a lighted area set into the hull farther on.

"Docking facility dead ahead, Captain," Worf reported. "It is a landing bay open to space, sir."

"Evacuated," Picard said, nodding. "So. Well, that gives us more of an understanding about the level of technology possessed by the Krann. The condition of the hull and much of the equipment on it suggests that the Krann have no shielding technology at all. They fly their ships completely exposed to the hazards of space."

"That's why the hulls of the ships look so abused," Troi realized. "I thought that perhaps they'd been in some sort of battle."

"They well may have been," Picard said, "but some of the damage I can see has clearly been caused by long-term travel erosion—micrometeoroid impacts, for example. If the Krann possessed shield technology, they'd no doubt use it to protect their ships from such." He scratched his chin. "Nevertheless, let's not underestimate these people," he continued. "From all appearances, they have completed an incredibly difficult interstellar journey and have not only survived it but, given the great number of these ships, they appear to have prospered."

Justman entered the Krann dock. A lighted red square was obviously their designated landing zone, and Worf set the shuttlecraft precisely in the center of it, killing the engines just as the shuttle touched the deck. Behind them, a heavy set of doors rumbled closed, and soon they heard a loud rush of air all around the shuttle as the landing bay was repressurized.

"Breathable atmosphere in the bay, Captain," Worf reported. "Pressure nominal."

"And here comes a greeting party," Troi added, pointing out the window. A group of seven Krann, all dressed in the same kind of dark, unadorned clothing, had entered the bay and were approaching the shuttle. "The one in the middle of the group is the Presider."

"Yes," Picard said. "I recognize him well enough. By any chance, are you getting anything?"

Troi shook her head. "Only what I can see from body language. Curiosity, confidence. Several of them seem quite apprehensive."

"One more thing," Picard said. "How would you judge what you're seeing against the impression you got from the Lethanta when we first met them?"

"Even though I can't read them, I can tell it's not at all the same," Troi said firmly. "Not at all. These people here seem much more secure to me. Understandably, we're a curiosity to them, and they want to learn what they can about us, but it's not much more than that. The Lethanta met with us because they were without hope."

"I see," Picard said, rising. "Thank you, Counselor. Mr. Worf, they seem to be waiting for us. I think it's time we cracked the hatch and met those people out there."

"Aye, sir," Worf said, leaving his seat to take position just behind Picard and Troi. He reached over their heads and pushed the DOOR OPEN button. As the hatch slid aside, the three *Enterprise* officers stepped down to the deck. The hatch closed behind them and locked itself as *Justman* automatically entered security mode.

Presider Hek was in the forefront of the reception

party. "Greetings, Captain Picard," he said, smiling. He bowed very slightly from the waist. "It is good to meet you face-to-face—again."

Picard bowed in exactly the same way and to the same meager extent as had Hek. "And I, Presider, am very pleased to meet you. If I may, permit me to introduce Counselor Deanna Troi, my closest advisor, and Lieutenant Worf, our chief of security."

Picard noticed that most of the six Krann who had accompanied the Presider to the landing bay were trying very hard not to be caught staring at Worf, while the one who seemed to be the oldest of them was happily leering at Deanna Troi.

"A pleasure to meet you all, Captain," Hek said. "These men here with me are the leaders of the six nations of Krann that comprise the fleet." As if on cue, all six national heads bowed somewhat more deeply than Hek had. The oldest Krann slyly added a wink for Troi.

Diplomatically, the counselor ignored it as she and Worf bowed from the waist precisely as the national chiefs had. Picard noticed that Hek seemed surprised and a touch irritated at that.

"The counselor and the lieutenant are my most trusted department heads," Picard said smoothly.

"Ah," Hek said, apparently mollified. The six Krann chieftains formed an impromptu reception line as Hek took Picard in hand. "Jean-Luc Captain Starship *Enterprise*," the Presider began in a more formal tone, "allow me to introduce Drappa Fuel Filter Examiner, Leader of the North Nation of Krann; Grek Heat Conductor Tester, Leader of the South Nation; Larkna Starboard Thruster Engine Wiper, Leader of the East Nation; Pwett Crop Grower, Leader of the West Nation; Scrodd Air Quality Boss, Leader of the High Nation; and Reckkel Metal Purity Guarantor, Leader of the Low Nation."

"I am honored to meet you all," Picard said. "Let me assure you that we have come here in friendship and amity, and we intend to form the basis of an enduring, rewarding, and peaceful relationship between the United Federation of Planets and the Krann Fleet as we meet here aboard your magnificent flagship."

"Quite gracious of you, Captain," Hek replied for them all. "We look forward to the creation of a lasting and rewarding friendship with your people as well. Now, we have a car waiting for us just outside the landing bay." He turned and gestured toward the open door ten meters away. "If you'll permit me—?"

"Of course," Picard said. "Thank you, Presider Hek. I must admit I'm looking forward to taking a look around your very impressive flagship. It makes ours seem quite small in comparison."

"That it does," Hek said, not without a certain pride. "Our flagship has grown quite a bit over the centuries, Captain. That's true of most of our older ships. The flagship is one of the oldest craft in the entire fleet, and one of the most revered. Many of her modules can be traced directly back to the Exodus."

"The Exodus?" Troi asked.

Hek smiled at her. "Part of our history, Commander—one might say the whole of it, up to now. We'll discuss it later, perhaps at our initial round of talks. Ah, here we are. Please step inside."

There was a wide hatch open in the wall directly across the narrow gangway just outside the landing bay. Interior lights clicked on to reveal about a dozen comfortable-looking seats set inside the shiny, windowless shell of some sort of conveyance.

"This is the car?" Picard asked.

"Yes," Hek replied. "We get around inside the flagship using these, when moving walkways and hanger lifts won't do—as in this case. We'll be going quite a distance. Please take a seat, everyone." He gestured around as they entered the car. "Anywhere at all, anywhere at all."

Worf held out his tricorder.

"Is that thing a weapon of some sort?" Hek asked pleasantly as the other Krann suddenly grew wary.

"No, Presider," Worf said. The Klingon looked at Picard, who nodded briefly. Worf handed the tricorder to Hek. "This is a tool we use for environmental analysis," he said.

The Presider turned the tricorder over and over in his hands. "Would you really feel better if you used it, Lieutenant?" he asked condescendingly.

"Yes," Worf replied, ignoring the Presider's tone.

"Then go right on ahead," Hek said, handing it back to him.

"Thank you," said Worf, and he did. He was quite thorough about it.

"I don't see a pilot anywhere," Troi said, looking around. She saw that the old man was still winking and smiling vapidly at her, and she tried to keep her expression blank.

"The car drives itself, Commander," Hek said. "We'll be traveling through a series of tubes to our destination."

"Like the old Paris Metro or the London Underground," Picard said, understanding. "I mean to say, this is a 'rapid transit' system of sorts."

The access door of the car closed and, after a moment, the vehicle began to move forward. Since there was nothing to look at, and no one was willing to risk starting what might prove to be an undiplomatic conversation, everyone aboard quickly settled into that special state of vaguely aware somnolence found among mass transit riders far and wide. Even Troi's superannuated admirer seemed to have surrendered love for sleep.

The acceleration was gentle enough to make Picard think for a moment that he had erred and that the Krann were technologically advanced enough after all to possess inertial dampeners. Then he felt the increasing vibration of their passage through the soles of his shoes, and he knew better. They were gaining speed slowly, and it was perceptible. From the clues his body was giving him, Picard guessed that the car was accelerating at about a twentieth of a gee. That was a minor amount, not enough to trouble those riding inside, but it was more than sufficient to build up an appreciable amount of speed in a relatively short time.

Picard spent a happy thirty seconds doing the math in his head. The car would be traveling at more than one hundred kilometers per hour just one minute after departure. No trip would last very long, since the length of the flagship was just a bit over four kilometers, stem to stern. Thus, the longest possible trip in this car should take about five minutes at a top speed of something like two hundred fifty kilometers per hour. Given the level of technology available to the Krann, Picard found those numbers quite impressive.

"Magnetic, is it?" Picard suddenly asked into the silence, and everyone's head spun around.

"What's that, Captain?" Hek asked.

"I was wondering if this car was magnetically propelled," he said, ignoring Worf's nod. "It gives a smooth and quite agreeable ride, and it certainly runs very quietly."

Hek nodded. "You're right, Captain," he said. "The car is driven by a series of electromagnetic rings set into the tube. The rings are turned off and on in series to draw the car forward, shunt it into a branching tube, or slow it down—which we should be doing about now, come to think of it." He paused for just a second. "I worked on building this portion of the system when I was a boy," he said, again with a quiet pride. "My first apprenticeship was on the ring joiner crew."

"You remember those days quite fondly," Troi remarked.

"Yes, Commander. Yes, I do."

The car came to a gentle halt and the door opened onto the platform of a small, unremarkable terminal nearly bare of ornamentation. There was a scattering of directional signs and nothing more. A few Krann, dressed in the same kind of dark clothing as Hek and the others, were standing around, idly waiting for a car to arrive so that they might begin their own journeys. They seemed curious when the national chiefs stepped out of the car, and they were startled by the presence of Picard and the other strangers from the *Enterprise,* but their reaction was altogether different when Presider Hek exited the car, the last to leave it. They were visibly frightened by him.

If Hek noticed the apprehension of the Krann passengers in the terminal, he gave no sign. "Captain Picard," the Presider said as he quickened his pace to take the lead, "this is the station that serves the inner government complex. Our ultimate destination, the hospitality module, is only a short distance from here. There is a passageway just outside this facility that will take us directly to it. There are facilities provided there for your comfort, if you should care to rest or refresh yourselves before we begin our formal meeting."

"That will be fine," Picard said agreeably as they walked toward a specially marked door. "I must say I'm looking forward to seeing something of your flagship on the way to the hospitality module, Presider Hek."

"I know you are, Captain. This way, please."

The passageway they came to was as narrow, bare,

and clueless as the area outside the landing bay had been. No one was around. Closed and dogged hatches were set every few meters on either side of the passageway, with no indication as to where the passages behind them—if any—might lead. There was another closed door at the far end of the passageway, some fifty meters away. Half the breadth of the corridor was given over to a moving walkway that clicked on at their approach and was soon jogging along at about a meter and a half per second, a brisk walking pace.

"Please step onto the walkway, everyone," Hek said, and they did so. "We'll be at the hospitality module in no time."

"Oh!" Troi cried, spinning around. She saw that Drappa, the oldest of the Krann, was standing right behind her. He was smiling insipidly.

"Sir," she told him, carefully keeping the anger from her voice, "please do *not* do that again." Drappa cackled at her and shook his head.

Picard frowned darkly. "Presider Hek—" he began.

"I'll have a word with him later, Captain," Hek said, holding up a hand. "My deepest apologies, Deanna Advisor to Captain. Drappa Fuel Filter Examiner has grown a bit—outlandish, let us say—as a result of his great age. Let me assure you that we do not regard this kind of behavior as proper conduct."

"Neither do we," Worf grated. "I believe the commander might appreciate a little more space in which to walk." His eyes narrowed as he looked straight at Drappa. "She would not want to tread on anyone's toes."

The old man blinked nervously and moved hastily away from Troi to the back of the group. Troi glanced at Worf and smiled her thanks.

The door at the end of the passage opened as they

approached, and they slid on through, the door closing silently behind them. Picard, Troi, and Worf found themselves in a large, warmly lit room decorated with wall fabrics and medallions of precious metals and etched glass.

"This is quite nice," Picard said approvingly. "Quite nice, indeed."

"What is this place, please?" Worf asked bluntly as he consulted his tricorder again.

"This is the core of our hospitality module," Hek replied. "You are standing in the reception area for arriving guests. We conduct our most important diplomatic business in other parts of this facility. Such talks have always involved agreements among our six nations. We've never had—others—here as our guests."

"We're the first?" Troi asked.

"That's right, Commander," Hek said, smiling again. "After all, whom would we have talked to? We've been in transit for generations. This module is the latest successor to a number of others we've constructed over the years. We pressurized it—when was that again, Reckkel? I believe you were a gang boss on the construction detail."

"Yes, Presider, I was," the Low Nation leader said. "We opened this facility thirty-two years ago. Nearly thirty-three now."

"Of course," Hek said. He looked around and sniffed. "Come to think of it, this kind of decor has long since gone out of favor. Perhaps we're due for a change. In any case—" Hek motioned to a group of half a dozen young Krann who were waiting patiently off to the side of the reception area.

"These people will take you to a place where you can rest and relax for a few moments," Hek said as the reception staff walked forward to join them. "I expect we'll begin our meeting in, say, an hour?"

"That will be fine," Picard agreed.

"I look forward to the beginning of our talks, then," Hek said, bowing perfunctorily along with the others. The *Enterprise* officers returned it and watched as the Krann officials turned and left the reception area through another door.

Picard turned to address the reception staff. "If you young people will lead on," he said, "we'll follow along."

"At your service, sir," one of the young Krann females said. The six reception staff workers were dressed in the same dark clothing that seemed to Picard to be *de rigueur* among all the Krann he had seen, and the oldest of them was no older than seventeen or so. The staffers all bowed very low and, without waiting for the obeisance to be returned, straightened and led Picard, Worf, and Troi through the reception area and down a short passage to a comfortably large room that contained a good number of plush chairs and sofas. Four of the six Krann went behind a partition and soon emerged with prepared trays laden with food and drink. They began serving.

Troi sipped from a small cup of light orange liquid. It seemed faintly alcoholic and was very tasty. Captain Picard accepted a tumbler of light brown liquid and something that looked like a ham sandwich. Worf took the same.

"If any of you needs to lie down," the same young female told them, "we can adjust one or two of the sofas to allow for that." She pointed. "There are recycling units behind those doors there, there, and over there."

"What is your name?" Troi asked.

The young female blinked, and the young male standing next to her plainly looked scared. "My name?" she asked. She sounded worried. "Have we done something to offend you or these others, Deanna Advisor to Captain? If so, I certainly do most sincerely apologize on behalf—"

"No, of course not," Picard said, interrupting her. "You've been most courteous, all of you." He paused to think; he'd seen this kind of thing before somewhere in his travels. "The exchange of names among our people is a friendly gesture," he continued. "It shows an intention to be amiable, to be approachable. It is one of the first things we do when we meet each other."

"No matter what one's duty station is?" the young male asked, perplexed. "Upper to lower, rising to falling?"

"We treat each other all the same," Picard replied. "Deanna Advisor to Captain was being friendly, and that is all." He smiled. "What *is* your name, young lady?"

"Hellek," she replied after a second. "Hellek Pool is my name. Thank you for asking, Jean-Luc Captain Starship *Enterprise.*"

"You're not going to put us on report?" the young male asked suspiciously.

"Certainly not," Picard told him. "We would never do such a thing."

"Tell him your name, Pragges," Hellek said.

"No need to, now," he groused. "I'm in the worker pool, same as Hellek. We're all still unconscripted, you see."

"Any day now, Pragges," Hellek told him reassuringly. "You just wait."

"These other four here are unconscripted, the same as yourselves?" Picard asked. "Do you mean to say that none of you has a permanently assigned function aboard this ship?"

"Oh, hull, no!" Hellek said, suddenly putting her hand over her mouth, and the other five young people looked equally horrified. Picard wondered what he might have said.

"Pardon my profanity," Hellek said, "but we're not *useless,* Jean-Luc Captain Starship *Enterprise!* We're among those who have been assigned to hospitality work for this period while we're waiting to be given our career assignments."

"We're *pool* workers, sir," Pragges said, looking insulted. "We work just as hard for the Fleet as any conscript."

"I'm sure that you do," Picard said placatingly. "I deeply apologize to all of you for my error. I intended no insult. We have a great deal to learn about each other's ways."

"Perhaps we were a bit quick to react," Hellek said diplomatically. "Well, then. You have the better part of an hour before Presider Hek will call the meeting. Are the refreshments satisfactory?"

"Quite," Worf said, working on his third sandwich.

"Do any of you require sexual release before the meeting?" Hellek asked politely.

Troi swallowed the wrong way and began coughing. "No, no, I'll be all right," she gasped, waving away several very concerned Krann.

"Er, I believe we'll be fine, Hellek," Captain Picard said. "That will be all for now."

"Is Deanna Advisor to Captain all right?" Hellek asked, concerned.

"I'm fine," Troi said, still red-faced and watery-eyed. "Really I am."

"Then we'll go for now and let you talk in private," Hellek said, a trifle doubtfully. "One of us will be back to escort you to the meeting room at the appointed time. Good-bye."

"Good-bye, then, and thank you for everything," Picard said. The six Krann bowed, turned, and left the reception lounge with polite haste.

"All right," Picard said after they were alone. "We have a number of things to discuss. Mr. Worf?"

The Klingon used the tricorder. "I am reading nothing except what should be here, sir—electrical current in the walls, environmental and maintenance systems in operation, and so forth. We are not being scanned—according to the tricorder."

"Excellent," Picard said, nodding. "Counselor, Lieutenant, do you recall our good friend Dathon?"

"Why, certainly, Captain," Troi replied. "Didn't he have two good friends, Darmok and Jalad, who met at—"

"Tenagra," Worf finished. "Yes, I remember them all quite well. They were to be emulated."

"Yes, they were," Picard said. "They were fine role models for Starfleet officers. Actually, I think of them quite often. I recall especially well their story of how Pinocchio's nose grew during his time inside the whale."

Both Troi and Worf nodded. It was helpful that both of them had been raised by at least one Earth parent, and so each had a working knowledge of some of that faraway world's more celebrated myths and legends.

"Yes," Troi said. "It grew quite long, didn't it?"

Worf nodded. "It had been given many reasons to do so." The Klingon thought hard for a moment. "Do you believe that Pinocchio had a taste for missionary stew?" he asked after a moment.

Picard thought about it. "No, I don't think so, Mr. Worf—at least, not as an appetizer. As I understood it, Pinocchio was quite a player of the game of cat and mouse."

"Pinocchio had friends, though," Worf said.

"Yes, and Aladdin needed exactly that kind of friend to patrol his harem, too," Troi said with a studied contempt. "Pinocchio called all the shots, believe me."

"I wonder whatever happened to Geppetto," Picard said. "I wish they'd told us that part of the story."

"It would be useful to know," Troi agreed. "John Wilkes Booth at the theater, perhaps—or maybe Hirohito in his bedchamber."

"Snow White and the apple," Picard put in. "Just a feeling."

"I think that was the way it worked," Worf confirmed. "That seemed to me to be the way Pinocchio went about things."

"What happened after that?" Troi asked.

"The shrink sat down and did her job," Picard said. "When it was over, she left, to return another day. You know something? I'm a bit hungry, after all, and we've got a little time left to us. How are those sandwiches, Mr. Worf?"

Not very far away, Presider Hek and Drappa were listening closely to the conversation between Picard, Troi, and Worf.

"What *is* this gibberish?" Hek fumed. "Pinocchio? What in hull is a Pinocchio? Aren't these people *ever* going to talk about anything important?"

"No one ever speaks about anything important in the reception lounge," Drappa said. "It's too thoroughly monitored for that, and everyone knows it. I don't bother my people about it anymore, except in special circumstances. Presider, either these people from the starship are mindless idiots capable of speaking of nothing but old stories, or they've assumed they're being monitored and are speaking in a kind of code."

"Fine, then. Break it."

"Oh, we're trying," Drappa said. "Our best cryptographers are already working on it—but they have no chance of success, Presider. The code clearly depends on cultural references with which we are not familiar—"

"Oh, shut up," Hek said tiredly. "We've got to meet with these people in half an hour, and I don't know a wasted thing more about them than I did when they first got here." He suddenly turned on Drappa. *"You* were supposed to keep that advisor of theirs off balance by making her nervous and keeping her preoccupied by harassing her."

"Perhaps you should have sent for the *real* Leader of the North Nation," Drappa shot back. "He'd have been more than fool enough to try again, even after that monster threatened him. It wouldn't have been in character for me to face this Worf down—not then." Drappa frowned darkly. "But I will, and sooner rather than later."

The Presider laughed. "Now *that's* more like the Drappa Chief of Intelligence I've long since come to respect." Hek glanced at the wall chronometer. "Not much time left," he said. "Call those five jackasses back in here, and we'll go over some basics for the meeting. I want our side of the table to at least *appear* to be negotiating in good faith. The more reasonable we seem, the more we sound like the Lethanta, the more effective we'll be in stalling these Federation people until we're ready to strike."

Entr'acte

KERAJEM WAS WORKING at his desk in Government House. He was alone for the moment. Less than two hours remained before he had to join Hattajek, Blakendet, and the others in the War Room, where he would stay throughout the remainder of the crisis.

The First Among Equals was clearing up the last of his paperwork while he waited for his visitors to arrive. There was someone special who he very much wanted to see before the Krann arrived, and this would be his last chance to do so. In the meantime, Kerajem was emptying his IN box. If this was indeed the last time he would be in his office, he intended to leave a clean desk behind.

There were a few documents that still needed his signature. For instance, an opposition party member in the Citizen Assembly had pushed through a resolution mandating a slowdown in the implementation schedule of the antipollution laws Kerajem's allies had passed the previous year. Kerajem knew that the idiot was secretly in the pay of the industrialists who had never done quite so well after the revolution as they had before it. Kerajem signed the veto and thumbprinted it with some satisfaction. He appended a brief memorandum explaining his veto.

The measure would be sent back to the Assembly by courier a little later that day. The Assembly was still in session, and most of its members were still in town and still meeting at the Citizen Palace. When the vetoed bill was received and posted, there would be scattered applause from his fickle friends on the left and predictable howls of outrage from his dedicated enemies on the right. More important, though, there would be the appearance of continuity, of policy being made, of mundane work getting done. There would be the appearance of normalcy. The veto would be the first item mentioned on the planetary information report to be broadcast that evening. The people would understand from it that their government expected things to continue much as they were, even after the arrival of the Krann fleet the next day.

Kerajem knew in his heart that the veto really didn't mean anything, that things could not continue as they were, that nothing would ever be the same again, that the arrival of the Krann would change everything forever, and that their coming might even bring the end of the world—but he nevertheless felt better for having cast his veto. He thought of the veto as a final affirmation of his principles, the last word on his hopes and dreams for his people. He placed the document in the OUT box.

The announcer on Kerajem's desk chimed softly for his attention just as he finished initialing the last pending document. "Yes?"

It was his primary receptionist. *"Citizen Magala and your granddaughter have just arrived, First."*

"Have them brought in, please."

"At once."

Kerajem reached into his desk and retrieved a small, gaily wrapped package which he placed on the desktop. A few seconds later, the door to the office was opened from the other side by one of Kerajem's personal aides, who stood back a slight but respectful distance as a young, attractive woman and her five-year-old daughter entered the office, hand in hand. The aide left the room, closing the door behind him.

"Hello, Daddy," the woman said, managing a smile for him. She looked tired and drawn.

"Grampa!" the child cried happily. She pulled away from her mother and ran to Kerajem as he came out from behind his desk.

"Ha!" Kerajem greeted her. The girl's feet gleefully kicked the air as Kerajem swept her up in a round-house embrace. "How's my precious little bug?" he asked, hugging her to him.

"I'm fine, Grampa," she said, kissing his cheek. "I missed you."

"I've missed you, too, Kara," he said, putting her down gently. "I've missed you very much. I'm sorry I've been so busy. I haven't had much of a chance to come see you and Mommy."

"I know. It's okay. Mommy told me you were busy. Mommy's missed you, too."

"And I've missed her," Kerajem said, putting his granddaughter down. "Hello, Seletina," he said to his daughter. He kissed her on the cheek, and they hugged each other very hard indeed. "Thanks for coming."

"As if you could have kept us away," she said into his shoulder. Her voice was thick with hidden tears. "We haven't seen you for so long, what with all this going on. I'm glad you sent for us."

"I'm glad you could get here." Kerajem hugged her even more tightly. After a moment, he stopped and took a step back. They looked at each other, red-eyed.

"Why are you crying, Mommy?" asked Kara.

"It's all right, honey," her mother replied. "I'm just happy to see Grampa, that's all."

"There's a little something for you over there on the desk, Bug," Kerajem said. "Go and see."

The girl hurried over and threw herself into Kerajem's plush office chair. She leaned forward in the seat and grasped the small package Kerajem had placed there. She began to unwrap it. "A music cube!" she cried. "Oh!"

"What do you say, Kara?" her mother called.

"Thank you, Grampa."

"You're welcome, Bug," he said. "Do you know how to work it?"

"Sure. See?" The girl pushed the black button on one side of the cube, and the device began playing a thin rendition of a simple children's song. She interrupted it after a few seconds by pushing the button again, allowing the cube to select another song at random.

"I remember that one very well," Seletina said. "'The Old Miner's Wife.' You don't hear it much anymore. You used to sing it to me."

"I remember," he said. "It would help you get to sleep after—"

"After Mother died," Seletina finished for him. She smiled. "I guess I should finally tell you I was shamming."

"Eh? You're kidding me."

"No." She hugged him again. "I knew you'd sit up all night trying to sing me to sleep if you had to, and I'd worry that you wouldn't get any rest at all. So I closed my eyes, and after a minute you would kiss me on the forehead and leave the room. When I heard your door close, I'd sit up and read until I could really fall asleep."

Kerajem shook his head ruefully. "Outfoxed by a seven-year-old," he said. "Please don't tell Jemmagar. It could ruin me."

"Don't worry, Daddy. He won't hear about it from me."

They laughed together. It was a good sound.

"Did you two have any trouble getting here?" he asked Seletina after a moment.

"Not with that escort you sent for us," she replied. "We got through the jams on the main roads without any trouble at all. We attracted an awful lot of attention, though. I hope no one asks you about it."

"I just wanted to make sure you got here in one piece. Besides, everyone's a little too busy right now to worry about my pulling a few strings for the benefit of my family. Did the movers get everything packed?"

"Everything we hadn't sent up already, yes. The 'spinner is full to bursting with the last-minute things." Seletina paused. "Going to the mountains isn't going to do much good, is it, Daddy?" she asked him, almost in a whisper, so her daughter wouldn't hear. "I mean, it really doesn't matter where we go, does it?"

Kerajem held up a hand. He glanced over at Kara, who was thoroughly occupied by the music cube and paying them no attention. "You never know," he said to Seletina quietly. "The situation may not become as bad as we've been fearing."

His daughter blinked. "You've heard from the Krann?"

Her father shook his head. "No. Not the Krann."

"Then who—?"

He gave her a small, mysterious smile. "There's someone else, daughter. Someone who might be able to help. I think they're friends, or they could become our friends if we're given time to form a friendship."

131

" 'Someone else'? What 'someone else'?"

"Others. People from very far away, people not unlike us."

"You mean, like, *aliens*? People from another planet?"

Kerajem nodded. "People from another star—from many other stars, explorers and scientists from many races, all working together for peaceful purposes. We met them yesterday, soon after they arrived in orbit. I've even been aboard their ship—I and some other members of the council, that is."

"Their ship? In orbit?" Her jaw dropped. "You mean you've actually been in *space?*"

"Mommy, is something wrong?" Kara called.

"No, darling. Everything's fine. You just play with the nice toy Grampa gave you, okay?"

"Okay."

"Sorry, Daddy," Seletina continued. "This is a lot to take in all at once—space people, and you being an astronaut. You know."

"I'll tell you all about it later," Kerajem promised her, hoping there would be a later. "Right now, just know that their leader and his associates are talking to the Krann, trying to find a way out of this for both our peoples."

"Can they do that?" Seletina wondered. "Do you think these aliens can actually get anywhere with the Krann?"

Kerajem saw hope dawn in his daughter's eyes. "We'll see," he told her.

"It's a miracle," Seletina said. "I remember that Grandmother used to speak of miracles."

"I remember, too. Maybe she had something there." He took his daughter by the hand. "Come," he said. "You two have to get going. I'd like you safe at the vacation house before it gets dark."

"All right," Seletina said reluctantly. "We'll leave

right away." Suddenly she reached for him and hugged him as hard as she ever had in her entire life, as hard as she had right after her mother had died. "I know you'll do your best for us all, Daddy. We'll see you after this is over."

"Count on it," Kerajem told her.

Chapter Ten

THE THREE STRANGERS from the *Enterprise* and the seven Krann officials gathered around a long, flat table of unpolished metal that had been covered from edge to edge with a thick, beautifully woven cloth of some natural material—cotton, Picard thought, or something very much like it.

The chairs they were sitting in were simple but ergonomically correct, and they were very comfortable. Several young Krann—different ones, this time—brought in refreshments and set them in strategic locations around the table. If these hospitality workers were as nervous in the presence of Presider Hek as some of their colleagues had been that day, Picard could see no sign of it.

Troi and Worf were sitting to either side of Picard, waiting as patiently as he for the meeting to begin.

A soft chime sounded from somewhere, and Presider Hek sat a bit straighter. "We may begin now, if that's all right with you, Jean-Luc Captain Starship *Enterprise*," he said. "Forgive my sudden formality, but this *is* official business, and I really should address you by your title."

Picard nodded. "As you choose, Hek Portside Hull Patcher, Presider of the Fleet Congress, but I highly value the friendship we have begun to form today, and I would deem it a great honor if you were to continue to accord us the privilege of addressing the three of us informally."

Hek looked surprised, and then pleased. "Very well, Captain Picard. My pleasure—and, please, do the same for us, if you would."

"Certainly, Presider." Picard paused for a moment and then plunged in. "Presider Hek, first I would like to thank you and these six national leaders of your great Krann Fleet for according us such a warm welcome today. We have been as impressed by your expressions of friendship as we have been by the beauty and grandeur of the ships in your mighty Fleet and especially of this truly magnificent flagship." Picard did not dare look at Worf, whom he knew was doing his best to keep his expression blank. "My officers and I are looking forward to what we feel sure will be a series of candid, productive talks."

"As are we, Captain Picard," Hek said for them all. "We know why you are here with us, and we should get right to it, don't you think?"

"Yes, we do," Picard said firmly. "The leading units of your fleet will be in standard orbit range of Nem Ma'ak Bratuna in less than two days. The Lethanta are sure to panic if large numbers of your spacecraft begin encircling their world, even if not a single shot is fired by your side."

Hek nodded. "You want to avert a war," he said. "To tell you the truth, Captain Picard, I don't see how you can possibly do that. We've come a long way and have been through too much."

"Tell us your side of it," Picard invited. "We

listened very closely to what the Lethanta had to say, Presider Hek. We will listen just as closely here, I assure you."

The Presider glanced left and right at the national leaders, who nodded. Hek returned his attention to Picard. "Very well, Captain," he said after a moment. "We'll trust you on that point. The story of our people has come down to us from generation to generation, parent to child. It is sacred to us, as I think you will come to understand. Grek, will you please begin?"

The leader of the South Nation nodded. "Yes, Presider," he said. "Captain, we know that long ago we were left to ourselves, and we lived in relative peace. There are legends about wars having been fought among us, but that was very long ago—so long ago, in fact, that there are no adequate records of who fought these wars, or when, or why. We do know that one day, at a time of relative peace, invaders came out of the sky and, soon, they made us slaves. They were the Lethanta, of course."

"We estimate that this occurred about seven thousand years ago," Scrodd put in. "We don't have a date *per se* for the invasion, but our heredity records are nearly complete despite everything, and they go back much farther than that. Given the number of generations that have passed between then and now, we're confident of that number."

"The Lethanta agree with you on that date," Picard said.

"How nice," Hek said dryly. "Please continue, Grek."

"Our people had no idea that there were others in the universe, much less others so nearby," Grek went on. "If we had been sufficiently technologically advanced, perhaps we would have known that the third planet of our home star was inhabited, but we did not even possess the telescope then."

"There were always stories about people being abducted and mysterious lights in the sky," Larkna said. "Who knows if they were true or not? There were also stories about dragons and giants and who-knows-what living in the unexplored areas of our world."

"Even if the stories were true and they had been believed," Pwett said, "there would have been nothing we could have done about staving off the invasion of the Lethanta. We were farmers, Captain—farmers and merchants. The Lethanta possessed spaceships and nuclear weapons. We had just invented gunpowder."

Reckkel picked up the story. "The Lethanta came to our world, slaughtered a sufficient number of us to cow any rebellion in the remainder of the population, and put us to work. We were adaptable, Captain Picard. Within less than a generation, we became an industrial army, mining and manufacturing at the command of the Lethanta. They stripped us of our resources, and they poisoned our world with their manufacturing."

"This went on for a thousand years," Hek said. "Thirty generations of my people were slaves, but we never forgot our freedom. There was an underground, always active and very effective in making the cost of our continuing occupation dear to the Lethanta. We waited, and learned, and bided our time. We knew that, eventually, our enslavers had to grow sloppy."

" 'Sloppy'?" Troi asked.

"Yes, Commander," Hek replied. "We had faith that their supervision of us would grow lax and that the Lethanta would gradually assign to us more technically sophisticated chores that they were no longer willing to do. We began to learn things, and we learned very quickly. Generations of my people with no hope of ever seeing liberation in their own lifetimes selflessly dedicated themselves to obtaining the eventual freedom of our people."

"Your eventual rebellion was successful, thanks to them," Picard said. "The Lethanta left your planet and did not return."

"They tried to return again and again," Scrodd said. "We drove them away every time, Captain, but at a terribly high cost. Finally they sued for a permanent peace, and we gave them one. It lasted for about a century and a half."

"What happened then?" Worf asked.

"Our people started dying," Hek said, and Picard and the others could see every Krann face at the table cloud over. "Our entire world was suddenly in the throes of an epidemic of unprecedented severity and mortality. All our people on Ma'ak Krannag were dead within two weeks."

"But some of you lived," Troi said.

Hek nodded. "Some of us were in space. There were a few thousand of us engaged in mining the moons of the fifth planet in our home system, and there were more thousands aboard military defense stations in orbit around our world. There were even a couple of hundred thousand of us who'd freely chosen to live on Eul Ma'ak Lethantana, and some of them left that world in time."

"In time for what?" Picard asked, already knowing what Hek would say.

"Our military defense stations still had control of our strategic weapons on Ma'ak Krannag," the Presider told him. "They could be launched by remote control. We responded to the bioweapon attack on us by unleashing a nuclear assault on Eul Ma'ak Lethantana. We intended the planet to be sterilized, and so it was."

"You were successful," Picard said, keeping his tone neutral. "But that left you nowhere to go."

"Precisely," Hek said. "Our people had to leave that star system. We had thousands of interplanetary-capable spacecraft, a population of perhaps eighty thousand people remaining, all the recycling and sustenance reprocessing equipment we could ever need, and a very powerful motive. We knew the Lethanta had launched an interstellar colonization effort using asteroid ships at some point not long before their attack on us. Our revenge would not be complete until we located and destroyed the last Lethanta—but we didn't know how fast their ships were going or in which direction. We formed the First Fleet and struck out for one of the more likely stars nearest Ma'ak Terrella, hoping that was the Lethanta's destination. It turned out not to be so, of course."

"There is a G_2-type star three point nine light-years from Ma'ak Terrella, Captain," Worf said. "It is uncatalogued at present. That may be the star system Presider Hek is speaking of."

"Thank you, Mr. Worf," Picard said. "Presider Hek, how long did it take your people to travel those nearly four light-years?"

"We don't know, Captain—not precisely, anyway. The trip is said to have taken twenty generations. The archived designs of those original ships seem to indicate that the slowest of them could maintain an acceleration of about a tenth of a gravity, and they had fuel reserves adequate for about two months of acceleration. If they used half their fuel to reach cruising speed and half to stop—and that leaves them no margin for maneuvering—then our First Fleet might have been able to reach a top speed of about twenty-three hundred kilometers per second."

"That would have made the trip about . . . about five hundred years long, at a minimum," Picard said.

"As you suggest, Presider Hek, it might well have been much longer."

"One can only imagine the privations, the sacrifices, our people made on that first long voyage," Pwett rasped. "They had fled their world in ramshackle spacecraft that were never intended to make an interstellar voyage. Many, many of us died—but most of us reached the uninhabited planet we still call Salvation, and we settled there for a long while."

"We were on Salvation for six hundred years," Grek continued. "We prospered there, and our numbers grew. We had the ability and, thanks to Salvation, the natural resources to build newer and better ships of different kinds. After all, some of our people were scientists working in space at the time of the Lethanta attack, and they and their trained successors had thought about little else other than how to improve the Fleet."

Drappa picked up the story. "It was determined at some point that we would not stay on Salvation but continue on in pursuit of the Lethanta once we had rebuilt the First Fleet into a newer, bigger and better Second Fleet."

"Didn't any of your people remain behind on Salvation?" Troi asked.

Larkna shrugged. "We don't know," he said. "Perhaps. If so, they're keeping their own records."

"We would certainly view any such stragglers as a disgrace to our people," Drappa said.

"Indeed we would," Hek said.

"So you went from star to star, looking for the Lethanta," Picard said. "You've been looking for them for about six thousand years."

"And now you've found them," Troi said.

Hek nodded. "The Fifth Fleet detected radio signals from this star system about seventy years ago, and we quickly determined that they were of Lethantan origin. You cannot imagine the celebration that erupted at the news, Commander Troi."

"Oh, I think I can."

"We were within several years of arriving in a star system about five light-years from here when we detected the signals," Hek continued. "Rather than divert, we stopped in that system briefly and, in an all-out effort, built our already vast Fifth Fleet into an even mightier Sixth Fleet. We would not be cheated of our vengeance again."

"How long were you in that other system?" Picard asked.

"Only thirty-two years," Hek replied. "We were in a hurry."

"It was a thirty-five-year trip, this time," Drappa said. "We boosted at a full one gee for as long as our newly designed engines could take it. I myself was only a boy when we heard the signals from this star system, Captain, the signals that told us the Lethanta were here. I'll never forget that day."

Hek nodded. "I was born in that system, Captain, and I was just a boy when we left it," the Presider said. "I'll never forget it—the anticipation, the sense of a long, long struggle coming to an end, of justice about to be done."

"Is this truly justice?" Picard asked. "Presider Hek, surely you must realize that the people living on Nem Ma'ak Bratuna are generations removed from those who did such great harm to your people. All this has been so long ago for the Lethanta that, before they detected your oncoming fleet, they had dismissed the age-old tales of oppression and flight as fiction born of superstition."

Hek's expression turned sour. "Superstition, eh? Well, we're bad luck for them—I'll give them that much."

Picard pressed his case. "We've met with the

Lethanta," he said. "We've talked with them, listened to them. We've seen the shock and horror in their eyes when they described to us what their ancestors had done to your people."

Hek looked at Picard for a moment. "They told you about that?" he asked. "All of it?"

"Yes, they did," replied Picard. "They were extremely frank with us about the matter."

Hek waved a hand in dismissal. "They're frightened," he said. "They'll say anything, do anything, to avoid retribution."

"Not anything," Picard pointed out. "They have not attacked you."

Hek almost laughed. "What can they do against us, Captain?" he said. "We've scanned them inch by inch, and we did a thorough job. We've charted every armament, counted every soldier, located every mine and missile. If the Lethanta deploy everything they've got as effectively as possible, and if they use every bit of it, they might make a small dent—a *very* small dent—in our numbers and strength." Hek shrugged. "We'll destroy them with the remainder."

"I believe they know that you cannot be stopped," Worf said. "They already know they are going to die."

"Presider Hek," Picard said quietly, "there are two billion people on Nem Ma'ak Bratuna, and not a single one of them has ever done you or your people any harm whatsoever."

"They are the inheritors of enormous guilt," Hek snapped. "They must pay for the crimes of their ancestors."

"These people have done nothing to you," the captain replied.

"Picard, how the hull can I tell the fleet that we are *not* going to attack the Lethanta?" the Presider suddenly shouted, his frustration clear. "They murdered our people without conscience! We have been pursuing them for that crime for *six thousand years!* We're now less than two days from our goal!"

"They have it coming," agreed Reckkel, and there was a murmur of assent from the others.

"Would *you* stop, Picard?" Grek challenged. "Would you withhold vengeance?"

"I hope I would have the wisdom to do so, yes," Picard replied calmly. "I hope I might have the courage to try."

"Don't accuse us of a lack of courage, Jean-Luc Captain Starship *Enterprise*," Pwett said, his teeth clenched. "We have been through more misery and deprivation than you will ever see—or so you should hope."

"I intended no offense," Picard said. "Surely, however, you must realize that there must be some alternative here, some way you can avoid murdering two billion people—men, women, and children— who have done you no injury? Cannot the past be pushed aside before it destroys the future?"

"The leading elements of our attack force will be in place in less than two days," Hek said.

"Divert them," Picard said urgently. "Stop them."

"No," Hek said flatly. "There is no reason to do so."

"There is every reason to do so," Picard insisted.

"Such as what?" Hek returned. "What could the Lethanta possibly have to offer to make us stop?"

Picard seized upon the opening. "Since I have been authorized by the Lethanta to approach you, I can, if you wish, find out what they'd offer. Shall I?"

Hek looked vaguely surprised. "Why, yes," the Presider said slowly. "Yes, why not? Go ahead."

"Then," Picard said, "if it is acceptable to you, I will go to establish some basis for negotiation, if possible. I will report back to you in twelve hours." He rose, and Troi and Worf rose with him.

"Wait a minute," Grek said, puzzled and angry. "Did we just make a peace overture? I never voted to authorize any such thing! We *attack!* That's *it!*" The other national leaders began to complain loudly over this latest turn of events.

"Quiet!" shouted Presider Hek in a very loud voice, and the leaders quickly settled down. "It will be *exactly* as I have said—or do I have to remind any of you who is in charge of this body? Captain Picard, please be back here in twelve hours with the offer from the Lethanta, if there is one."

"Excellent," smiled Picard. "I shall be here at that time. Presider Hek, we were a bit disappointed that we did not get to see much of your flagship on our way here to this chamber."

Hek spread his hands. "Well, Captain, I'm sorry, but we did go straight from a landing bay to a car tube and then to the hospitality module. Time was of the essence, or so you told us."

"Yes, but we are also very interested in learning all we can about your people," Picard said. "Yours is a fascinating story, indeed, and we have never before encountered a culture such as yours. I wonder if we might exchange observers over the next day or so. We might learn a great deal about each other that way."

Hek waved a hand. "We don't have the time right now to send anyone over to your ship," he said almost disdainfully. "Frankly, I don't know whom we'd send. Everyone is tied up right now, as I suppose you can imagine."

"I regret that, Presider Hek. Then might I send an observer aboard your flagship and take a look around, to meet with your people and walk about at will without interference? Perhaps in disguise?"

Hek shrugged. "We have nothing to hide, Captain. Feel free to have your observer come aboard. Send two, in fact. They can go anywhere you like, see anything you care to have them see without hindrance."

"Very well," Picard said. "That's very generous of you, Presider Hek. Thank you."

"You're welcome, Captain Picard," Hek replied, "but for what, I don't know. One of the hospitality workers waiting just outside the door will escort the three of you back to the landing bay. If you need to contact me before our next meeting, just call." He smiled tightly. "I'll answer this time."

"I'd appreciate that," Picard said. "Until next time, then."

"Until next time," Hek echoed, and he and the six national leaders rose from their seats as Picard, Troi, and Worf filed out of the room.

When they had gone, Hek turned to his colleagues. "Well done," he said. "That went better than we'd planned."

Drappa looked puzzled. "I thought we were going to—"

"No," Hek interrupted, holding up a finger. "Not yet. There was a last-minute change of plans, dictated by circumstance. It's just as well, as this observer nonsense gives us a little extra time—which reminds me, Drappa. I want an updated report in my hands within the hour."

"Yes, Presider."

"We're still on schedule?"

"Yes, we are," the intelligence chief replied confidently.

"Good." Hek held up his right hand, holding the thumb and forefinger about a centimeter apart. "We are *that* close now, Drappa," he said, smiling dangerously. "I don't want any mistakes made."

Chapter Eleven

"CLOSE YOUR EYES," Beverly Crusher ordered, and Troi did.

The doctor closely studied Troi's left eyelid under a lighted magnification lens she had swung into place.

"Hmmm. Captain, I don't care what the analyzer says. This shading looks a little off to me."

"Fix it, then," Picard told her. "I trust your eye more than I do that analyzer, Doctor."

Will Riker was sitting up on the next bed over, watching what was going on. He now looked like a Krann male. The bridge of Riker's nose had been built up, but not much, and the filtrum above his upper lip had been filled in. His beard had been removed and its roots inhibited, and his skin color had been changed to a shade the color of rich cream containing just the barest splash of coffee. Riker's hair was its normal color, but the irises of his eyes had been dyed a warm yellow. He, like Troi, was already dressed in dark clothing identical in style and color to the attire the *Enterprise* party had seen the Krann wearing during their time aboard the flagship.

Dr. Crusher set down the epidermal infiltrator she'd been using on Troi's eyelid. "You can open your eyes now, Deanna," she said after a last, long look. "I'm done."

Troi now looked much like Riker, except that her skin was a touch darker than his, and her newly shortened black hair had been given golden highlights. The irises of her eyes were now a pale green.

Looking over, Troi saw Riker and grinned. "'Light he was, and golden-eyed,'" she misquoted. "Will, it's been years since I've seen you without your beard."

"I'll have it back soon enough, don't worry," Riker said, stroking his chin. "Feels pretty bare, though; it's been a while. Too bad you didn't see any Krann with facial hair, Captain."

"They may not be able to grow any," Picard said, "or the Krann might consider it out of fashion or taboo. We can't take the chance of you being the only person aboard the flagship with a beard, Will."

"Losing my beard is a small price to pay for galactic peace," Riker replied bravely. "What a waste, though. Maybe I should have donated it to Data. He seemed a little uncomfortable when he left."

"Oh, stop," Beverly Crusher told him. "Data seemed pleased enough when I got through with him. Ro, too. Nice job, Bev." She reached around and patted herself on the back.

"Don't dislocate that shoulder, Doctor," Riker said. "I don't know what we'd do without you."

"Transporter room three to captain."

"Go ahead," said Picard.

"Commander Data and Ensign Ro have beamed down to the surface of Planet Three, sir."

The captain nodded. "Very good. Bridge, take us back to our position off the Krann Fleet. Best speed."

Two sets of Krann clothing had been placed in neat piles on one of the unused beds. "Mr. Worf did an admirably thorough job of recording the physical characteristics of the Krann we saw and met with while we were aboard the flagship," Picard said. "The clothing is a copy of the usual Krann style of dress—a two-piece black suit varying little in ornamentation from individual to individual. Everyone we saw was wearing the same thing, more or less."

"You only see that in totalitarian cultures," Beverly observed. "It's a bad sign, Captain."

"Indeed," Picard said. "However, keep in mind that we saw hardly anything aboard that flagship—rather, we were not permitted by the Krann authorities to see much of anything. That's a lack that you two will correct, I hope. We need to know a great deal more about these people than we do."

The door to sickbay opened, and Geordi La Forge entered the room. "They're ready now, Captain," the chief engineer said. He handed Picard two shiny, silver-colored buckles about six centimeters by four.

Picard took one of them and held it up, studying it closely. "Excellent, Mr. La Forge," the captain said approvingly. "This is very good work."

"Thank you, sir."

"We've been worried about the Krann being able to listen in on our message traffic," Riker said. "I assume you've dealt with that problem, Geordi."

La Forge nodded. "That we have," he said. "These communicators operate on subspace frequencies we presume the Krann don't know about, can't detect, and won't be able to monitor. These units have a shorter range than standard communicators, and they require more power, but that shouldn't be trouble-some." He held a small, dull object between his forefinger and thumb. It looked like a cough lozenge. "The buckles themselves run silent, for security reasons. This is the audio pickup. It fits in the canal of your left ear and is visually undetectable, unless you're being body-searched."

"In which case, the jig is up anyway," Riker said wryly.

"That's what I thought," said Geordi. "With this pickup bug, those around you won't be able to hear message traffic from this end. To transmit, tap the buckle and talk as you normally do."

"How long is the power cell good for?" Riker asked.

"Two days at this range," Geordi replied. "Less if the range increases, but it won't. We'll be maintaining station close by, and in any case, you and Counselor Troi won't be away that long. Since we don't care whether the Krann can monitor our message traffic with Nem Ma'ak Bratuna, Data and Ro have standard-issue communicators disguised as belt buckles compatible with their Lethantan clothing. These subspace models I've rigged for you and the counselor don't have nearly enough range to reach us here from Nem Ma'ak Bratuna. The power pack alone would be about the size of your head."

"How closely do you think the Krann are monitoring our communications, Captain?" Troi asked.

"Several of the things Presider Hek said clearly indicated to me that he knew the content of our space-to-ground radio communications with the Lethanta," Picard replied. "I think they are probably unable to monitor our normal communicator traffic, Counselor, but 'probably' is not good enough for the sort of operation you and Will are to be conducting. We have to be cautious. The Krann have had centuries to play with signal interception techniques, and I imagine that by now they've become rather good at it. If we use subspace frequencies, I don't expect the Krann will be able to listen in. Up to this point, after all, they've had no experience with subspace—not even any knowledge of it."

"How do we wear these things?" Riker asked, taking them from Picard and handing one to Deanna.

"The buckles attach electrostatically to a treated area of your Krann jacket just below the collar on the left side," La Forge replied, touching an area around his collarbone and just to the left of his throat. "That's where the Krann have an extra fastener, apparently so they can close the top of their jackets if they want to. These buckles work like standard communicators—tap them to open a channel, or just answer if you're called. They'll also let us keep track of both of you with no trouble—and, just in case, an emergency transporter recall routine has been built into the ROMware." Geordi suddenly grinned. "You can even use them as buckles, if you want to."

"Worf to Captain Picard."

"Yes, Lieutenant?"

"Sir, I have completed the latest sensor probe of the flagship."

"Pipe the results down to sickbay, if you will."

"Aye, sir."

Picard walked a few steps over to a convenient display unit and, after a very brief delay, the screen glowed and a three-dimensional matchstick representation of the flagship built up quickly. Cubes and squares and blobs of color then began popping up here and there, denoting the apparent purpose of that particular area of the flagship. Text flowed rapidly up the right side of the display.

Picard looked at a huge red area at the tail of the craft. "Half the aft section of the ship must consist of engine and engine alone," he mused. "Remarkable."

Riker studied the diagram. "I don't see any indication of fuel storage, Captain," he said. "I suspect they don't have much fuel left. They may have drained themselves dry to get here as quickly as they did, figuring they could refuel after they'd dealt with the Lethanta. I expect that the fuel tanks were carried outboard and rebuilt into something else as they were emptied."

"I agree," Picard said. "The Krann waste nothing." He pointed at a large gray area roughly amidships. "What have you been making of this, Will? We've seen it after every sensor sweep. The configuration remains remarkably consistent between our probes."

"The gray color indicates 'no important function,' of course," Riker said, scratching his bare chin. "I don't believe that for a moment, though. That area reads just like empty cargo space but, as you say, the Krann aren't wasteful. They couldn't afford to be. They'd soon turn an empty cargo bay into additional living space or something else useful. That whole area looks *too* innocent."

"Are they somehow shielding whatever's really there from our sensors?" Troi hazarded.

"I believe they are, Counselor," Picard said, "but I couldn't begin to tell you how they're going about it. Makes you think, though."

"That should be where you put us, Captain," Riker said, tapping the screen. "Right on the edge of that gray area—in that small alcove there."

"Agreed," Troi added. "We need to take a look around in there for ourselves."

"I concur," Picard said. "If that area contains some sort of a threat to us, we need to prepare ourselves for it. Further, we still haven't managed to find an explanation concerning the origin of the three warp blips that brought us here in the first place. We need to know if the Krann have cracked the secret of warp drive. The answer to all our questions may lie right there, somewhere in that gray area."

"If it does, Captain, we'll find it," Riker said.

"I know," Picard told him. "I'd like you two to be ready to beam over to the Krann flagship in ten minutes. I've still some arrangements to make with the operator on duty in Transporter Room Three."

They materialized in a confined area filled with neatly marked and labeled storage bins. The area was utterly clean.

They listened carefully. No one else was anywhere around.

Riker sniffed. "This smells like fresh air," he said, surprised. "If I didn't know any better, I'd swear I was smelling some weather coming in—rain, I mean." He sniffed again. "That's exactly it. It smells like it's going to rain. I think I can even smell flowers."

"They may do that on purpose, Will," Troi guessed. "The Krann may find it helpful or even necessary to have their environmental conditions mimic planetary ambient factors as closely as possible. It may be a public health measure—physical, mental, or both. There's a great deal we don't know. After all, we don't make multigenerational star trips. I wonder what Beverly might have to say about it?"

"Maybe we can get her over here later to take a look," Riker said. "Look—every wall I can see is painted a bright color, and the lighting is warm and indirect, even in this utility area. I don't see us going to that kind of trouble, not in what amounts to a locker room." He paused, smiling a little. "Damned if it doesn't feel like spring in here," he said after a moment. "I feel like going for a walk in the woods."

"They've got nothing but time, Will, hundreds of years between planetfalls," Troi said. "You can do a lot of finicky maintenance when you've got that kind of time, even on a huge ship such as this one."

"I suppose," Riker said. "Well, shall we? The exit should be over this way. Our survey showed this portal leads to a short passage—*here* we are—that opens up onto a large gangway that eventually takes us into the gray zone. There's the hatch." He grinned. "I'm actually looking forward to this."

"Don't expect too much, Will," Troi cautioned him. "Every passageway we saw on our way to the conference with the Presider was stark, confining, and utterly functional. Everything was bare metal. We didn't see a lick of ornamentation between the landing bay and the meeting room."

"This may be more of the same," Riker said. "Despite what we saw back there in the storage room, I wouldn't expect the Krann to spend much of their time on cosmetics. From what you and the captain said at the mission briefing, they seem to be an austere people—all business, no time for frills."

They now stood in front of the hatch. There was a small, tapered red handle set into the middle of the door. "See that?" Riker asked. "I think it should open for us if I do *this*—"

"Will?" Troi suddenly said. "Be careful—"

The door smoothly slid aside, and there was a sudden blast of light and a roar of noise.

"Eh?" Riker grunted, poking his head through the hatchway. He was looking at a high, wide, brightly lighted and colorful corridor filled with hundreds upon hundreds of gaily dressed people of all ages bound on unknown errands or no errands at all. A broad, grassy strip dotted with benches divided one side of the corridor from the other. There seemed to be a convention that everyone heading in the same direction walked on the left. Open areas of various sizes were set into the walls and ran up and down the sides of the corridor. The people inside the stalls were conducting some sort of business—retail sales, mostly, from the look of things.

"Deanna?" Riker's tone was puzzled. "I was expecting something a little bit different from this. It looks like Mardi Gras out here."

"I don't understand it," Troi said, shaking her head. She looked up and down the corridor. The ceiling was at least twenty meters over their heads, and there was no knowing how long the corridor was, as both ends curved gently up and away into the distance. "We saw nothing even remotely like this on our way in or out. We must have been prevented from seeing it."

"I think this corridor must circle the entire flagship, just under the hull," Riker said. "Notice the curvature? It seems just about right for this section of the ship. You could walk around the whole thing, if you wanted to."

A casually dressed older man strolling by the open hatchway caught sight of Riker and Troi standing there. "Hey, you two!" he called to them happily. "Aren't you just a *little* overdressed?"

Not knowing what else to do, Riker smiled and waved at him, and Troi followed suit. The man waved back and walked on. "We're going to have to get out of these clothes," Riker told Troi in low tones. "None of these people is wearing an outfit anything like these. Everyone's dressed very casually. We're way too conspicuous. Perhaps we've broken some cultural rule without knowing it—like wearing a tuxedo to the beach, maybe." He sighed. "We could have beamed over wearing our off-duty clothes, and we'd have been all right. They'd have been close enough."

"Do you want to transport back?" Troi asked him.

"No," came Riker's quick reply. "You don't learn anything that way. Let's find out what we can do about our situation first." He pointed. "I think I may see something helpful about sixty, seventy meters down that way."

"What—oh, yes," Troi said with some relief. "I do, too, now that you mention it."

Off in the near distance, two Krann dressed in the same dark outfits as Riker and Troi were heading down the broad arcade in their direction. They were as conspicuous as a pair of burned-out bulbs in the center of one of those garish antique signs that cultural anthropologists kept on exhibit at the Las Vegas Cultural Preserve. Despite their somber dress, the Krann couple was chatting animatedly and, obviously, laughing at something one of them had just said. Suddenly the two drifted off the causeway and into one of the open stalls that lined it.

Riker and Troi began walking in that direction. Despite their initial apprehension, their dark, confining attire attracted hardly more than a glance as they passed several score gaudily dressed Krann.

They quickly spotted the two Krann they were seeking.

"One male, one female," Troi said.

"Not so hard to tell them apart, either," Riker said.

The darkly dressed Krann were standing around the largest of several bins inside the stall. The male was holding up a blue and yellow garment dyed in colors that almost seemed to glow in the ambient light. The item of clothing looked to Riker like a pullover shirt. There were other Krann in the stall—men, women, and a few children—but all of them were dressed in comfortable-looking clothes dyed in bright, clashing colors. As they watched, a Krann family—it could only have been that—gathered together a number of items and walked out of the store.

"It's a clothing outlet," Riker said. "Something like that, anyway. These people are shopping."

"Yes," Troi said. "I can see related goods on those shelves lining the walls. It's like a bazaar, but with a lot less commotion." She thought about it. "Maybe this is the kind of thing you do when you have a large population, but you don't have replicators. You put everything in a central location and pick out what you need—and only what you need."

As the two *Enterprise* officers watched, the Krann male in dark dress suddenly turned away from the bin and, noticing them, gave them a grin and a big wave. Seeing that, the woman with him turned too and, smiling, gestured them over in friendly fashion.

"Well, here goes nothing," Riker muttered.

"Right behind you," said Troi.

Smiling as broadly as he could manage, Riker strode into the stall, Troi close behind him. "Hello," he called out.

"Greetings," the Krann woman replied. "Off shift a bit early, I see. Your distributor must be down, too."

"Yes," Riker said, nodding ruefully. "They're working on it but, you know . . ."

"Sure," the woman said. "Second time this year for us. We didn't want to wait for them to get ours running again, either. Last time it took them the whole next shift. We have somewhere to go." She looked around. "I think there must be a facilitator around here *somewhere* . . ."

Riker looked around. "There's never one around when you need one," he said knowingly.

The Krann woman laughed. "Isn't that the truth?" She looked through the bin, fussing. "Hull, this thing is a mess. How are you supposed to retrieve the samples you want? I mean, look. The *pasterjacks* are all mixed in with the *opinopps!*"

"Told you we should have done this yesterwatch," the man with her said mildly.

There was suddenly a gentle voice behind them. "Does anyone see anything they like?"

Riker turned. The voice belonged to a short, balding Krann male who was dressed in an elaborately casual outfit dyed in colors only slightly less bright than most of the clothing in the bins. He was smiling pleasantly at Riker.

"Maybe that green and yellow item over there," Riker said, pointing.

The man blinked. "For *you?*"

Riker realized he had made a mistake of some sort. "No, of course not," he said, thinking quickly. "For her." He indicated Troi, who was not standing at his side.

"Oh. Oh, well, certainly! My apologies." The facilitator handed Troi the garment. It was cut much like a jacket, and it seemed to be about her size. "It's a fine choice for your spouse."

"I like it," Troi said. She looked around. "Where?"

"Over there," the man said pointing toward the back of the stall. There were a couple of doors set into the wall. "You two are going to want some other things first, though, aren't you?" He smiled again. "Can't fly on just one jet, you know."

"Certainly not," Riker said, chuckling. "We're far from done, of course. Perhaps you could, er, show us something? If these others don't mind? They were here first, after all."

"Oh, no, go ahead," the Krann woman called over her shoulder. She was already digging through another bin as her mate stood by. "We're doing just fine."

"Very well, then." The facilitator led Riker and Troi over to a set of smaller bins. "Anything here would be appropriate spontaneous wear for you, as I'm sure you'll realize. Those repositories over there contain some more items your spouse might want to take a look at. We have a fine selection immediately available, as you can see, or you might be interested in our programming something for you while you wait . . . ?"

"You know what?" Riker said suddenly. "If you've got the time, I'd really like you to outfit my spouse. I'm sure you could do a terrific job. After all, it's a special occasion for us."

The facilitator blinked again. "You mean—"

Riker grinned widely. "That's right."

"Wonderful!" the facilitator said, genuinely pleased. "Well, of *course* I'll help. This is a very, very special day for you two. I'm just sorry your distributor failed. What a time for *that* to happen!"

"Don't we know it," Riker said ruefully. "Anything you can do—"

"—will be done. Don't give it another thought. Now let me see." The facilitator put a finger to his lips and squinted at Troi, who tried to relax and look pleasant. "I think I know what I want to do," the facilitator finally said, "but it'll take a bit of programming."

"We wouldn't want to put you to any trouble," Riker said hastily.

"No trouble at all," the facilitator said. "First, I'll need some basic patterns. You'll both need a lot of red, of course. That bin over there should have a few things I can work with. Excuse me. I'll be right back." He walked quickly toward the other end of the stall.

"Will?" Troi whispered. "What are you two talking about?"

"I have no idea," Riker replied pleasantly, "but it's our very, very special day, and we're getting exactly what we need—or at least I hope we will. Just play along."

The Krann woman in dark dress came over to them. "I couldn't help but overhear," she said. Clearly, she was pleased for them. "The lists are just so *long,* and especially at a time like this—well, you're fortunate people, you two. You and your spouse must be very happy."

"We are," Riker said. "Aren't we, dear?"

"Oh, ecstatically," Troi agreed.

"Bet you can't wait for all this to be over, eh?" the Krann male with her said. He winked at Riker.

"Uh, right," said Riker.

"Permit us to introduce ourselves," the man said, bowing slightly. "I am Kerrn Starboard Atmosphere Monitor. This is my spouse, Nawha Starboard Gas Analyzer."

"As you can see, Kerrn and I have a lot in common," Nawha said.

Riker bowed and identified himself. "Dex Portside Sanitation Systems Supervisor. This is my spouse, Pralla Portside Consumables Monitor."

"Ah," Nawha said. "You have a lot in common, too."

"Like attracts like, I suppose," Troi said. "We're very pleased to meet you."

"A pleasure to encounter you," Kerrn said. He bowed again, this time more deeply, and Nawha followed suit. "We're honored by your presence here," he continued. "Supervisory personnel usually don't frequent this corridor."

"I think we might have been missing something," Riker said, making a show of looking around. "This is a very pleasant place."

"Well," said the facilitator, coming back, "my little pavilion here *does* try to give the best service in this entire module, and word *does* get around." He held up something that looked very much like a skirt that had been splattered with fifteen colors of paint and smiled. "What do you think?" he said, sure of an enthusiastic response.

"Perfect!" Nawha said, clapping her hands together. "Pralla, he's found the *very* thing!"

"Oh, I agree," Troi replied enthusiastically. "It's perfect! Now what could possibly go with it—?"

"Well, I'll take care of *that,*" the facilitator said. "If you'll just come back this way—?"

"I just don't understand fashion," Kerrn said as the facilitator led them all toward the other end of the stall. "Just give me a simple nine-color outfit suitable for any occasion, and I'd be out of here before the old one hit the recycler. Can't stand shopping, myself. Know anything about floatball, Dex?"

"Haven't been following it lately, no," said Riker. "I've been too busy lately. Used to be a big sports fan, though." He watched as Troi stood on a small platform at the back of the stall. There was a gentle hum as bright lights bathed her from above and below. The facilitator then entered a series of numbers onto a touchpad set into the wall, using some sort of tag on the fifteen-color skirt as a reference. He then punched in another series of numbers without referring to anything at all, entering the digits and commands as if by instinct.

"Well, we're all set," the facilitator said, pleased. "I've added a few excusable frills, purely in the spirit of the day." After a moment, a small display lit up next to the touchpad. It showed a miniature female figure draped in the outfit that had just been designed by the facilitator. The outfit looked like something designed by a Highlander on hallucinogenics, but here, among the Krann, it seemed to represent the height of fashion.

"Rosco, you are a *genius!*" Nawha cried. "It's *just* the thing! Pralla, Rosco's outdone himself, don't you think?"

"Oh, yes," Troi said as enthusiastically as she could. "I've never seen anything like it. And so effortlessly, too!"

"Well, now," the facilitator said modestly. "Mustn't give me my own boat just yet, you know."

Kerrn and Nawha laughed, and Riker and Troi joined them close behind.

"I take it, then, that you like it?" the facilitator asked Troi. "Do you wish to order this ensemble?" His hand hovered near the touchpad.

"Can we think about it?" Riker asked quickly. "I mean, this is our special day."

"Well, yes, it is," Rosco said, a hint of huffiness coming into his voice, "and it's not getting any younger, you know. Why, it's almost celebration hour."

"What's the problem?" Kerrn asked, puzzled. "He's done the work."

"Well, we need to talk it over anyway," Riker insisted gently. "It's beautiful work, Rosco. You can be proud of it. Very proud indeed."

"We'll be back soon," Troi said.

Rosco pursed his lips. "Return here or not, it doesn't matter," he said haughtily. He punched a series of commands into the touchpad, and the display went blank. "I've randomized the design, and I shan't recreate it. Go somewhere else if you need such services today." He waved them out of his stall. "Please leave. Go. Have a good watch, but *go.*"

"We're leaving," Riker said abruptly. "Good-bye to you, Kerrn, Nawha."

"Er, good-bye, you two," Nawha said for both of them. She seemed as puzzled as her spouse.

Riker and Troi left the stall and began walking up the concourse.

"I don't understand," Kerrn said to Nawha as they watched them go. "Did we offend them somehow?"

"Supervisors," Rosco sniffed. "Came down here to slum, I think, and have a little fun with us. Well, we don't need that kind around *here.* We work hard, and we plot a direct course. Not like them." He shook his head sadly. "I've never had this kind of thing happen to me in my entire life. Shows you what the fleet's coming to, so close to planetfall. There are no standards anymore." He paused and then, with an effort, brightened. "Well, then," the facilitator said pleasantly. "What can I do for you good people?"

The first thing Riker and Troi noticed as they walked down the concourse was that there were now a good many more Krann dressed in dark clothing.

"I've got it," Troi said. "The dark clothing is a standard work uniform. Remember what Nawha said about coming off shift a little early? Apparently the shift she was talking about is over now. That explains why the same dark uniform was all we saw people wearing in the hospitality module. Everyone there was at work."

"We'll blend in a lot better now," Riker said. "I'm glad we weren't breaking some sort of taboo."

"There may be taboos to break, Will. It seems to me that these people have a love of ritual costuming. For instance, according to Rosco back there, we're supposed to wear 'a lot of red' for whatever celebration we're supposed to be celebrating today. Not many people are, though."

"Damn," Riker said. "I wish we hadn't offended that shopkeeper. He'd done us no harm, and he'd gone to some trouble for us. We insulted him somehow without realizing it."

"And we shocked Kerrn and Nawha, too," Troi pointed out. "I don't know what we did. Whatever it was, it must have been quite a gaffe."

"Perhaps Rosco thought we were questioning his skill somehow," Riker said. "We didn't let him deliver the goods. I had to get us out of there, though. He'd already scanned you—to get your sizes, maybe. I thought some sort of an identity check must be coming up next, and we're a little shy of proper ID right now. I also didn't know how we'd pay for the clothes or Rosco's services—or even if we had to, for that matter. Leaving seemed to me to be the wisest course. I don't know what else we could have done."

"I thought we were doing rather well up to that point, considering we didn't know what anyone was talking about," Troi said. "Today is our 'special day.' I wonder what the occasion is supposed to be."

Riker shook his head. "Believe me, I wish I knew. At first I thought that they took us for an engaged couple who'd set the date, but then they seemed to expect you to be my wife—or spouse—already, and so I played it that way. At first Rosco was showing both of us the general merchandise he had to offer, and then he started concentrating on the way *you* were supposed to look for your special day." He smiled. "My guess is that they thought we'd just found out that you're pregnant. Anyway, I tried to act like a proud papa, and they all accepted it."

"Pregnancy was my first guess, too, but it just doesn't fit," Troi said. "Why is *everybody* celebrating today? Look around, Will. *Everybody's* happy. Couples are going here and there, arm in arm and hand in hand, but it's clear that some people are happier than others." She indicated a couple walking together a few meters away, seemingly in their own world, holding each other closely. "See? Their celebration is a special one, a celebration within a celebration. Even the single people are happy, Will, and they have no obvious reason to be. It's a holiday of some sort, an important one, and it can't be because everybody got pregnant on the same day. To belabor the obvious— and no pun intended, Will, so don't you go smirking at me—humanoids don't work that way. We're still missing the point of all this."

"Maybe they're happy they're about to invade Nem

Ma'ak Bratuna," Riker guessed. "After all, they've been waiting to do so for a pretty long time. Whatever celebration *we're* supposed to be having might just happen to coincide with this larger celebration by the Krann of their impeding victory."

"I think they'd be off somewhere preparing for the invasion, in that case," Troi remarked. "They should be off practicing their space raid drills or something. Surely they wouldn't be here, enjoying themselves."

"Not everybody fights in a war," Riker pointed out.

"True, but these people don't look like they're even expecting one," Troi said. "There should be an element of sobriety in a wartime population, a bit of reserve, and there just isn't one here. Maybe that's what's bothering me. It just doesn't jibe, Will." She sighed in frustration. "I wish I were able to read them. I *hate* being blind."

"Hold on a second," Riker said, interrupting her. "See that? The hatchway over there?"

"Certainly." There was an uncharacteristically wide hatch set into the wall between two stalls. It was closed, and there was a guard standing in front of it. Unlike the other hatchways they had seen, this one was not marked in any way. Indeed, the door and collar had been painted the same color as the wall to either side in an effort to make the hatchway blend into its surroundings.

"It looks to me as if it might lead into the gray area," Riker said.

"The guard has a weapon," Troi pointed out.

"I don't intend to do anything right now," Riker told her. "There may be another way in, further on— but I think we're getting warm. Let's keep looking around."

Data and Ro had been beamed into an alley between two small buildings located not very far from

Government House. The first thing they noticed was the smell.

"Interesting," Data said, sniffing.

"Awful," Ro replied, looking around at the trash. "It smells like the plumbing's backed up. At least the weather's been cold. That should help to keep the stink down. Of course, I've been in worse places."

When the Lethanta had learned that Picard was sending observers to the Krann, they had all but insisted that he send observers to their planet as well. For the moment, the impending war seemed limited to a battle of openess, which, Data thought, was the only kind of battle he could whole-heartedly support.

"We did not see any such accumulations of detritus on our way to Government House," Data said. "I am sure I would have noticed them."

Ro nodded. "You were given the grand tour, Commander," she said. "They weren't likely to take you on the garbage run. But one dirty alley does not a civilization make. Shall we—?"

"Of course." They walked together to the mouth of the alley and stepped onto the narrow street beyond.

Data and Ro were dressed in nondescript outfits designed to allow them to blend in with the rest of the Lethantan population. Beverly Crusher had altered their appearances. Ro Laren had needed little cosmetic work, as her hair, eye, and skin colors were already compatible with the Lethantan mainstream. The bridge of her nose had been smoothed out and her eyebrows corrected slightly, and she had been given a haircut. She thought she looked odd, but not nearly as odd as Data.

Data looked like a human male built along terrestrial lines. While the Lethanta came in the wide range of colors and body types typical of humanoid races, it had been faster and easier for Dr. Crusher to make Data look like a terrestrial Caucasian, and so that was what she had done. Data's skin color and texture had been changed, and his eyes were now a warm brown. He had also been given the receding hairline possessed by many Lethantan males of Data's apparent age, and what hair he still had was cut and combed into an agreeably Lethantan style.

Back in sickbay, Ro had watched as Data had taken a hand mirror and studied his new face this way and that for a long, long moment right after Beverly Crusher had finished with him. No one, not even the captain, had said a word. Then the android had blinked, set the mirror down, and gotten on with the business at hand.

The street they were walking on was fairly nondescript. Low, decrepit-looking buildings lined it on both sides, and there was trash scattered everywhere. There were a number of people walking about, but no one seemed to be going anywhere special. A few were standing around talking. There was no vehicular traffic, but the curbside was almost solid with parked ground vehicles in various stages of disrepair. Off in the distance, there was the raucous sound of several people yelling curses and threats at each other, and then there was the sudden sound of breaking glass, and then silence.

"I think these buildings might be dwellings," Data said. "Because of the number of people standing nearby, however, I am not free to use my tricorder to prove or disprove my theory."

"Don't worry about it, Commander," Ro said. "They are. I know a slum when I see one."

"'Slum'?" The android thought about it. "Ah. I understand. You look thoughtful, Ensign. Might I inquire—?"

"Hmmm? Oh. Probably nothing, Commander." Ro shook her head. "Something we saw back there was bothering me, that's all. Something that didn't fit somehow, something that didn't seem right. I just can't put my finger on it."

"I understand. Please inform me if you do." They walked on and soon rounded a corner that opened onto a wide boulevard.

"Do you see what I see?" Ro asked.

"It would be quite difficult to overlook it," Data said.

The buildings along the boulevard were much taller, and a huge sign had been strung across the full forty-meter width of the busy boulevard between two of them. The banner was made of a light, strong, and utterly white fabric that billowed in the wind like the sail of a gigantic schooner, and on its face it bore a single word in blazing red letters five meters tall:

PREPARE!

"I don't think we have to wonder much about what we're supposed to 'prepare' for," Ro said dryly. "At least we know that the presence of the Krann in this system is no secret to the populace." She looked down the boulevard. "That big building in the distance is Government House, isn't it?"

"Yes, it is."

Ro nodded. "This avenue we're on leads directly to it, so this is the street we want. The Lethanta must consider this a major thoroughfare. There's a ton of traffic and lots of people. If I had to hang up a sign, this'd be the place I'd want to do it."

"The banner has not been up for very long," Data observed. "It shows no evidence of having been degraded by the weather or the pollution emitted by the internal combustion engines of the many ground vehicles on the boulevard. Perhaps this means that the common people were told about the impending attack only a short time ago."

"Good point, Commander," Ro said. "Let's go see if we can find out."

"That is my intention." They began walking in the general direction of Government House, which was several kilometers away and almost invisible through the haze of airborne grit and grime that hung over the capital city. In contrast to the side street they had just quit, the boulevard bore heavy traffic heading in both directions.

The people they passed on the sidewalk seemed subdued. There were a number of small stores and shops fronting the boulevard, and most of them were open, but they did not seem to be doing very much business.

They had not gone more than a block or two when they suddenly heard the cry of sirens. Data looked behind them. "There are a small number of ground vehicles attempting to work their way through traffic," he told Ro. "They are still some distance away."

"I can see flashing lights," Ro said. "The law is the law the galaxy over. Think they're looking for us?"

"Unknown as yet. I would not worry, however. We can beam back to the ship instantly if we encounter trouble. We might as well stand here and watch what happens."

They looked on as three large ground vehicles—clearly belonging to some emergency or security force—fought their way through traffic and squealed to a stop just short of the giant banner, blocking the boulevard and bringing all traffic to a halt. Uniformed men swarmed out of two of the vehicles and to both sides of the boulevard, where they disappeared into two buildings, each opposite the other, from which the banner had been hung. More uniforms popped out of the third vehicle. These men—Data thought of them as police, as Ro had suggested they were—took up position along the street.

A minute or two later, the huge banner was cut loose from its pinnings on the roofs and upper floors of the two buildings. The sign sank to the street in slow motion, trapping air in its folds as it fell. It finally settled on the boulevard, tentlike, covering a large number of stalled vehicles and evoking angry shouts and cries from the people inside them. Several policemen began pulling at the fallen banner, gathering it together and dragging it to one side of the street, where it lay in a heap.

"I'm beginning to get the idea that PREPARE! is not a message condoned by the government," Ro said.

"I think you are correct," Data replied. "I wonder who is responsible for—"

"*Just* a minute, you two!" one of the policemen called. He began walking toward them, and he was scowling. "Stop right there!"

Data looked around. The small crowd that had been standing there with them to watch what was going on had melted away, and he and Ro were the only onlookers still on the street. "I believe he is speaking to us," he said to Ro.

"No kidding," the ensign returned. "Well, Commander? Do we run down the street? Do we beam up? Do we slug him?"

"None of those courses of action seems necessary at this time, Ensign. Let us simply remain here and see what happens."

The policeman came up to them and thrust his face about ten centimeters from Data's nose. He looked angry. "All right, citizen," he said. "What did you see? Who put up that thing?"

"I do not know, sir," Data said politely. "My friend and I were out walking." He pointed down the boulevard in the direction from which they had come. "When we came around the corner two blocks down

169

that way, the sign was already hanging over the boulevard. We saw no one who might have been responsible for its placement there."

The policeman looked closely and intimidatingly at Data. "You from around here, citizen?" he asked the android. "You talk funny."

"I am from a place not far from here, sir," Data said. "However, I have done some traveling."

"And you say you saw nothing."

"That is correct."

"What about you?" the policeman shot at Ro.

"I didn't see anything, sir."

The policeman sighed wearily. Suddenly, he seemed resigned. "Yeah, I know," he said. "Whoever put that thing up is long gone. Look, are you two sure you didn't see anyone or anything? There been a preacher around here?"

"No, sir," Ro said. "We haven't seen any preachers."

The policeman looked around on the sidewalk. "No, I guess not," he said after a moment. "I don't see any tracts scattered around. Usually people drop 'em as soon as the preachers or their cohorts hand them out. This time they just strung up the sign and beat it." He looked at the white heap in the gutter. "It's gigantic," he said, shaking his head. "What a waste of time and talent. I wonder how they managed to get it up there?"

"How do they ever?" Ro asked knowingly.

"You said it." The policeman unclipped and took in his hand a small device attached to the belt of his uniform. "Well, let me register your identification cards, you two, and you can be on your way."

"I have mine right here," said Ro as she reached for her belt buckle.

Suddenly there was a low, terrible growl all around them. The policeman looked quickly around the sky as the sound rose rapidly in pitch and volume to become the ear-splitting, soul-shaking alert of a siren, of a hundred sirens.

The entire city was howling.

"Air raid!" the policeman snapped at them. "Get out of here! Head for the nearest shelter!"

"Where is it?" Ro asked.

The policeman cursed and pointed half a block farther down the street. "The symbol's right there over that door, you idiots. Get going!" He hurried away, calling to his comrades, who were quickly climbing into their ground vehicles. "Wait for me!"

"Shelter or home base?" Ro asked Data.

"Let us conceal ourselves in that doorway for a moment," Data told her. "I wish to contact the ship."

They hurried over to the doorway and stepped inside its shade. The arrival of the police a few minutes before had effectively cleared the street, and the air raid alert would keep them from returning for a while. No one would see them.

Data tapped his belt buckle. "Data to Captain Picard."

"Picard here."

"Captain, is there any sign of a Krann attack on our location or anywhere in proximity to it?"

"No. No, there isn't. The reason for this alert is a mystery to us. We're reading no sign of any unusual Krann activity. Their lead ships continue on course for Nem Ma'ak Bratuna, but they are still a day away. What's going on, Mr. Data? We're noticing a great deal of sudden Lethantan military activity in your part of the continent. And are those air raid sirens I hear in the background?"

"Yes, sir, they are," Data said. "The Lethanta appear to believe that they are under attack."

"Captain, this is Ro. We had been stopped for routine questioning by a local security official when

171

the sirens went off. The official clearly believed that an attack was imminent, and he ordered us to go to a shelter."

"How far away is this shelter, Ensign?"

"A few meters down the street from us, sir."

"What do you want to do, Mr. Data?"

"I believe we should go to the shelter and see what happens, Captain. We will not learn anything by returning to the ship at this time."

"I agree, sir," Ro said.

"Then go ahead. We'll keep a transporter lock on you and have you both out of there in an instant, if need be."

"Understood, Captain. Data out."

Together, Data and Ro hurried the short distance to the shelter entrance. It was fairly narrow and was obviously not intended to handle great numbers of people heading in or out at the same time. There was a red diamond-shaped sign centered over the entrance. There was a small bit of white lettering on it: HERE.

Data and Ro passed through the doorway and into a small, bare lobby. The only light came from outside.

"This *can't* be it," Ro said, frowning. "It's wide open to the street."

"There is a stairway in that direction," Data said, pointing into the dimness at the back of the lobby. "It leads down." Seeing there was no one around, he took out his tricorder. "There are two people located in a confined area some ten meters below us. That must be the shelter."

Ro nodded. "That sounds more like what we're looking for, sir. I've been in a few of these things in my time." She took out her own tricorder. "There's a reinforced shell of metal and concrete surrounding the shelter on all sides, but it shouldn't interfere with our beaming out, if we need to. Shall I lead, Commander?"

"As you like."

When they were halfway down the stairs, they heard a heavy rumbling behind them. Data hurried back upstairs just far enough to be able to see what was happening.

A heavy blast door was descending from a hidden pocket located above the entryway. The grayish light from the street above disappeared, leaving them only a small scattering of artificial light that managed to find its way up the winding stairway from the shelter below them.

"Hey!" came a rough female voice. "Is there still somebody up there?"

"Yes," Data called. "There are two of us. We will be down there directly."

"Well, hurry the hell up, then," the voice complained. "I want to close this damn hatch, and we haven't got all damn day."

Chapter Twelve

"I'M JUST ASTONISHED," Riker said finally. "As they used to say down in the Big Easy, this joint is jumpin'. You wouldn't think there was a war on."

Whatever holiday celebration Riker and Troi had stumbled upon was continuing unabated. The happy crowds in the corridor had grown substantially since their arrival. Everyone seemed to be buying something. Some of the Krann were absolutely loaded down with sacks and packages.

"Ever see those old films?" Troi asked. "The ones with a lot of holiday shopping in them? *Miracle on Tenth Avenue,* or something like that. This reminds me of that. Shopping was part of the religious ritual, wasn't it?"

"You think all this is somehow religious? It doesn't seem that way to me."

"I don't know," said Troi. "Probably not, as the usual symbology is absent. They all seem to be celebrating *something,* though, and it's a major celebration."

Riker and Troi had been walking along the arcade for more than three hours, taking their time and looking at everything worth noticing. No one had challenged them. They were now about halfway around the nine-kilometer concourse from Rosco's clothing stall. They now knew that Rosco's was only one of literally thousands of shops, restaurants, and other kinds of outlets of various sizes that lined both sides of the promenade.

"I certainly wouldn't have expected to find entrepreneurial capitalism here," Troi remarked. "I thought a closed society would have chosen another way—communal economics, perhaps."

"Not a chance, Deanna. These people would give the Ferengi a run for their gold-plated latinum."

"They surely would. To tell you the truth, I was expecting to find the Krann living like ants in a colony."

"We've been making a big mistake," Riker said after a moment. "We've been looking at things the wrong way. Deanna, we have a planetary bias."

"What do you mean?"

"We're biased by our own environment and experiences, Deanna. We think people *have* to live on planets. We've been seeing the Krann only as wanderers, as rootless transients. We've been thinking that Krann society must have been affected in any number of bad ways by their ceaseless traveling. We forgot that the Krann *live* here. They're used to being transients—except that they don't think of themselves as that. The Fleet *is* their planet, moving through space on a steady course, just as any of our worlds does. The only difference is, they get to pick the course they take."

"That part may not mean very much," Troi cautioned. "The Krann usually take generations to get where they're going, and a journey that lasts for generations is not at all voluntary for the descendants of those who began the trip. It may be that even at the outset of a star trip, the destination is picked by the leadership, and everyone else finds themselves forced to go along."

"Good point," Riker allowed. "That makes this mode of living even more planetlike, if you look at it in a certain way." He thought about it for a moment as they walked on. "This race boasts a population of three billion people," he finally said. "The Krann live scattered among a hundred and sixty thousand space-craft of every imaginable configuration. That repre-sents a lot more geographical diversity than you're likely to find on any given planet."

"It's like a Dyson sphere without the sphere," Troi realized. "Over time, the Krann have created their own vast planet out of this collection of ships. In a way, they've terraformed space itself by wrapping metal around it. It's amazing." She shook her head in disbelief. "We've never met anyone else who lives like this. I'm not sure we've ever met anyone else who *could*. We have a lot to learn from these people."

"I hope they give us the time," said Riker. "If we can't talk the Krann out of attacking the Lethanta, the war could destroy much of the Krann fleet. Maybe all of it. As we used to say in Alaska, the Lethanta are armed for bear, and we don't know everything we need to know about them, either."

"There are a great many bears out here, Will—a hundred and sixty thousand ships filled with more than three billion people, bent on murdering a race of two billion that possesses its own unique history and culture. All we have to do is figure out how to stop the Krann from trying to destroy the Lethanta."

"Yeah," Riker said, a touch wearily. "That's all we have to do, and we haven't done much about finding out how." He looked around. "Wait a minute. Are you hungry?"

"Now that you mention it, yes. Did you want to return to the ship?"

"No. Don't have to. How do you feel about crashing a party?"

"A party? Where?"

"Down that way a bit," he answered, pointing. "See the crowd? It's spilling out of one of the shops near that intersection. That must be one of the restaurants."

"It looks like a party, all right," Troi admitted. "We've passed a few today, but this is the biggest we've seen so far."

"That crowd looks big enough to get lost in, and I don't think anyone is going to ask us for our ID, either. Come on."

"Do we just walk in?"

"Watch me." Riker took Troi by the hand and led her into the periphery of the crowd around the restaurant. The facility was a small, brightly lit place that was packed to the rafters with happy people of all ages. They were cooking something inside. It smelled good.

The party inside had spilled out onto the concourse, where it continued unabated. Many of the partygoers seemed to know each other, and the mood was relaxed and convivial. Passersby took a look as they walked by the restaurant, many of them waved, and almost all of them smiled. Some tapped the area over their hearts once-twice-thrice, using the first two fingers of their right hands. It was a private sort of gesture, quickly and almost furtively done. Riker noted it and filed it away for later investigation.

Many of the Krann attending the party were dressed in the same kind of dark clothing that he and Troi were wearing. Riker assumed that those particular Krann had come straight to the party from their duty shifts.

"I'll be right back," Troi said.

"Good hunting." Now part of the crowd, Riker looked around unobtrusively. A woman across the way gave him an interested look, which he returned with a smile, a shrug, and a tilt of his head toward Troi, who was heading inside the restaurant. The woman gave Riker a slight, somewhat sad smile and turned away.

Riker found what he was looking for a few steps away. An informally dressed young Krann male was talking a mile a minute to a small knot of males and females. Everyone was laughing. Riker inserted himself into the cluster of listeners and, when the next laugh came, he joined in heartily.

"Ah!" cried the male who was the center of attention. "New blood! I take it, shipmate, that you're a friend of the happy couple?"

"That I am," Riker said with gusto. "What a great day this is!"

"It is indeed!" the male cried. "And that calls for another drink!" There was a rousing chorus of agreement. "Here you go," he said to Riker, handing him two empty pitchers. "These are for you, my friend—you and your good spouse, that is." The group with him laughed good-naturedly.

Riker smiled. "I see," he said. "Any preferences?"

"Sure," someone else said, pointing at the two big pitchers. "Just get those refilled. That'll do it!" More laughter.

"That's fine, Bitt, but what are the *rest* of us going to drink?" the first male said, and everyone laughed again.

"See you later," Riker said. Pitchers in hand, Riker threaded his way through the crowd and into the crowded restaurant. He saw that it was not quite a restaurant. It was more like a bistro, one of those dark, tavernlike places that were still popular in some nation-states on Earth and on worlds colonized by Earth humans. This one had two hundred people crowded into a space that could hold perhaps fifty comfortably. Everyone was jabbering, and the resulting noise level was rather incredible. There was soft music coming from somewhere, but it was nearly impossible to hear. Riker probably would not have noticed it at all had he not passed right by a hidden speaker placed in a wall next to the entryway.

There was a young female standing near the door. Her expression was one of expectation and willingness to help. Riker guessed that she was a worker assigned to the bistro. He raised the two pitchers and gave her a help-me look. She smiled. "Do you need those refilled?" she asked.

"Actually, they belong to a person named Bitt, who's standing in that group right over there." He pointed. "Could you—?"

"Of course." She took the pitchers and began threading her way through the crowd toward something that Riker thought looked very much like a bar.

"I'm back," Troi said, coming up beside him.

"Did you have a chance to check in?" Riker asked.

"No. There were others there with me."

Riker nodded. "We're not in any particular hurry. We'll try later."

Troi knew there was no chance they could be overheard above the babble surrounding them. "Did you notice that no one in that group outside did any bowing when we met them?" she asked Riker. "Now *that's* a first."

"Sure is. I'm still sorting out who bows to whom and when. I've just put 'drunken bums at parties' on the Don't Bow list."

"Drunkenness may have nothing to do with it,"

Troi said, taking him seriously. "Perhaps the usual rules of protocol are suspended at affairs like these—whatever this affair is, I mean."

"Maybe," Riker said. "We'll just keep feeling our way along. We've been doing all right so far. By the way, I see something interesting over there."

"Helps to be tall. I can't see a thing above standard chest level. What is it?"

"There's a big table near the back of the main room that seems to be the center of everyone's attention. Lots of people are sitting there. Know what else?"

"What?"

"There's a young couple sitting at the table, too."

"And?"

"They're the only ones here wearing a lot of red."

"Ah."

"Let's drift over thataway."

"Lead on, Dex."

Together, they moved slowly through the crowd, taking their time and nodding pleasantly at everyone who looked their way. No one questioned their presence.

The crowd was thickest at the room side of the main table, which was long and ran the width of the bistro at that end. The couple in red was sitting in the center of the far side, and each was talking with the people sitting nearest to them. The male suddenly looked up briefly and, spotting Riker, gave him an uncertain smile. Riker returned it with a broad grin. That seemed to reassure the male in red, who returned to the conversation he was having with the person on his right.

"I just made eye contact with the groom," Riker muttered to Troi.

"Do you still think this is a wedding party? Are you sure we're properly dressed for it?"

"Very funny."

"I thought we'd established that red didn't have anything to do with weddings," Troi reminded him. "Rosco thought we were already married, remember? This celebration must have something to do with the coming attack on the Lethanta."

"No, it doesn't," said Riker. "It's something else, something important to these people, and there's only one remaining possibility that seems likely. Damn. I wish I could use the tricorder just for a second."

"Let's try to get a little closer to the table," Troi said. "Maybe we'll overhear something."

Suddenly there was a cry of pain. "Ouch!"

Riker had stepped on someone's foot—was still stepping on it, as a matter of fact. He moved back quickly. "I'm terribly sorry," he apologized. "My fault entirely."

The foot belonged to a young male. "Hull, you could hardly help yourself in here," he replied in friendly fashion. He was slurring his words a bit. "What a mob!"

"You're very gracious."

"Gracious?" the young male said. He grinned. "That's not a word I hear very often, at least as applied to my own unworthy self. No, I'm just in a good mood, I guess. How do you happen to know the delighted dyad?"

He had to mean the couple in red. "We've worked together," Riker said carefully.

"Ah, too bad. You've gone ahead and mentioned work." The young male wagged a finger at Riker in mock warning. "Well, I won't report you to the porty palice—sorry, I mean the party police—as long as you promise not to do it again."

Riker chuckled appropriately. "All right, I won't."

"Excellent. By the way, I'm Wiggin Ship's Defense

Design Maker Journeyman, not that I want to talk about work." He bowed slightly.

"Pleased to meet you, Wiggin," Riker said. "I'm Dex Portside Sanitation Systems Supervisor, and this is my spouse, Pralla Portside Consumables Monitor."

"Oh, hull," Wiggin said, straightening. "I beg your pardon, Dex Portside Sanitation Systems Supervisor. I assumed—well, never mind. Blame the *sinarrtha*. I sometimes have a little too much for my own good." The young male bowed again, this time more deeply.

"It's a party, Wiggin," Riker said quickly. "Relax. Please think of Pralla and me as friends."

"Yes, please do," Troi said quickly.

Wiggin looked up. "Really?" He seemed surprised. "Well, if you shay so—say show, I mean. I'd be pleased to, actually. I guess it *is* a special day. I didn't know Agrell and Twesla knew, er, I should say 'were acquainted with,' supervisory personnel."

"We value all our friendships," Riker said vaguely. "We're very happy for Agrell and Twesla, of course."

"We surely are," Troi said brightly. She decided to risk it. "They've waited a long time for this."

"I'll say they have!" Wiggin said, perhaps a little too loudly. Heads began turning in their direction. "Everybody stands around and waits while the wasted protocol board decides when and where we can eat, sleep, and break wind!"

"Let's leave," Troi said quietly to Riker.

"I agree." The drunken Wiggin had suddenly grown rather obnoxious, and Riker knew that the one thing he and Troi did not need now was to be noticed. They slowly began moving away from Wiggin, as if the press of the crowd were forcing them apart.

"Look!" Wiggin suddenly cried. A group of Krann were rising from their seats at a table not two meters away. "Come on, let's go sit down!" The young male darted through the crowd and claimed the table before anyone else had a chance. "Dex! Pralla! Come *on!* I got us a *table!*"

"Our newfound friend has gotten us a table," Riker said resignedly. "He'll probably keep yelling for us until hell freezes over. Well, maybe sitting down with us will keep him quiet."

"Maybe we'll learn something from him," Troi added. "He's already rather defenseless, the poor boy."

"Think so?" Riker seemed amused by that.

"Dex?" came a plaintive voice. *"Pralla?!?* Where *are* you?"

"We really should go sit down," Troi insisted. "People are starting to stare."

"All right," Riker decided. "We'll stay with him for as long as it's doing us some good. We haven't really talked with any of these people yet. We might as well start with this one."

"I think this young man might be helpful," Troi said.

"There's a grand tradition in old spy novels where the good guys—that's us—pump drunks for information," Riker said.

"There is?"

"Yes, there is—even when the drunk is a phony, like our friend over there."

"He is?"

"I'm sure he is. I'm assuming he's a plant and that our cover is blown. We ran into him too easily, and he's sticking around us way too long. We should play along and see what happens."

"Dex! Pralla! Where *are* you?"

"There he goes again," Troi said. "I gather we shouldn't let Wiggin know that we know that he knows—I mean—"

"You've got it."

"My, you're sneaky."

Riker grinned at her. "You knew that already. Let's rejoin our friend over there. And one more thing—"

"What is it?"

"Put 'when introduced by name' on the Do Bow list."

"Right." Together, they crossed the distance to the table where Wiggin was waiting for them. "Ah, *there* you are," he said, pleased. "Facilitator's been by already. I've ordered a couple of pitchers of green stuff for us, and there's a free meal ration that comes along with it. Special occasion, you know."

"Why, thank you, Wiggin," Troi said as she and Riker seated themselves. Wiggin winked at her. Troi pretended not to notice.

"'Green stuff'?" Riker asked. He'd already noticed that many in the room were drinking something that was colored a light, almost pearlescent green.

Wiggin gave him a strange look. "Sure, Dex," he said. "Green stuff. Standard alcoholic beverage, category three." He suddenly grinned. "Or four. Hull, I forget. It's my favorite, anyway."

"Of course," Riker said smoothly. "We usually call it something else, though. Hey, this is a pretty good party, isn't it?"

"Sure is," Wiggin said happily. "Not too many get held on the flagship concourse itself on Posting Day, but I hear Agrell is a systems analyzer who's on his way up. That's got to have greased some gangways for him. He's one lucky son of a tube cleaner—oops. Pardon me, Pralla."

"Quite all right," Troi said politely.

"There they are!" someone cried from the front of the bistro.

Riker and Troi looked around quickly. Riker kept his hand ready to slap his emergency recall signal. He glanced quickly at Wiggin. Riker half expected the young Krann to pull a weapon in an attempt to arrest him and Troi, but Wiggin merely looked annoyed and a bit dazed. For the first time, Riker felt a flicker of doubt about Wiggin's motives.

"Nice, quiet time we're having here," Troi muttered.

"Don't I know it," Riker said. "Excuse me." He stood and looked above the heads of the crowd for the source of the commotion. He quickly found it. An angry-looking group of four Krann had spotted Riker and were coming straight for him—and they were being led by Bitt, the male who'd given Riker the two empty pitchers to fill.

The party was definitely getting livelier.

Riker frowned. "It's our friends from outside," he told Troi.

"What friends?" Wiggin asked, clearly puzzled. "I thought you two came here alone—?"

Riker ignored him. "I'll take care of it," he told Troi. He rose from his seat, and, turning to face Bitt and his companions, stood by the table, waiting calmly.

Bitt was obviously, clearly, magnificently angry at Riker. His pale face was orange with emotion, and his aquamarine eyes flashed with anger. The Krann male, his several friends close behind him, pushed his way through the remainder of the crowd in the bistro and planted himself before Riker. Bitt's friends seemed merely irritated. They also seemed expectant.

"What's the matter, Bitt?" Riker asked mildly. "Is there something wrong?"

"Tube cleaner!" Bitt shouted into Riker's face. "Shirker! What piece of wasted hull did they scrape *you* off, you functionless knob?"

"I really don't think this kind of language is called for," Wiggin said, his eyes wide. "After all, this is a—"

"Quiet, wreckage!" Bitt roared, not bothering to

look at Wiggin. "I'm talking to the garbage master here. Listen, you lump of used protein, you stuck us for a double pitcher back there, and I mean to collect!"

A gasp seemed to run all around the bistro, and the crowd quieted. The soft background music continued to drift easily through the sound system for a moment or two until someone finally thought to stop it.

The bistro was silent. "A double pitcher?" Riker asked Bitt. "Do you mean the two empty—ah. I see. Are you somehow under the impression that I intended to supply you with two pitchers of, uh, whatever had been in the pitcher?"

"You took them from me, slag," Bitt spat. "Then the facilitator came to me a few minutes later with two filled pitchers and a debit notice, and I see you sitting in here with *this* dead weight."

"Hey, wait a minute—" Wiggin began.

"Spin down, waste bag," Bitt told him. "You're not involved in this—yet."

"That's more than enough," Riker interrupted. He allowed his own expression to darken by tapping into his lingering resentment of an unfortunate and embarrassing incident that had happened during his plebe year at the Academy. Riker's controlled anger welled up so strongly that Troi, sensing it, blinked at its suddenness.

"First, you are mistaken," Riker said bitingly. "Neither my spouse nor I ever intended to join you or your friends. Second, you thrust the pitchers on me. I incurred no obligation to you or anyone else. I did more than I had to do when I gave the pitchers to the facilitator and directed her to return them to you."

"Wait a minute," Bitt said. "That's not the way—"

"Quiet!" Riker barked. "Your breach of etiquette in this matter is obvious. Even a child knows better."

"'Breach of etiquette'?" Bitt cried, outraged.

"You're babbling nonsense, shaft scraper. *You took the pitchers!* Just who in hull do you think you are?"

Wiggin rose quickly. "How glad I am that you asked," he said. "Allow me to present my friends Dex Portside Sanitation Systems Supervisor and his spouse, Pralla Portside Consumables Monitor."

Bitt's color faded. "Supervisor?" he echoed in a small voice. His friends took a step back.

"And his spouse," Wiggin said cheerfully. "Dex and Pralla, I call them, seeing as how we're friends and all."

"But he isn't wearing his insigne," Bitt said weakly. "Neither is she."

"Are you now presuming to tell us how we're to dress off watch?" Riker said in a threatening tone. "I didn't intend to bring rank into this, but—"

"No!" Bitt said hastily. "Not at all, Dex Portside Sanitation Systems Supervisor!" He looked very worried indeed.

Riker pursued it. "Can't my spouse and I enjoy a party on this great day without some drunken idiot like you ruining it for us? What in—in hull is your designation, anyway?"

"Bitt Portside Ship's Stores Accountant Journeyman," the Krann stammered. "Forgive me, Supervisor. I—I did not know w-who you were." One of the females with Bitt looked stricken.

"You were never introduced, Bitt?" Wiggin asked, marveling. "You didn't even know their names, and yet you think they were under some sort of obligation to buy you a round? It does appear that the breach of protocol isn't on my friend Dex's side, not at all."

"Quiet, scuttler," hissed Bitt.

"No, *you* be quiet," Riker grated. "Now listen to this. You've disgraced yourself, and you've embarrassed our hosts on this great and special day. You will apologize to me, you will apologize to my spouse, you will apologize to our friend Wiggin for your last remark, and you will most certainly apologize to our hosts at the main table for this egregious disturbance you have caused."

Bitt paused. "Agreed," he finally said, tight-lipped. "Dex Portside Sanitation Systems Supervisor, I apologize to you for my conduct. Pralla Portside Consumables Monitor, I offer my apologies to you as well."

"I'm not finished," Riker continued. "You will now buy a round for everyone in the place."

"Everyone?" Bitt asked.

"Everyone," Riker replied. "Your friends will help you pay for it, of course. You'll pay half, and they'll make up the rest. You've all offended everyone here by your boorish behavior. Your friends participated in your little game with us just outside, and they followed you in here to see a fight. They share your blame—and they'll pay, just as you will."

"'The detail shares the duty,'" quoted Wiggin with a smirk.

Bitt nodded. "Agreed, Supervisor," he said, as the others mumbled their assent.

"Very well," Riker said in dismissal. "Apology accepted. Wiggin, call over a facilitator and put all that into motion, will you?" He suddenly grinned. "Everyone here seems pretty thirsty to me."

"Right away!" Wiggin chirped. He held up a hand with two fingers extended, and one of the female facilitators hurried through the crowd.

Bitt stood silently before Riker. "Well?" Riker finally asked. "Are you waiting for something, Bitt?"

"I was wondering if, er, that would be all, Supervisor," the Krann asked quietly.

"Oh," Riker replied. Clearly, he could impose yet another penalty on Bitt, but he had no idea of what it might be or of how to enforce it—and something in his gut told him that, in any case, enough was enough. "Yes," he said, his tone magnanimous. "That will be all."

There was a roar of approval from everyone present, and the music began playing again. Bitt was clearly relieved. One of Bitt's female friends hugged him hard while the two others, a male and a female, thanked Riker profusely.

Troi saw an opportunity and took it. She bent her head against the renewed clamor to speak to Wiggin. "Would you mind if these people joined us?" she asked him.

"Why, no, not at all," Wiggin replied grandly. "Plenty of room, *plenty* of room—and it's a great day, after all. C'mon, you pot cleaners, drag over some chairs and sit down with me and my friends Dex and Pralla." He clumsily patted Troi's hand, and she frowned at the uninvited approach. Wiggin blinked and withdrew his hand quickly.

Understandably, Bitt and his friends seemed hesitant to sit down. "Are you sure, Supervisor?" Bitt asked, ignoring Wiggin.

"Certainly," Riker told him. "I don't hold a grudge—and, after all, it's a great day."

"It certainly is," Bitt acknowledged. "Well, thank you, Dex Portside Sanitation Systems Supervisor. I and my friends would be pleased to join you." Bitt pulled back one of the chairs and sat down. "Come on, all of you," he said to his friends, a note of surprise in his voice. "We've been invited."

"That you have," Riker said. "Courtesy of our good friend Wiggin, here."

"Eh?" Wiggin asked. Then he shrugged and grinned. "Oh, well, a day like this one comes only once every couple of years, and I suppose my account can stand it." He looked at Troi and winked. "After all, the company is more than worth it."

Troi thought about it for a split second and then winked back, adding a slow and meaningful smile. Wiggin looked drunkenly blank at her for a moment and then, realizing that she had returned his volley in kind, seemed startled and confused.

Bitt cleared his throat and addressed Riker politely. "Permit me, Supervisor, to introduce my friends."

"Please," Riker said. "Call me Dex. And my wife is Pralla."

Bitt looked uncomfortable. "Uh, well, certainly, Dex and, uh, Pralla. Going antispinward around the table, I am pleased to introduce to you my friends Sharra Portside Electrician Journeyman, Nozz Portside Shaftway Maintainer Journeyman, and Lettana Starboard Plumbing Specialist Journeyman. As you can guess, Lettana recently transferred to our section."

"We're pledged," Lettana said, taking Bitt's hand. She smiled. "We're to be mated soon."

"Congratulations." Troi beamed. "That's wonderful." She took Riker's hand and looked very sincere. "I hope you and Bitt will always be as happy as Dex and I are now."

"Thank you," Bitt said uncomfortably.

"We decided we wanted to work in the same gang, too," Lettana added. "You know what they say: 'The couple that maintains together remains together.'"

"How very true," Riker commented.

"That's what *I* always say," slurred Wiggin.

"We wanted to be together as much as possible," Lettana said. "That's why I transferred from my duty station on the starboard side." She smiled at Bitt, who responded with a self-conscious, sheepish sort of grin.

"That's nice," Troi said, smiling. "Just the kind of story that puts you in the mood for a day like today. It *is* a great day, isn't it?"

"Sure is," Lettana said brightly. "A *great* day!

Posting Days usually are, of course—and it's been a long time since the last one." She patted Bitt's hand. "I hope we'll be as fortunate as Agrell and Twesla are, when our turn comes."

"How long do you think it'll take them to catch?" Bitt wondered.

"Not long, I bet," Nozz said. "I mean, just look at 'em. They probably can't wait for the party to be over so they can get started." He laughed. "Two months, tops. I'll put five work credits on it."

"There you guys go again," Sharra complained. "I swear you two have waste tubes for brains. Can't you ever behave?"

"Who? Us?" grinned Nozz. "When a lucky couple gets a fleet permit to breed, how and when they go about it is a fit subject for public speculation."

Ah, thought Riker. He glanced at Troi, who nodded.

"And private profit, too," Bitt said.

Lettana blinked. "Private profit? Are you guys betting on Agrell and Twesla? Our *friends?* I'm ashamed of you both."

"Good for you, Let," Sharra said approvingly.

"Thanks, Shar," Lettana said. "You know, you boys should have let us in on it from the beginning. Is there a pool yet? I've got seven work credits that say it'll take them six months."

"Oh, Let!" Sharra said, frowning. "Not you, too! Well, at least you and Bitt-for-brains over there are compatible."

Lettana ignored her. "I hear Agrell is working lots of extra watches, some of them on outside maintenance. Let's face it. Walking the hull every watch doesn't do much for your fertility."

"Hey, that's good information," Nozz said. "Thanks, Shar. Bitt, I hereby retract my wager."

Bitt looked properly regretful. "Can't let you do that, shipmate. Wouldn't be quite ethical."

"Ethics," complained Nozz. "Phooey."

"Uh, guys," Sharra began. "I don't quite think—" She gave a sidelong glance at Riker and Troi.

"Don't mind us," Riker said quickly.

Bitt frowned. "Actually, Supervisor—I mean, Dex—under fleet regulations, wagering is pretty high on the list of unauthorized financial transactions. We really shouldn't be—"

"Put me down for ten work credits on one month," Riker interrupted, a glint in his eye. "Agrell doesn't look like the type who'd let a few stray wavicles bother him any."

"My," Troi said mildly. "Relative of yours?"

The five young people erupted in loud laughter. "Oh, you're bad, Pralla," Wiggin said, wagging a finger.

"Why is Agrell going outside?" Sharra asked, puzzled. "His station doesn't require it."

"He's pulling extra duty," Lettana explained. "Hazard pay. It's voluntary on his part, of course. He's trying to finance a private module aboard the Upper Nation."

Nozz whistled, his eyes wide. "I didn't know that. Their own mod? At *their* age?"

"That kind of thing is a pretty expensive proposition for a young couple," Riker said knowingly.

"Tell me about it," Bitt shrugged. "Well, Agrell's connected. You know. He might just be able to pull it off soon. Hull, he and Twesla made the breeding list on the first try." The Krann shook his head. "Nice to be born in high orbit instead of having to boost yourself there, if you know what I mean."

Lettana looked a little sad. "A private module would be a nice thing to have," she said quietly.

"Just try and get one these days," Nozz said. "Restrictions on everything. Fill this out. Wait here. You wind up not doing anything except what you did yesterwatch and the watch before that. Never mind that you can't afford to do anything anyway, what with half your accrued credit balance being grabbed off every year for the military preparedness budget. Preparedness for what? Boogie men from the void?" He sighed, disgusted. "It's insane."

Wiggin nodded. "My grandfather says it was a lot different in his day, before the last planetfall."

"Mine says the same thing," Sharra said. "Things were a lot looser in the old days." She looked at Riker. "Do you remember the last planetfall, Dex?"

Riker guessed that he and Presider Hek might be taken for the same age. "Not really," he said. "I was very young then. I think I might remember a little about it."

"Weather," Bitt breathed. "I think I'd like to experience weather. I've read all about it. I wonder what it's really like."

"Maybe soon, shipmate," Nozz said. "This system we've entered is a promising one, or so I hear. We might find a planet we can run around on for a few years while we stock up."

Riker thought about it and decided to take the plunge. "What would you say if I told you there is such a planet here?" he asked.

Bitt looked at him blankly. "Excuse me, Dex?"

"There's such a planet here in this system. In fact, there are two of them."

The five Krann stared at Riker. "You're serious," Bitt said with something like wonder.

"I am."

"How do you—oh. I forgot. You're a supervisor. You'd know, if anyone would."

"Remember now," Riker warned them all. "You mustn't tell anybody."

Bitt shook his head emphatically. "There's not a chance we're going to tell anyone else, Dex—but this alone was worth the price of all those drinks."

"I don't believe it," Sharra said breathlessly. *"Two* planets! Maybe we'll finally settle down here."

"Dream on, Shar," Nozz said discouragingly. "We'll stay a while and then move on, just as usual. Look at your history tapes."

Sharra looked toward some distant point. "I wish we could stay anyway," she said. "I think I'd like to live by the water—an *ocean,* it's called. More water than you can imagine, so much so that things *live* in it."

"The old folks hate it when you talk about settling down," Nozz pointed out.

"Cycle 'em," Sharra grunted.

Troi spoke up. "Do you think you could live at peace in the same system with the Lethanta?"

The five Krann looked at her. "Excuse me?" Bitt asked.

The counselor tried again. "I said, do you think—?"

"Oh, we heard you all right, Pralla," Bitt said for them all. He looked puzzled. "But who in hull are the Lethanta?"

"Do you mean to say—" Troi began.

Just then every light in the bistro began blinking in a one-two-three rhythm. Riker stood quickly and, looking over the heads of the crowd and through the front window of the establishment, saw that all the big overhead lights in the concourse outside were blinking in exactly the same manner. People were milling about, confused. "What the hell—hull—is this?" he wondered out loud.

The Krann at the table seemed mystified. "Oh, hull," Bitt said softly. "One-two-three. It's one of the old-fashioned alert signals. We all had to learn them before becoming apprentices. Remember?"

"An alert signal?" Wiggin asked. "Are you sure? Maybe it's just a power interrupt."

"I'm sure," Bitt replied. "One-two-three means 'combat imminent.'"

"It's a drill of some sort," Nozz said. "It *must* be."

"No," Bitt said. "They wouldn't do something like that on Posting Day. This is no drill." He suddenly looked horrified. "Does this mean we're actually about to *fight* somebody?"

Chapter Thirteen

THE OLD WOMAN clutched the small book to her chest as she sat on the floor of the dimly lit shelter, her back to a crate marked CIVIL DEFENSE. The stained, ragged cloth cover of the book she was holding flapped to and fro as the woman rocked back and forth while mumbling something unintelligible, her eyes tightly closed. Data had long since analyzed what she was saying. It was a prayer.

The four of them—Data, Ro, a young man and the old woman—were seated in the middle of the small underground shelter, surrounded by crates and barrels. "She's beginning to get on my nerves," the man suddenly said.

"Excuse me, Tarrajel?" Ro asked.

"I said—oh, never mind," he said, sighing and waving a hand. "That was rude of me, Fessalahka," he said to Ro. "I'm sorry. I shouldn't have said anything. The old lady can't help it. It's just that some of the old folks still buy into all the crap the monks used to sell, and I'm tired of hearing about it." The young man shifted his weight and frowned more deeply. "I wonder when we'll be able to get out of here? This has been a pretty long alert. I wonder when they're coming?"

"This may be merely a drill," Data said.

"I hope you're right, Porratorat," Tarrajel told him.

"He might be," Ro said. "We haven't heard any explosions or anything."

"That doesn't necessarily mean much," Tarrajel said. "The Krann could be vaporizing the other side of the world. We'd never know."

"Perhaps we could leave the shelter," Data said. "I would like to go outside and look around. Perhaps we could learn something."

Tarrajel snorted. "The only thing you'd learn, my friend, is that being out on the street during an alert is a shoot-on-sight offense, like everything else is these days. Say, I saw somebody raising an illegal banner over the avenue just before I came down here. Did they catch anybody?"

"I do not know," Data replied. "The banner was cut down, but I did not see the authorities apprehend anyone."

"Well, that's good," Tarrajel said, settling back. "I don't have any use for the old religion, but I don't want to see anybody wind up in the hands of the police, either—not for putting up a sign, anyway. There are better reasons to go to jail."

The old woman stopped mumbling and opened her rheumy eyes. She wagged a finger at Tarrajel. "Prepare!" she said urgently. "The agents of vengeance are coming, and there can be no escape!"

"Prepare how?" Ro asked politely. "Please tell me."

The old woman looked at her suspiciously. "You're no Follower," she said. "Few of you young people are."

"No, I'm not a Follower," Ro said, putting on her most sincere look. "But I bear Followers no ill will, and I really want to know how to prepare for what's to come. The banner we've been talking about warned us to prepare. I'd like to know what that means." The ensign took the old woman's hand. "What's your name, mother?"

The old woman smiled timidly. Ro saw that she didn't have very many teeth, and the few she had were not in good shape. "Ilsewidna," she answered. "I work here. I work for the landlord. I clean up inside the building."

"Hello, Ilsewidna," Ro said. "I am Fessalahka, and this is my spouse, Porratorat."

"How do you do?" Data said politely.

"Do you already know the heretic in here with us?" Ilsewidna said sourly.

"My name is Tarrajel," the young man said. "I practice law. I have an office in the building. I see Ilsewidna just about every day. Hello again, mother."

"Don't you call me that," Ilsewidna grated. She refused to look at him. "You're always calling me that, and you're no son of mine." She held up her book and shook it approximately in Tarrajel's direction. "You mock the truth," she said, nodding vigorously. "You mock it with your disbelief, even when the truth is all around you, even when it is about to strike you dead. Well, it's all in here, every bit of it, no matter what the government says, or how many of us they imprison and torture."

"As you say, Ilsewidna," Tarrajel said mildly. "The truth is yours."

Ilsewidna moved closer to Ro. "Daughter," she began, "have you ever been given the truth? Was your mother a Follower? Or your grandmother, perhaps?"

Ro shook her head. "I'm afraid not, mother. I've never even heard of this book before."

"How terrible for you," Ilsewidna clucked. "What a wicked world this has become." She held the book up. "When I was a little girl, we had to read from the book for two hours each night after our work shifts were over. Oh, we could read, all right, no matter what stories the government tells you. We could read and write, and there was plenty to eat. Me and my brothers and sisters would sit by the firelight as one of us read the verses aloud. My mother would tell us what they meant if we didn't understand them. Life wasn't near as terrible as Kerajem and his crowd would like you to think."

"I'm sure it wasn't," Ro prompted. "What does the book say, mother?"

"It's truth," Ilsewidna said again. "That's all it is, and that's all it has to be."

Tarrajel cleared his throat. "Uh, Fessalahka, if I might try to explain—?"

Ilsewidna frowned as Ro shifted to face the young man. "Yes?"

"Actually, Ilsewidna is right," Tarrajel said. "The book *is* truth, or at least it's truth of a sort. It's truth as viewed through a distorting glass of time and tradition, but it's truth nevertheless—unfortunately for us."

"Truth," Ilsewidna insisted. *"Truth!"*

Tarrajel waved a hand. "Yes, Ilsewidna. It's truthful enough. The book—*The Holy Book of the Exile*—tells in very obscure and confusing language the story of how, thousands of years ago, our people enslaved and abused an innocent race, which eventually rebelled against our rule and forced us to leave our native world."

"That would be the Krann," Data observed.

"So it seems," Tarrajel said. "Historical events are not stated in straightforward terms in the *Book of Exile,* but the ancient writings can be interpreted to

199

foretell the Krann invasion. I'm not surprised you and your spouse haven't heard of the book, Porratorat. Few people our age have, and fewer still have read it. The *Book of Exile* has been suppressed since the revolution."

"I have read it," Data said. "An acquaintance of ours recently gave me a copy."

"How unusual, Porratorat," Tarrajel said. "Well, what did you think of it?"

"I believe the ancient writings in the book can be interpreted in any number of ways," Data told him matter-of-factly. "They can certainly be interpreted in a manner that predicts the present crisis."

"How did you come to know of the book, Tarrajel?" Ro asked.

The young man grinned. "I was a history student before I went into law, and I decided that I needed to read the *Book of Exile* to understand my chosen subject more fully. I've always believed in doing as many illegal things as possible, and I don't believe in the government's right to tell me what I can and cannot read. I've studied the *Book of Exile* very closely—as an historical text, of course, not a religious one. As religion, it's pretty thin stew."

"Truth!"

"Yes, Ilsewidna," Tarrajel said. "As I've said, it is truth—but only of a sort." He addressed Data and Ro again. "The book is apparently based on our earliest written records, the ones we brought with us from our homeworld. Those records, of course, were all lost during the dark centuries that followed our arrival here. We think the book was written from oral histories that were developed during that time. That made the text subject to corruption."

"The 'dark centuries'?" Ro asked. "Um, I'm sorry, Tarrajel. I was never very good at history."

"Not much to remember, in this case," Tarrajel

said. "When we arrived here, the civilization that had been maintained throughout the long journey from the homeworld aboard the asteroid ships broke apart quickly. People spread out all over the planet. It took centuries for our people to draw together again and start building a planetary civilization. The *Book of Exile* dates from the beginning of that era."

"You said the book represented truth, Tarrajel," Data said. "Why did you say that?"

"The book has been proven correct in one very important way," the young man said. "The most important thing that's in the book, the thing that concerns all of us now, is its promise that one day, should we not repent our sins against the enslaved race, that race would find us and annihilate us."

"And we did *not* repent and it *has* found us and we are all going to *die!*" cried Ilsewidna. She pointed a finger at Tarrajel. "The monks were keeping the beast at bay with their holy sacrifices, but your radical friends in the government killed or imprisoned all of them."

"Now, Ilsewidna—" Tarrajel began.

The old woman ignored him. "The radicals destroyed the church," she continued bitterly. "They pulled down all our institutions and replaced them with lies and more lies. They changed the holy way we lived, where adults and children worked together, worked hard, to build a holy world full of hope and free from fear. They destroyed truth and created a false paradise that drew the ultimate evil of the Krann to us like a magnet draws iron. And now we're all going to die in flame and fire and horror, just as the holy book promises."

"The Krann will not necessarily attack, Ilsewidna," Data said. "There is still reason to hope for a peaceful solution."

"No," Ilsewidna said dully, clutching the book to

her. "No, there's no hope left. The Krann are here, and they're bringing war and death to us all, and it'll be the price for our sins. We didn't obey the law, and so we'll die. It's in the book." Ilsewidna's eyes filled with tears. "I have three grandchildren," she said thickly. "Don't they have a right to grow up? Don't they? They haven't hurt nobody. They never enslaved no one, they never did nothing wrong. They're good little kiddies, mindful of their manners and always nice to their grandma. I taught them their prayers, too, even when their mother didn't want me to and their father hit me and threatened to call the police on me, to put me in jail. They're so little. So little . . ." Her voice trailed off.

"Ilsewidna is only one of millions," Tarrajel said. "You've seen them around recently, no doubt. The Followers see our doom at the hands of the Krann as assured, and even deserved. It's been hushed up, but some Followers have been caught engaging in acts of sabotage against the defense effort. They believe they're helping to fulfill the promise of the *Book of Exile*. That's why the interpretation of the prophecy is so important. If enough people believe it and act upon it, it will hamper any effort we may make to defend ourselves against the Krann."

"The prophecy of doom thus becomes a self-fulfilling one," Data observed.

"But how can a book written by primitive people be so correct about what's happening to us right now?" Ro wondered. "That's not possible, is it?"

Tarrajel closed his eyes and leaned back against one of the crates. "I wouldn't have thought so myself," Tarrajel said sadly. "Given the horrible crimes our people committed so long ago, though, prophesying the vengeance of the Krann might be pretty much like predicting tomorrow's sunrise. You'd have a high probability of being right."

"The Krann are going to kill us," the old woman mumbled. "They're going to kill us with fire and flame."

"I know, mother," Tarrajel said quietly. He closed his eyes. The shelter was silent then, except for the soft crying of Ilsewidna and the sympathetic, hollow sound from somewhere of dripping water.

Suddenly, distantly, there was a quick series of thuds. The four of them could feel the vibration as they sat on the thick concrete floor.

Ro took a chance and tapped her communicator. "Ro to *Enterprise*," she called. There was no response.

"What are you doing, Fessalahka?" Tarrajel asked Ro.

The ensign ignored him. "Please try yours, sir," she asked Data.

The android activated his own communicator. "Data to *Enterprise*," he said. Nothing.

"I am not getting any response," he told Ro after a moment. "I do not believe the signal is getting through. Perhaps it is being blocked somehow, or the ship may no longer be in range."

"Or it may have been destroyed," Ro frowned.

"That possibility exists."

"What are you two *talking* about—?" Tarrajel demanded.

The building they were in suddenly rocked back and forth like flotsam caught in heavy surf, and things went flying. A terrible noise came an instant later and remained. The rolling went on for some time.

"Judgment!" Ilsewidna screamed. *"Judgment has come at last!"*

Ro looked at Data. "I'd like to use the tricorder now, Commander. Permission to operate openly at this point?"

"Permission granted. Your scalp is bleeding, Ensign. Are you in any pain?"

"Not so you'd notice." Ro took out her tricorder and, in plain view of Tarrajel and Ilsewidna, began scanning over their heads. After a moment, she sighed heavily. "I was afraid of that," she said. "It was nuclear, all right. Wasn't a very big blast, though, since we're still around to talk about it. Ground zero was six point three kilometers east of here."

"I believe there is—was—an airport at that location," Data said.

"More bad news," Ro continued. "The building above us is on fire and is threatening to collapse. We can't stay here, sir."

"Agreed," Data said. "We will leave at once."

"I'm not leaving," Tarrajel said flatly. "It's not safe out there."

"Maybe you didn't hear me," Ro said. "It's not too safe down here, either."

Tarrajel shook his head firmly. "They're still bombing us, Fessalahka—or whatever your real name is." He put the palm of his hand flat on the concrete floor. "You can even feel it."

"You'll bake like bread, stupid," Ro told him. *"The building is on fire!* You and us and the old woman will have a chance of living through this mess if we all leave here *right now."* She studied her tricorder again. "We're upwind from the airport, so unless there's another nuclear strike near here—"

"How do *you* know?" Tarrajel snorted. "Who *are* you people, anyway?"

"Little visitors from heaven," Ro returned sarcastically. "What'd you think?"

"I *knew* it!" Ilsewidna shouted. "I was not forgotten, even at the last. All praise to the monks!"

"Fine, mother," Ro said distractedly. "Commander, I say we head for Government House."

"Would that not be a priority target for the Krann?" Data asked.

"Not necessarily, sir. The strike at the airport was a tactical hit. If the Krann were going to attack the entire city, they'd have done so by now. I think they'll refrain from hitting the political headquarters too hard, if only so there's someone left among the Lethantan leadership to surrender to them when all this is over. I wouldn't give you two strips of latinum for the rest of the planet, though."

"I see." Data tapped his communicator again. There was no response. "Very well. We shall go to Government House."

"You can't get out of here," Tarrajel said. "The blast door up on street level won't roll back until the all clear is sounded—and if they catch you on the street during an alert, they'll shoot you."

"They'll have to catch us first," Ro said. "The door won't be a problem. How do you open the door down here, anyway?"

"That red crank right there to the left of the hatch, child," Ilsewidna told her. "See it?"

"Yes. Thank you, mother. Are you two coming along or not?"

"No," Tarrajel said. "I'll take my chances here. Whatever else you two are, you're also crazy."

"I'll stay and take care of him, daughter," Ilsewidna said. "After all, nothing bad's going to happen to *me.*"

"I hope you're right, Mother," Ro told her. Almost embarrassed, she bent and quickly kissed Ilsewidna on the top of her head. "Mother Ilsewidna, you take care of yourself."

"You, too, child," the old woman said. "Take care of that husband of yours, too. He's a quiet one, but he's as smart as all get-out. You watch out that someone else don't grab him."

205

"Oh, don't worry," Ro said, hiding a smile. "I won't let that happen."

"Good for you." Ilsewidna looked into Ro's eyes and raised a hand to stroke her cheek. "I had a one like you once," she said. "Gone these many years now. Just up and disappeared one day. Lively, smart, and pretty as a sunrise. Then she was gone. Ran off, I guess, but I don't know why. I don't think she's dead, but she never wrote me, not even once." Her eyes filled, and then she blinked rapidly. "Well, you take care, daughter," she finished, patting Ro's cheek.

"Stay safe, mother. We'll leave the upstairs door open for you, just in case you change your mind." Ro spun the crank, and the shelter door smoothly rolled aside.

"Thanks, dear," the old woman chirped, "but everything will be fine now. You'll see."

Ro did not look at her again. "Commander?" she called. "I'm ready. Meet you topside." She left the shelter and headed up the stairs.

"Very well," Data replied. He turned to the other two. "I wish you both luck," he said. "However, your luck will be enhanced if you do not remain here too long."

Tarrajel remained stubbornly silent. "Thanks, son," Ilsewidna said, "but we'll be fine. Get along, now. You go take care of your wife."

"Ah. Yes. Yes, so I shall. Good-bye." Data left the shelter and, hurrying up the dark stairs, met Ro at the top landing. Smoke was beginning to fill the place.

"Do you want to do the honors, sir?" Ro asked.

Data nodded, drew his phaser, and fired at the blast door. It crumpled and fell with a loud crash into the street. They stepped over it and looked around.

"Wait a moment," Data said, holding up a hand. A second later, from below, they heard the downstairs shelter door roll back into place. "Very well," he said. "Let us leave."

Data and Ro looked up and down the boulevard as they hurried away from the building. The street was strewn with the wreckage of buildings and cars. Despite the strict civil defense regulations, not everyone had bothered to go to a shelter; there were bodies everywhere. They could see other people, still alive, hurrying through the fire and smoke and wreckage along the boulevard. They were heading no one knew where—to homes that perhaps no longer existed.

The fighting was still going on. In the distance there were dozens of bright flashes as conventional weapons were brought to bear on the civilian population of the capital. Through the smoke and haze that now hung over the city, Data and Ro could see Government House, still intact, sticking up like a black finger of defiance against a blood-red sky.

Ro studied her tricorder again. "The Krann must be attacking from orbit, sir," she reported as they continued down the boulevard. "The only aircraft overhead are not bombing the city—therefore, I assume they're friendly."

"Reasonable, Ensign." Data looked around. "I think we had better hurry to Government House—" He was interrupted by a tearing, grinding sound behind them. The two *Enterprise* officers whirled around just in time to see the building in which they had taken shelter shudder and collapse, crushing and burying whoever and whatever was inside.

Ro's scan for life signs was negative.

They moved on.

Chapter Fourteen

FIVE OF THE SIX surviving members of the Council of Ministers of Nem Ma'ak Bratuna were seated around the table in the conference room at Government House, which still stood. One or two of the men at the table looked determined, while the others seemed frightened and uncertain. Three of their number were dead or missing as a result of the Krann raid—a raid that the Council itself seemed to have precipitated.

For his part, Picard was seething, but he was hiding it well. He remained seated in his chair in the bridge command area, hoping that doing so would send an unspoken message that would soothe the Lethantan leadership and calm the ministers down a bit. It was the kind of subtle thing that had worked before—the Picard touch. Unfortunately, it was not working very well now.

"First Among Equals," the captain began, "it was not helpful for you to have declared a planetwide military alert—even if, as you say, it was for defensive purposes only. As I have told you, Presider Hek of the Krann took your move as an aggressive one and authorized an initial strike on Nem Ma'ak Bratuna. That offensive continues even now with heavy losses on both sides. I must also tell you that a promising avenue for negotiations to resolve this crisis peacefully has simply evaporated away. The most that can be done now is to try to stop the fighting. I suggest a truce in place—"

Kerajem opened his mouth to speak, but Security Minister Jemmagar interrupted him. "Pardon me, First, but the captain has issued a direct challenge to the authority of this body, and I must respond to it." Kerajem nodded without looking at Jemmagar.

"Captain Picard," the security minister began, "I'm sure we all appreciate your efforts on behalf of peace—"

"I'm certain you do, Minister Jemmagar," Picard said blandly.

"Er, yes, yes, we do, but we of the Council of Ministers have a grave responsibility to assure that our people are prepared to deal with the undeniable threat from the Krann. The defense drill was long scheduled—"

Picard's mouth tightened. "Minister Jemmagar, your practice alert was sheerest folly. It appeared to the Krann that you were undertaking a preemptive strike on the forward units of their fleet—units *you* could detect, although we could not, because you chose not to share with us your discovery that the Krann had adjusted their camouflage techniques to foil our sensors. We might have been able to avert this war if you had." He paused. "I must ask you to refrain from declaring military alerts and taking similar actions from here on. I cannot be held responsible for the consequences if you do."

"The council has a responsibility to the people,"

Jemmagar said ponderously. "We will not be, be scolded by you, Picard, as if we were schoolboys."

"Yes," Picard replied bitingly. "Yes, you do have a responsibility to your people, Minister Jemmagar. Let me suggest to you that it lies in getting them through this crisis and out the other end as safely as possible while your civilization remains relatively intact." He shifted his attention to Kerajem. "First Among Equals, which is it to be? Do we get the chance to resolve this situation without further loss of life, or do we abandon all hope, thanks to sheer stubbornness? Peace is still possible, but not if either party continues to act precipitously."

Kerajem paused for a moment, and then nodded. "There will be no more drills," he said. "We will provoke the Krann no further. You have my word on it, Picard."

"But, First—" Jemmager began.

Kerajem held up a hand. "No more. You have my word on it, Captain Picard—but this concession on our part presupposes that the Krann will cease hostilities and offer no further aggressive moves of their own." He hesitated. "Please offer the respects of the High Council to Presider Hek and the members of the Fleet Congress."

"I will certainly do so," Picard said quickly. "Thank you, Kerajem. I will relay this news to Presider Hek immediately. Picard out." The captain did not allow himself a sigh of relief until the view of the conference room was replaced by the usual starfield. "Mr. Worf," he said after a moment, "hail the Krann flagship. I want to talk to Presider Hek."

The crowd in the bistro was mumbling again, but for a different reason. "Hull, the rhythm's changed," Bitt said, looking up at the lights. "Three-three-three now. I think that means—"

"Alert canceled," Wiggin slurred. "Everything's over. You're not the only one who knows his alert signals, my friend. Hey, what's the alert for an empty pitcher, anyway?" He held it up and waved it around. "C'mon, facilitator. *Facilitator!* Show's over, and my friends here want another drink."

"Actually," Bitt said, "I think Lettana and I would like to leave now." He glanced up at the lights. "I just realized I haven't talked to my parents for quite a while, and I expect the lines will be tied up." He addressed Wiggin. "If you'll excuse us——?"

"Oh, sure, sure," Wiggin replied. "Thanks for the gift of your company, and all that. Happy Posting Day. 'Bye."

"I think we'll leave, too," Nozz said, taking Sharra's hand. "We thank you for your hospitality, Wiggin, and we hope we can repay it in kind before long."

Bitt turned to Riker and Troi. He tapped his breast one-twice-thrice. "I am glad we met, Dex, Pralla. I am glad we have formed a friendship."

The two disguised *Enterprise* officers rose from their seats and returned the tapping gesture. "So are we, Bitt. Happy Posting Day to you and Lettana. Nozz and Sharra, the same to you."

"And to you, Dex and Pralla. Good-bye." The two couples turned and began to snake their way through the crowd.

"Nice folks," Wiggin said. "Too bad they had to rush off like that." He winked at Troi. She smiled and winked back.

Riker bent close to Troi's ear. "What's going on *now?*" he asked her, his voice low.

"Our friend Wiggin wants to get me alone," Troi replied, "and I intend to let him. Go to the bathroom, Will. It's in the back, just to the right of the bar. There are two of them. They're sexually segregated here.

211

Yours has a symbol on the door that looks like a figure eight."

"Good idea. It'll give me a chance to call the captain and find out what's been happening." He raised his voice. "If you will excuse me, Wiggin," he said pleasantly, "I'll be back in a few minutes. How about getting that pitcher refilled while I'm gone?"

"Got to see a journeyman about the plumbing, eh?" Wiggin said loudly, and heads turned. "Hope everything comes out all right, Dex." He laughed hysterically at his own joke.

Riker glanced at Troi and, shrugging, gave her a wan smile as he walked away.

Wiggin smiled drunkenly at Troi, which somehow made him look even more boyish. He suddenly leaned forward, putting his elbows on the table and resting his chin in his hands. "Hello, Pralla," he said. "Fancy meeting *you* here. I'm glad."

Troi smiled. "I'm glad I met you, too, Wiggin. It's a great day all around."

"Best Posting Day I've ever had, that's for sure. Look, do you mind if I tell you something?"

"Go ahead."

"You are the most beautiful woman I've ever seen." Wiggin gave Troi what he must have thought was a sensual look, but it was all the counselor could do to keep from laughing.

"You know, Wiggin," Troi said after a moment, "there's an empty chair right here next to me. I don't think Dex will be back for a while."

Wiggin seemed startled, and then he smiled. "All right." He shifted over. "This is better."

"Yes, it is." She patted Wiggin's hand. "This is *much* better."

"You were worried during the alert," Wiggin told her. "I could tell."

"A little," Troi said, putting just the right amount

of nervousness into her voice. "It was very unusual, wasn't it?"

"It sure was," he replied. "I've never been through an alert before."

Troi smiled. "Well, to tell you the truth, neither have I."

Wiggin waved a hand. "No need to be scared. There's nothing that can hurt us." He moved closer to her. "I wish I could talk about it, but I can't." He put a finger to his lips.

"Oh? Well, I can certainly respect your privacy—"

"Nope," Wiggin said, shaking his head firmly. "Can't talk about it, not even a little. Orders. They've got us working heel-and-toe watches in weapons design, you know. They'd get pretty mad at me if I ever talked about it. You know, I've got no social life at all."

"I'm sorry about that. I really am."

Wiggin seemed to be lost in thought. "Maybe I could show you."

"Excuse me?"

"Maybe I could show you the section where I work, I mean. People are brought through sometimes. Relatives, people like that. You know. Wait a minute. How much trouble could I get into? Hull, you're the spouse of a supervisor. You must have a security clearance, right?"

Troi nodded quickly. "Uh, that's right. Of course I do."

"And the watch is young," Wiggin said. He winked at Troi again. "It could be a magic one."

"It might be," Troi admitted. "Why, I might disappear into thin air before it's over, just like *that.*" She snapped her fingers.

"Oh, not you," the young Krann said. "You're a hot-blooded one, you are."

"Now, Wiggin," Troi said, patting his hand gently. "Stop that. What would my spouse say?"

"Hull if I know," the young Krann replied. "Want to stick around long enough to find out?"

Troi paused. "No, not really," she said, finishing her drink. "Let's get out of here."

"Debit stub!" Wiggin cried, and a facilitator quickly appeared at his elbow. She gave him a chit, which Wiggin thumbprinted in a corner. "All right," he said, grinning. "Done! Let's *blow* this *lagga* stand!"

Troi tapped her communicator. "I'm right behind you."

There was what appeared to be a delivery entrance toward the back of the bistro, just beyond the bathrooms and very near the kitchen. Since the heavily used bathrooms were far from private, Riker walked past them and through a door marked NO EXIT.

He found himself in a narrow, unoccupied passage that ran for a dozen meters in both directions before making abrupt turns to port and starboard. There were doors similar to the one he had just gone through spotted here and there along both sides of the corridor. Riker thought the corridor must be part of some sort of cargo delivery system that was designed to keep freight vehicles off the concourse.

Riker reached into the pocket of his Krann clothing and slipped the audio pickup bug into his left ear. He then tapped the communicator. "Riker to *Enterprise*," he said quietly. "Are you receiving me?"

"Loud and clear, Commander," came Geordi's voice. *"Are you receiving us?"*

"You're coming through five by five."

"Good. Patching in the captain now."

There was a very brief pause. *"Hello, Will,"* Picard greeted him. *"Is Counselor Troi there with you?"*

"No, sir. She's not far away, however. We're in no danger. I'd like to make my report."

"Go ahead."

Riker gathered his thoughts. "Captain, the people on this flagship apparently have no idea that the fleet is about to go to war with the Lethanta. There is a major holiday in progress aboard this ship, and virtually everyone seems to be celebrating it. I've seen the way civilian populations conduct themselves during wartime, and what I'm seeing here is in no way similar. These people are at peace, or at least they think they are. The only sign of impeding hostilities was the declaration of a combat alert some two hours ago, and it took everyone around us completely by surprise. They were all frightened and shocked."

"We know about that alert, Will. The Lethanta held a planetary defense drill, and the Krann took it as a provocation. In response, elements of the Krann fleet carried out an attack on various Lethantan targets, civilian and military alike. The losses on both sides have been high, but the effect on Nem Ma'ak Bratuna has been nothing short of devastating. I've arranged a truce in place, pending negotiations between the Lethanta and the Krann, again with us acting as mediator. All Krann forces are returning or have already returned to their original stations. I must also tell you, Will, that Commander Data and Ensign Ro are missing, following an attack on the Lethantan capital. We have not been able to raise them."

Riker stroked his chin in thought. "I see. All of this explains a great deal, sir—but it does *not* explain why none of the Krann we were with understood what was happening, or why."

"Where have you been, by the way?"

"At a party. Sir."

"Oh. Excellent way to meet people. What did you find out?"

"Today is an important Krann holiday called Posting Day, Captain. It is the day upon which Krann authorities grant married couples permits to have babies."

"I see," Picard said. *"Procreation is very strictly controlled, then."*

"I believe so, sir. The permits are issued only every few years and are apparently hard to come by even then. Influence appears to count. Couples who receive one throw a big party, the bigger the better. We dropped in on one of those. The size and location of the couple's Posting Day celebration confer status upon them, according to what we've heard."

"Rather like an Earth wedding, I suppose. Your point, Number One?"

"Sir, it seems to me that these people don't have a clue as to what's going on between the Krann and the Lethanta. There were a lot of people where we were, all of them in a relaxed social situation. Counselor Troi and I talked to young people who have never even *heard* of the Lethanta. The Krann we've met know they've arrived in a new star system, but they have not been told that it contains two class-M planets." He paused. "Captain, Presider Hek said we'd see his intentions were peaceful if we came aboard. I wonder if he was telling the truth, after all?"

"Sir?" came Geordi's voice, interrupting. *"Counselor Troi's subspace communicator link has just been opened, but she isn't talking to us. I've got her located."*

"Is she in trouble, Geordi?" Riker asked quickly.

"I don't think so, Commander. From what I'm hearing, the counselor is engaged in normal conversation with a person named Wiggin. And she's on the move—now thirty meters from your position, bearing four fifty-four mark five. Distance from your position is increasing at normal walking speed."

"She hasn't set off her emergency recall signal, has she, Mr. La Forge?" Picard asked.

"No, sir, she has not."

"I don't believe she's being kidnapped, then," Picard said. *"If she was able to activate the communicator for audio pickup, she could just as easily have actuated the recall signal. No, the counselor simply wanted to let us know that she was going somewhere. Number One, tell me quickly about this Wiggin."*

"We met him at the party," Riker replied. "He's a young Krann who claims to be a weapons designer of some sort. I think he may not be what he claims to be."

"You think he may have been a plant."

"Yes, sir. I believe he arrived at the celebration just after we did and only pretended he'd been there all along."

"I see. So you believe your location aboard the flagship has been detected."

"Yes, sir. I do."

"If that's true, then the Krann want you to be there, at least for now," Picard observed. *"They haven't done a thing to remove you. I wonder why?"*

"We do have their agreement to board their ships and take a look around, sir."

Riker heard Picard chuckle. *"Yes, but I hardly expected them to live up to it quite this diligently. Well, we'll take advantage of Presider Hek's apparent generosity for as long as possible. Number One, Mr. La Forge will guide you to Counselor Troi's present position. Follow her and this Wiggin person, but don't be caught at it. I'll now leave you in the hands of Mr. La Forge. Picard out."*

"Aye, sir. Geordi?"

"Locked on to you, Will."

"Good." Riker opened the service door and, looking around, stepped inside the bistro. "I'm heading for the concourse just outside the restaurant," he said very quietly. "How far away are they now?"

Troi and Wiggin were heading down the concourse. The crowds swarming through the passageways had not ebbed. If anything, they had grown, despite—or perhaps due to—the combat alert not long before. The counselor considered that some of the Krann might be celebrating their relief.

"*Wait'll* you see this!" Wiggin said enthusiastically. "Anybody who has is really impressed—and I helped substantially with the design, of course."

"So I assume you're going to show me a weapon of some sort?" Troi asked lightly.

"Maybe, maybe not," the young Krann said, grinning. "It's supposed to be a secret. You'll see."

"*Counselor, this is Picard,*" came a voice in Troi's ear. "*We have been listening in and are tracking your movements via your communicator. I assume you are wearing your audio pickup. If you are, tap the communicator once.*"

Troi did so unobtrusively.

"*Very good. We have you heading for an area that we've marked on our maps as one of the main mass transit stations aboard the flagship. Tap once if you understand.*"

Troi did so.

"*All right,*" Picard said. "*We see that the inbound portion of the tube system leads directly into the area of the flagship that we have been unable to probe with our sensors. Wiggin may be taking you there, and Mr. La Forge says we will likely lose communication with you when you enter that zone. Commander Riker is trailing you at a distance. He will follow you into the sensor-proof zone, and he'll be there to render assist-*"

ance, should you need it. Good luck to you, Counselor. Picard out."

The tube car stopped in a station marked BAY FOURTEEN, and Troi and Wiggin pushed their way out onto the platform. The station was choked with passengers.

"Sorry, Pralla," Wiggin said. "We've hit the end-of-watch commuter hour. It's the worst time to be here. Just push your way through. Go *that* way." He pointed.

Troi did so. "Today was *supposed* to be a holiday," Troi complained.

"Oh, it's no holiday *here,* and especially not *now,* with all that's going on." Wiggin moved through the crowd toward Troi and took her hand again. "I'll show you what I mean," he said, pulling her along. "Come on."

There were two exits from Bay Fourteen—a large, open arch through which commuters could move freely into yet another concourse, and a small, closed door that appeared to be a security gate. Wiggin was leading Troi there.

The gate was closed and had two armed guards stationed at a booth just to its side. Troi's talents gave her no ability to learn anything useful from their body language. The guards *seemed* relaxed, but—

Troi hoped Will had caught the same tube car that she and Wiggin had, and that he was still following her. Geordi had been right about the communicator blackout. She had not heard from the *Enterprise* since shortly after the car had entered the gray zone. In fact, the communicator was completely dead within the zone, thanks to whatever kind of sensor-killing field it was that was blanketing everything here. With her communicator nonfunctional, she could not even attempt to contact Will. Troi was tempted to look around the platform for him, but Wiggin might catch her at it and grow suspicious.

This whole idea was mad, she fretted. She chastised herself for stupidly allowing herself to be mouse-trapped so neatly by this besotted boy. She had only Will Riker's conjecture that their presence aboard the flagship had been detected, and that this young Krann was actually an operative who had been assigned to them. If Wiggin was genuine, it meant that Troi was trapped in what appeared to be a high-security area with no possibility of beaming out. Just how was she supposed to get inside a Krann security zone without being caught, anyway? Wiggin had apparently assumed right off the bat that she had one, since she was the spouse of a supervisor.

Troi knew she had put Will at risk, too, if he had managed to follow her here. Given the circumstances, she hoped he had not. Thinking about it carefully, the counselor decided that she might have a chance to make a break for it while the guards processed Wiggin at the security entrance. Just a quick lunge through the open archway nearby and on into the concourse just off the station, and she'd be away, lost in the crowds. Then she'd try to head out of the gray area and contact the ship. If Will was still following her, he would figure it all out and do the same thing.

But Troi also knew that if Wiggin was a Krann operative after all, then everything would be fine because he was doing an excellent job of leading her around by the nose. It meant that she was being taken to Bay Fourteen for a reason. She was being taken to see something, and a little thing like a security clearance wouldn't matter. If the Krann already knew of her presence aboard their flagship and wanted to arrest and detain her, they'd have done so by now.

It was odd, but Troi knew that her continued safety

depended on Wiggin being a complete phony. If he was genuine, she was dead. Either way, she'd soon find out.

"Here's where I work," Wiggin said. "It's a lot more impressive inside, let me tell you."

The first thing Troi noticed as she and Wiggin drew closer to the security gate was that the guards were waving people through rather casually. That was a good sign.

"Is it always this crowded?" Troi asked as they slowly oozed their way toward the security gate with the rest of the crowd.

"The next watch is arriving for duty," Wiggin told her. "Like I said, it's a bad time." He fished in one of his pockets and extracted a small, round object that looked like a coin. "Get your disk ready, and we'll go right on through."

"Uh, Wiggin, I don't know quite how to tell you this, but I don't have my disk with me."

"Huh?"

"I don't have my disk. I must have, uh, dropped it somewhere. Perhaps I lost it somehow at the party. You know how it is. I'm sorry."

"Hull, wait a minute. We're almost at the gate." Wiggin called over to one of the guards, an older Krann in a green uniform. "Guss! *Guss!*" He waved, and the guard spotted him. Wiggin took Troi's hand again and sidled over to the guard post.

"Hello, Wiggin," the guard said. "What are you doing here? Pulling some extra duty?" He looked Troi up and down, and his eyes seemed to say, *Another one, Wiggin?*

"No, nothing so selfless," Wiggin replied. "I was bringing this beautiful friend of mine over to see the shop, but she's lost her disk somewhere. Is it okay to get her a visitor's pass?"

The guard shrugged. "We're not under alert any

longer, and I got no orders to the contrary, so I guess it's okay." He grinned. "You a spy, lady?"

Troi smiled at him. "Do I look like a spy?"

"Matter of fact, you do, but never mind." The guard reached under his desk for something and came up with a glass plate about thirty centimeters long and fifteen wide. "Gimme your name and thumbprint on here. Bureaucrats. Gotta have a record of everything. You know." He passed the plate over.

On closer inspection, Troi saw that it was actually a glass sandwich. There was the lightest tracing of internal circuitry between the two panes. A stylus was clipped along one long side of the glass.

"Thankful she'd studied Krann writing, Troi carefully signed "Pralla Portside Consumables Monitor" across the face of the glass. The stylus left a golden glowing trace as she wrote. She then placed her right thumbprint within an engraved square and handed the glass back to the guard with a smile.

"Boy, you sure do write big," he said. "You vouch for her, Wiggin?"

"Sure do."

"Put your print here, then." Wiggin did, and Guss took the stylus and scribbled something on the glass. He then handed Troi a button. "Okay, hon, this is a visitor's badge. Stick it somewhere on your collar so the sensors can see it, and go on ahead inside. Give it back when you leave." He grinned. "Otherwise, we have to chase you."

Troi clipped the button next to her throat. "Thank you, Guss."

"Any time."

"Let's go," Wiggin said to her, and they went on through.

Chapter Fifteen

HEK'S FACE FILLED THE VIEWSCREEN on the bridge of the *Enterprise*. He looked very much like a man who'd just pulled off a rather complicated and very convincing card trick. His bright, aquamarine eyes seemed to be dancing.

For his part, Captain Picard was a bit bewildered. "This is very good news indeed, Presider Hek," he said, rising from his seat. Practiced as Picard was in hiding his personal emotions while conducting the necessary business of diplomacy, he was not quite successful at doing so this time. There was a note of surprise in his voice as he continued, "I am certain that the Council of Ministers will welcome your offer of a tentative peace settlement while formal negotiations between your two peoples get under way."

Hek shrugged. "Didn't expect us to be so reasonable, eh, Captain Picard?" He laughed. "I suppose I should have expected that. Perhaps we have not been very reasonable up to now on our side."

Picard shook his head. "It's not that, Presider Hek. I simply had no idea that your Fleet Congress desired to open negotiations with the Lethanta quite so soon—or to conduct such wide-ranging talks with them, once you did."

Hek nodded. "I can see why," he said. "I'm not a stupid man, Captain. I know we are perceived as the aggressor here. We came to this system with the intent of avenging crimes against us, of settling scores that are millennia old, of finding our oppressors and destroying them. It remains true that many of our people still seek vengeance against the Lethanta. However, the outbreak of open hostilities between our people and theirs has scared enough members of our Congress into seeking another, peaceful solution. I, of course, am the agent of the will of the Fleet Congress."

"Of course," Picard said. "Might I inquire as to your terms, sir?"

Hek paused for a moment to study his fingernails. "There was mention made of an uninhabited class-M planet in this system," he finally said. "I think we might profitably explore what happens to that planet, for a start."

"I will broach that subject with the Council of Ministers at the earliest opportunity," Picard said. "Might I ask you when our own next meeting is to take place?"

"In ten hours," Hek said, stifling a yawn. "It's been a long watch, Captain Picard. I need some sleep before we begin this next phase. This next session will be aboard our flagship, if that's agreeable to you. I don't feel free to leave the flagship while the crisis continues."

"I quite understand, Presider Hek," Picard said. "May I tell the council that you will order the Fleet to maintain, say, a million-kilometer distance from standard orbit at Nem Ma'ak Bratuna, as a sign of your good will? The second wave of your Fleet is quickly approaching that limit."

Hek frowned darkly. "I'd like to see how the talks with the Lethanta go first," he said. "Our ships will do them no harm, so long as the talks between us remain worthwhile. Is that all for now, Captain?"

"I think so," Picard replied. "Thank you again, Presider Hek."

"I will see you in ten hours, then. Out." The screen returned to showing the view forward as Picard reseated himself. "Well," he said to himself. "That was a rather remarkable performance, I must say. Of course, I don't believe a word of it. Mr. Worf?" the captain asked over his shoulder. "What do you think?"

"He is stalling for time, Captain. He has made his decision. He intends to fight. He will fight *us* if need be."

Picard nodded. "I agree. This stuff about him being the agent of his Congress is all so much blown smoke. Hek makes the decisions, not the Fleet Congress. So what's going on here? *Why* is Hek stalling for time?"

"Sir," Worf said, "if they maintain their present rate of deceleration, the main elements of the Krann attack force will arrive at standard orbit, Nem Ma'ak Bratuna, in ten hours. That is when you are supposed to meet next with Presider Hek—at his suggestion."

Picard rubbed his eyes wearily. "Mr. Worf," he said after a moment, "I want to speak with First Among Equals Kerajem."

"Aye, sir."

Troi and Wiggin entered a large room with scores of cubicles. Men and women of various ages walked briskly here and there. Everyone seemed to have something important to do, or at least they believed that they did. The buzz of activity was unrelenting.

"This is where I work," the young Krann said with no little pride. "The design section."

"My, it's impressive," Troi observed. "How long have you been assigned here?"

"Since I was an apprentice. I was assigned here by chance. Luckiest thing that ever happened to me. I love this work."

"I can tell. And what exactly do you do?"

Wiggin shook his head and smiled. "I can't say, really. Fleet security. You know. 'Weapons designer' will have to do."

"I quite understand," Troi said.

"Come this way," Wiggin said. "I'll show you my work area." Together, Troi and Wiggin threaded their way between cubicles, almost every one of which housed a person sitting at a smallish desk, bent closely to his or her work. Some were drawing freehand on larger versions of the glass plate Troi had seen at the security entrance to Bay Fourteen, while others were working at computer terminals and other similar devices. Troi thought it was interesting that no one looked up as they passed.

"Everyone's quite busy," she said.

"Well, you know," Wiggin said. "That big ship sitting out there. Quite a problem."

Troi was all innocence. "'Big ship'?"

"The aliens, I mean." Wiggin waved a hand. "They're supposed to be a big secret, but you're a supervisor's spouse, so you've been briefed. Right?"

Troi nodded. "Oh, certainly."

"We don't know a wasted thing about them, and that's the problem. Here's my cubicle." As they entered, Wiggin pressed a button on the surface of his small desk and a terminal mounted on the shelf above it came to life. There was a chair in front of the terminal, and Wiggin sat down. "Have a seat while I check my messages. Won't take long."

There was a covered stool to the side of Wiggin's desk, and Troi seated herself. She looked around. The cubicle was efficient but hardly sterile. There were pictures of young women taped here and there on the textured metal walls—some of Wiggin's previous conquests, Troi supposed. Wiggin's desk held not much more than a terminal and a thing that would do for a coffee mug until one came along. The place looked normal, lived in, comfortable. Troi wondered whose cubicle it really was.

"There's nothing worth talking about," Wiggin said after a moment, and then he smiled. "Now where were we?" He moved his chair a little closer to Troi.

"You were telling me about the aliens," she reminded him. "You said they were a problem for you."

"They sure are," Wiggin said. "Trying to prepare for an attack from them is impossible when you don't know what to expect," he said. "What kind of weapons do they have? How many? Will they fight to destroy us? To capture us? Or just to incapacitate us? Maybe I shouldn't say this, but rumor has it that the aliens have faster-than-light drive."

Troi kept her expression blank. "That's not supposed to be possible, is it?" she asked.

"No, it's not, and it makes you wonder what else they've got. But I think we might have an answer. It's something we've been working on for a long time for—for other applications. Crash priority, especially recently, and it's ready to go. The final checkout's taken up most of our time lately." He grinned. "I can't show you the specs on it, of course, but you can see the thing itself if you want—from a distance, anyway. We brought a school group through just yesterwatch to see it."

"The 'thing'? What is it?"

"An answer to whatever it is that's out there. We hope. Come on, Pralla. It's in a converted cargo bay that's just the other side of the next bulkhead."

Troi and Wiggin left the cubicle area and went down a small, spare gangway to a heavy metal door. There were large red and green lights mounted overhead. The green one was lit.

"What are the lights for?" Troi asked.

"Vacuum warning," Wiggin replied. "We're just one level away from the hull. The cargo bay can be opened to space. This door is actually an air lock." Wiggin put his hand against a slick metal panel mounted on the wall to the right of the door, and after several seconds the door began to roll aside slowly.

"Getting in and out of here is not a very quick process, I'm afraid," Wiggin said, "but this is one of the smaller air locks. There's a much bigger one for watch changes and so forth a few levels spinward. We can move hundreds of people in and out in just a few minutes. Ah, here we go."

Wiggin and Troi entered the air lock. It was big enough to hold six people, if they crowded in. Wiggin reached past Troi's shoulder and pressed his hand against another metal plate. The door behind them began to roll shut.

"Now where were we?" Wiggin asked Troi as the door behind them closed fully. He was not quite leering.

"You were about to open this other door here," the counselor said firmly.

"Oh." He sounded disappointed. "Are you sure?"

"Very." Her tone brooked no nonsense. "You were about to open this door."

Wiggin nodded. "As you say," he said resignedly, "that was what I was about to do." He put his hand on the plate for the inner air lock door, and it rumbled aside.

Troi gasped when she saw it. The cargo bay was huge, but the device inside nearly filled it.

"Well?" Wiggin asked, grinning as if he'd built the thing all by himself. "Whaddaya think?"

Troi was wide-eyed. "I'm impressed," she said. "I'm very, very impressed." They entered the cargo bay and began walking slowly toward the device.

The weapon looked something like an ancient anti-aircraft gun combined with the fat, smooth barrel of one of the old planet-based optical telescopes. It was pointed right at the wall of the cargo bay—or, rather, at two large doors that were apparently designed to swing open so that the weapon could be extended into space and fired. The barrel was mounted on long, gimbaled legs that would allow the device to be pointed up, down, left, and right. Thick cables led from the weapon into the cargo bay floor. Scores of Krann technicians were swarming and clambering over, around and through the device, adjusting, repairing, replacing, fine-tuning. The activity seemed very nearly frantic.

Troi wished desperately that she could have brought a tricorder along with her on this mission. Instead, she tried to memorize every visual detail that she could. "What does this thing *do?*" she asked Wiggin, still a bit breathless. "I mean, how does it work? Does it fire a death ray or something?"

"It defends the fleet," Wiggin said boastfully. "That's all I can tell you." He pointed. "See the big hinge between the first and second sections of the right rear leg? That's mine."

"Oh, it's quite nice," Troi said distractedly.

"So you're impressed?"

"Hmmm?" Troi asked. "Oh. Yes. Yes, I'll say I'm impressed. The hinge and everything."

"Knew you would be. You still worried about those big bad aliens now, Pralla?"

"More than ever, actually."

Wiggin laughed. "Well, I guess there's no help for it, then. Seen enough?"

"I think so."

"Then let's go," Wiggin said. "I don't have to go back to my desk, so we can leave through the main air lock. It's right over there. Then we can go anywhere you want. It's still Posting Day, after all, and the night's pretty young."

All Troi wanted to do now was report back to the *Enterprise,* and that meant getting out of the sensor-proof gray zone as quickly as possible. She also wanted to find Will, and if he was likely to be anywhere, it would be—

"Perhaps we can go back to that nice restaurant we were at before," Troi said.

"Well, maybe we could," Wiggin responded. "For now."

"So let's leave the way we came, shall we?"

The young Krann shrugged. "Well, all right."

Troi and Wiggin quickly walked back to the small air lock and, once through, they retraced their steps back to the security gate.

That was where Will had been all along, standing there, waiting for her. He looked very angry. He was getting rather good at it.

"Dex!" Troi yiped. "Wiggin, it's *Dex!*"

"Oh, hull," Wiggin muttered. "It would be."

Riker walked up to the two of them and confronted them right in front of the guard booth. A crowd began to collect.

"Where in hull have you two been?" Riker spat. "I swear, every time I turn my back on you, Pralla, you're off with some young punk—"

"Hey, wait a minute—" Wiggin began.

"Shut up!" Riker spat.

"Hey, Wiggin," Guss called from the booth. "You want me to call security?"

Riker turned to address him. "Guard, I am Dex Portside Sanitation Systems Supervisor." There was an intake of breath from the collecting crowd. "This incident is under control. There is no need for security personnel here."

Guss blinked. "Of course not, Supervisor."

"Then, as you were." Riker turned back to Troi. "You're coming home with me, Pralla. Right now."

"Yes, Dex," Troi said sheepishly.

"We'll forget about it this time," Riker continued, his lips tight. "We'll charge this little incident off to too much celebrating. Too much Posting Day."

"Yes, Dex." Troi looked quite penitent.

"And *you,*" Riker said, turning to Wiggin. "If I ever catch you near my spouse again, I will stuff you out the nearest waste hole. Is that clear?"

"Yes, Dex," Wiggin replied quickly.

"What did you call me, Journeyman?" Riker snapped. "That mode of address is reserved for friends and equals only, and you are neither of those to me."

Wiggin straightened up. "I apologize for my conduct, Dex Portside Sanitation Systems Supervisor. I intended no offense."

Riker nodded slowly. "None taken, then. Back to your routine, Journeyman, and do it fast."

"Yes, Supervisor." Wiggin spun on his heel and left quickly, hurrying back through the security gate for Bay Fourteen.

"Let's get out of here," Riker muttered. "There's a tube car coming. We need to get out of the gray zone so we can touch base with the captain."

"We also need to talk," Troi said into his ear as the car arrived and slowly drew to a halt. "Do we want to return to the ship?"

Riker shook his head. "I don't think we're quite done aboard here yet. We'll at least call in first, let the captain know we're still alive and kicking." He suddenly smiled. "I found us a place. We can go there."

"A place? Do you mean a place to stay?"

"Yes. It's kind of like a hotel room, but free of charge. They let me sign for it, so I did. Reminds me of one of those inexpensive little bed-and-breakfast places in Europe, whatever they're called—oh, yes. A *pension.* I think the one I found is meant for drunks, so they can sleep it off. Maybe that's why it's free. It's provided as some kind of public service." He paused. "Deanna, you do realize we're being led around—"

"—by the nose? Yes, I do. And wait'll I tell you about what *I* saw."

They boarded the tube car. As it pulled away, Wiggin reemerged from the security gate and, standing there, watched as the train departed. When it was finally gone, he allowed himself a tight, brief smile. He then rapped his knuckles on the side of Guss's guard booth and walked onto the tube station platform to wait for the arrival of the next car. It had been a job well done, but he was off duty now and, after all, it *was* Posting Day, and there were drinks and a woman or two out there somewhere with his name on them.

Chapter Sixteen

PICARD WAS IN HIS READY ROOM, taking another call from the First Among Equals.

"Things are tense here, Captain Picard," Kerajem said. He was in his office at Government House. *"The Cabinet is increasingly restive. The older ministers are almost too scared to speak, and the younger ones want to teach the Krann a lesson, as that idiot Jemmagar put it during our last emergency meeting."* Kerajem nearly spat. *"How could we ever hope to teach the Krann a lesson?"*

"And where are you on this, First?" Picard asked.

"In the middle, as usual, and hoping for some sort of miracle. Captain Picard, do you have any *hope that Presider Hek is open to some sort of peaceful settlement?"*

Picard considered his words carefully. "I'm not sure, First," he said. "I cannot tell what's on his mind or what kind of settlement he might accept. I have been trying to find out all along, but the man is extraordinarily difficult to read."

"*So you think he is insincere about seeking a peaceful resolution to this crisis?*"

"As I said, I'm not sure," Picard said. "But I do think he is a practical man. If a peaceful settlement is attractive enough, if it allows him to maintain his authority, then he might agree to one."

Kerajem nodded. "*I hope you're right, Captain.*"

"There is one practical reason for hope, First Among Equals," Picard said. "In my last conversation with him, Presider Hek seemed to bring up the possibility that the Krann might want to settle on the fourth planet of this system."

"*Settle down? And abandon their fleet in space?*" Kerajem shook his head. "*I doubt they would ever do such a thing, Captain Picard. They've been living a spaceborne existence for thousands of years, and they're used to it. Oh, some of them might like to live planetside, but I can't believe* all *of them would. It's just not their way.*"

"They lived on a world once," Picard pointed out.

"*That was a long time ago.*" Kerajem sighed. "*Captain, our Cabinet session resumes in a minute. I'll call you at the next recess.*"

"Very well," Picard said. "Good luck to you, First Among Equals."

"*And may good fortune find you, Captain. I know you're doing your best.*" The terminal went dark.

"I just hope it's enough," muttered Picard.

"*Captain,*" came Worf's deep voice, "*Commander Riker is calling.*"

"Ah. Thank you, Lieutenant." Picard pressed a button. "Hello, Number One," he said into the air. "Is everything all right?"

"*Yes, sir. We're both fine. Is there any word yet from Commander Data or Ensign Ro?*"

"I'm afraid not."

"Understood, sir. Deanna is right here and will communicate through my pickup."

"Fine. Are you two reasonably private? Can you talk freely?"

"Yes, sir," Riker replied. *"We're in what amounts to a cheap hotel room just outside the gray zone. No one else is in the room with us."*

"Excellent. I can have you beamed directly here to the ready room to make your report in person—"

"Excuse me, Captain, but I don't think that would be wise. I have reason to believe that the Krann can detect our use of the transporter. If we beam out, they may know it, and I'd rather have them realize we're still here, keeping an eye on them."

"Understood. Your findings since your last report, then."

"With your permission, Captain, I'll let Commander Troi make her report first. She reconnoitered well inside the zone."

"Go ahead, Counselor."

"—and so, Captain, I agree with Commander Riker's assessment. I was being shown something we were meant to see, and I was intended to get away with it." Troi motioned to Riker to pass her what was left of a glass of water that was sitting on the nightstand, and he did so. *Thanks,* she mouthed. "I was meant to see the weapon in Bay Fourteen and, I presume, I was intended to report its presence to you." She took a sip of water.

"But what is it?"

"I couldn't tell, sir. It looked like no weapons system I am familiar with."

"Did your Krann friend say this whatever-it-is could hurt us? Did he give you any indication of what it could do? Fire a missile or shell at us, that sort of thing?"

235

"Wiggin would not tell me, Captain. I made some silly comment about a death ray, which he ignored."

"Was there only one of these things?"

"I got that impression, yes, sir."

"Good Lord. I feel as if I'm playing 'Twenty Questions.' All right. Clearly the Krann wanted to ensure that you saw the device, whatever it is and whatever it can do. Perhaps its presence is intended to intimidate us, or at least make us more uncertain about the capabilities of the Krann. What do you think, Will?"

"I agree we're being scammed, Captain," the first officer replied. "I'm not sure about the reason. It may just be that the Krann are attempting—rather successfully, I think—to distract us. Perhaps there is something going on aboard this ship that we are *not* supposed to notice."

There was a brief silence as Picard thought about that. *"I don't believe any single weapon possessed by the Krann can do anything of consequence against us,"* he finally said, and Troi saw Riker nod.

"If I may, sir," Riker added, "I think it's important to note that Wiggin made contact with us not very long after we were beamed aboard the flagship. Somehow the Krann realized we were there. We can't have been recognized."

"I agree, Will. They know about the transporter, or they deduced its use somehow. Either way, I agree that the secret is blown, but I think we'll maintain appearances anyway. We'll travel to the flagship via shuttlecraft for the next round of talks. Sometimes there's great value in not letting them know that you know that they know."

Riker looked confused. "Er, yes, sir."

"In line with all that, Will, I want you and the counselor to remain aboard the flagship until the next round of talks begins in about, um, eight hours.

Presider Hek set the schedule, and the timing happens to coincide with the arrival of the main elements of the Krann attack force in standard orbit around Nem Ma'ak Bratuna."

"That doesn't sound on the level," Troi said.

"No, it doesn't. I want you two there so you can keep me informed about what you see aboard the flagship— assuming the Krann allow you to make such reports, that is. The transporter chief will keep a lock on both of you until you're safely back, so don't go into the gray zone unless it is absolutely necessary. Now, anything else?"

"I don't think so, Captain," said Riker.

"Not from me, sir," Troi added.

"Get some rest, then. Good night. Picard out."

"Good night, sir. Recon party out."

"No word from Data or Ro yet," Deanna fretted. "That can't be good, Will."

"If anyone can make it through, they can," Riker told her. "Don't give up on them yet, Counselor. I haven't—and neither has the captain."

Deanna tried to stifle a yawn and failed. "Been a long day," she said. She closed her eyes.

"I hate the holidays," Will joked. "Don't you?" He looked around the room, rubbing the back of his neck. It was small but neat, it had been painted not long before, and it was carpeted. All there was for furniture was a narrow but comfortable bed, a small bureau, and an even smaller table. There was no chair for the table. "At least there's a head," Riker observed. "There's a shower stall in there, too, of all things. A water shower, I mean. Haven't seen one of those in a while."

Deanna's eyes opened. "A water shower? Oh, I *love* those. Is the water hot?"

"Let me check." Will ducked inside and ran the tap

for a moment, and there came the sudden sound of a hard rain. "Yep," he reported. "Hot as all hell. Good pressure, too. There's a container of thick liquid stuff that I think is soap, or a good excuse for soap. There's also a couple of towels."

"Sounds grand," Troi said, stretching. "Will, would you mind very much if—?"

"Hmmm? Oh. No. No, not at all."

Deanna gave him a tired grin. "Thanks, Will. Uh, I'll toss you for the bed, assuming we can find something to toss."

"No. It's yours."

"But—"

"I won't discuss it," Will insisted. "Just lend me one of the pillows. I'll be fine on the floor. Actually, I'm a little tired myself."

"With pleasure," Deanna smiled. "Thank you. Uh, there's an extra blanket, too. Here." She tossed it across the room to him. "These people thought of everything."

"Very hospitable." As Deanna disappeared into the bathroom, Will spread the blanket on the floor alongside the bed, doubled it over the long way, and dropped the pillow where it belonged. He quickly doffed his Krann garb, retrieved the audio pickup bug from the trouser pocket, and inserted it into his left ear, in case the *Enterprise* called during the night. Dropping down to the carpet, Will crawled inside the folded blanket and made himself comfortable. The padding under the carpet proved to be soft and agreeable, and he dozed off quickly.

About twenty minutes later, a soothed and satisfied Deanna emerged from the bathroom, one bath towel wrapped around her and the other around her hair. She heard the once-familiar sound of Will's determined snoring coming from just beyond the bed. *Not quite like the old days,* she thought kindly, *but close enough.* Deanna smiled at the gentle memory as she killed the room lights, dropped one of the towels close by the nightstand, clipped her communicator to the remaining towel, and got into bed. She was asleep within minutes. Will's snoring had never bothered her in the old days, and it did not bother her now.

Chapter Seventeen

"ASTONISHING," PRESIDER HEK SAID some hours later. "They're still aboard the flagship, Graff. Why is that?"

"Their captain has ordered them to remain here for the present," his attaché told him. "Captain Picard wants them to be on board with us at the time our initial attack force reaches Nem Ma'ak Bratuna and to report to him on what is going on aboard the ship."

"How do you know all this?" Hek asked. "I thought you told me yesterwatch that we were unable to monitor their communications."

"Yes, Presider, but I had their room bugged. We recorded their half of the conversation and easily extrapolated the rest of it from context."

Hek grinned. "Now *that's* what I like," he said jovially. "Initiative. I thought they'd stymied us."

"They may have, in a way," Graff said.

"Eh? I don't like hearing that kind of thing, Graff."

"And I don't like reporting it to you. However, I had thought that they would return to their ship shortly after Deanna Troi rejoined Commander Riker outside Bay Fourteen, and both returned to the unshielded part of the flagship."

"Oh, is that all?" Hek waved a hand. "Well, we can get rid of them easily enough. As long as they're back where they belong by T-Time, I'll be satisfied."

"Then that's the way it shall be, Presider."

"Good enough."

"Good morning," Deanna called.

"Umph," Will replied from the floor. He roused and, after a moment, blinked and sat up. His hair was spiky and his mouth tasted like soap. "I'll bet there isn't a cup of coffee within a million kilometers."

"You're probably right about that," Deanna told him. She was adjusting the buckles on her Krann clothing. "The bathroom's all yours this morning, Will. I'm done with it."

"Oh. Well, thanks. One of those hot showers of yours sounds like a great idea right now."

Deanna tossed him a towel. "Thanks," he said. "See you in a bit."

"Will?" she called. "Do you want me to check in with the ship?"

The water was running now, and steam was spilling through the door and into the bedroom. "Just call in," Will shouted back. "Let whoever answers know that we're all right. The captain's got enough going on right now without our interrupting him to say 'good morning.' If he needs to talk with us, he can always call us back. Oh, *dammit!*"

"What's the matter, Will?"

"Nothing much," he called back. "I forgot to take the stupid pickup bug out of my ear before I got water in it, that's all. Anyway, go ahead and make the call to the ship, all right?"

"Will do," Deanna said, and she did.

About five minutes later, Will emerged from the bathroom in significantly improved condition. He dressed quickly.

"My," Deanna said. "You clean up really well, Commander."

"Well, thank *you,*" Will replied. "The day is looking better and brighter, after all." He glanced at the chrono he'd brought along. "Well, it's about that time. The captain should be about ready to leave the *Enterprise* for this ship, so we're on duty. You hungry?"

"Now that you mention it, no. I usually skip breakfast anyway."

"Good. I'm not hungry, either." He looked around to see if they'd left anything. "As I understand it, we don't have to check out. Let's just get back on the concourse, and see what we can see."

"Fine. Uh, Will?"

"Yes?"

"Thanks for the use of the bed. It was kind of you."

Will bowed in perfect Krann fashion. "My pleasure."

Together, Riker and Troi left their room and walked down a short hallway to the lobby of the *pension.* They were a little surprised to find that no one was around, not even the lobby security guard. "I don't like this," Riker said. "It's as if the place has been cleared out on purpose."

"Let's go, Will," said Troi. "If you're right, we're sitting ducks here."

They left the *pension* and walked down the concourse, heading away from the gray zone.

"There are a lot fewer people out and about today," Troi observed.

"This might be more like what a normal day is

like," Riker said. "Things seem calm enough—whoops!"

Lights everywhere were blinking again—four-four-four, over and over again.

"I wonder what *that* means?" Troi wondered.

"I don't know," Riker replied, "but this is the third time in two days that the Krann have dragged one of these alerts out of mothballs. It's got to mean trouble."

Troi turned around and looked the other way up the concourse, in the general direction of the gray zone. "Will? Look."

"Eh?" Riker swung around. In the far distance, he could see a swarm of black-garbed people running down the concourse right toward them. He could also see that their pursuers were armed, as the blinking alert lights glinted madly off the silver barrels of their weapons.

"I think four-four-four might mean 'let's go chase the Federation spies,'" Troi said.

"Fat chance," Riker said, tapping his communicator buckle.

There was no response. He tapped it again.

"Mine doesn't work either," Troi said.

"They've expanded the gray zone," Riker said tersely. "Let's move." He grabbed Troi's arm and, together, they quickly headed down a narrow passage that opened up onto another concourse. Riker took a moment to try the communicator again. This time, he heard a faint buzzing in his ear.

He threw a glance behind him and saw that other Krann were coming after them. Some of them were drawing fairly close.

"Let's keep going in this direction," he told Troi. "The interference seems to be weaker this way." They zipped down a passage toward another concourse,

243

always heading away from the original boundary of the gray zone.

Captain Picard and Worf were in the main shuttlebay and were about to board *Justman* for their return to the Krann flagship when a call came through for Picard. *"La Forge to Captain."*

"Go ahead."

"Commander Riker and the counselor seem to be in trouble."

"What kind of trouble?" Picard snapped.

"They're trying to contact us via the subspace communicator, but the Krann are jamming the signal with whatever it is they've been using to establish the gray zone. We're getting only intermittent contact. The transporter lock we've been maintaining on them is gone, too."

"Can you re-establish the lock?"

"Not without more signal, Captain. They're moving around the flagship—running is more like it, with the sketchy speed readings I'm getting. I think they're being pursued."

"Stand by, Mr. La Forge. Captain to Transporter Room Two."

"Aye, sir. Dodson here."

"Dodson, confer with Chief Engineer La Forge about getting Commander Riker and Counselor Troi off the Krann flagship. I want you two working hand in glove."

"Yes, sir!"

"Picard out." He turned to Worf. "Mr. Worf, please return to the bridge. Kindly send my apologies to Presider Hek and inform him that our arrival aboard the flagship will be delayed indefinitely."

"I'm sure he already knows that, sir."

"I'm certain he does, too, Lieutenant. Nevertheless, let's play the hand out. I also think I know why we haven't been able to locate Commander Data and Ensign Ro. I'll bet the capital's been 'gray-zoned' by the Krann, everywhere but Government House, in order to distract us. Mr. Worf, I want a search party to go down and look for the two of them on a line between the bomb shelter and Government House."

"Government House, sir?"

"Yes. If I know Data, he'll reason that Government House is probably the safest place to be in the entire city. I just hope he and Ro evaded harm on their way there."

Worf braced. "Permission to lead the search party, Captain," he said formally.

"Granted. Use a shuttlecraft, Mr. Worf. This one's ready to go. We have to assume that all our communication frequencies are subject to jamming at will by the Krann, which makes the transporter nearly useless. I'll have the bridge advise the Lethanta that someone's coming down. Don't take too long at this." Picard smiled slightly. "This is one of those times when I really do need you to be in two places at once. I'll be in Transporter Room Two if you need me."

The Klingon nodded. "Aye, sir." He turned and quickly left the shuttlebay to organize his team.

"Damn!" Riker exclaimed as he and Troi came to a sudden stop. "Dead end." He looked around quickly. There was one door, which proved to be securely locked.

Their pursuers were about a hundred meters away and getting closer quickly.

"Will!" Troi cried. "I think I can hear something!" She cupped her hand to her left ear and tapped her communicator again.

"—stand with——Riker—combine—" came a familiar voice through heavy static. *"Emerg—signal——lock—"*

"Will!" she cried. "Come over here and hold on to me! We both have to send our recall signals at the same time so they can get a lock on us!"

Riker hurried over and put an arm around her. "One, two, three, *now!*" Riker said as one of the Krann security guards drew close enough to leap at him. They both tapped their communicators at the same time.

And they disappeared.

And they reappeared.

"Man, are we glad to see *you!*" Riker said. "That was pretty close."

"Welcome aboard, Number One, Counselor—" Picard began.

The transporter suddenly began complaining loudly.

"Captain," Dodson reported, "the transporter has detected biological contamination involving the commander and the counselor. I've established a containment field."

"Dr. Crusher to Transporter Room Two, on the double," Picard called.

"On my way, sir."

"Ops to Captain Picard."

"Picard here."

"Sir, the leading elements of the Krann fleet have opened fire on several Lethantan facilities in orbit around their planet. Lethantan forces are rushing to engage the attacking Krann ships."

"I'll be right there. Open a channel to Presider Hek and *keep* it open. I intend to talk to that—person. Will, Deanna, we'll soon get to the bottom of all this. I suspect I know what was going on now."

"So do I," Riker said, his teeth clenched. "A pretty gutsy gambit on their part."

"And it will cost them dearly. See you later." With

that, Captain Picard left the transporter room and headed at a brisk pace for the turbolift, which the bridge had already thoughtfully sent down for him. He entered it and fumed quietly as the 'lift made its quick, nonstop way to the bridge.

There they were. At last.

"Worf to landing party," the Klingon said into the air. "I've located the commander and the ensign. Report back to the shuttlecraft immediately."

"About time you got here," Ro managed through bloodied lips.

"You have been wounded," Worf said. He had a medical kit in hand. "Allow me to assist you."

"I guess I could use a pain pill," Ro allowed. "It's been a long night."

"Ensign Ro was shot by the police on our way here," Data reported. "We were violating a local regulation by being on the street during an attack. I did not feel comfortable moving the ensign in her condition, so we did not continue to Government House. I remained with her here, discouraging passersby from inflicting more harm on her."

"You'll find some used-up Lethanta here and there," Ro said. "Thanks, Commander."

"Why did you leave safety?" Worf asked.

"The building we were in was on fire and about to collapse," Data said. "We took a chance. I was shot at while I retrieved the ensign from where she had fallen."

"I can see that," Worf said. "Are you damaged, Commander?"

"Not significantly, thank you. How is Ensign Ro?"

"Not too bad." Worf looked through the medical kit. "I will stabilize her condition before we bring her to the shuttle."

"That is a relief," Data said. "I was concerned."

"I'm touched," Ro said, grimacing again. "What happened to the communicators, Worf? We never heard from the ship after the bombings began."

"The captain believes they were jammed by the Krann, except for communications between us and Government House. We believe the Krann cut off communications between us in order to create more uncertainty. No doubt the Krann thought that allowing us to talk to Government House, but not to you two, might lead us to think that communications were clear and that you were dead. It certainly did make us uncertain." Worf frowned darkly. "Much has happened in the last few hours, and none of it is good. I will brief you on the way back."

The turbolift doors opened onto the bridge, and Picard walked briskly to his chair. Harkey was at Ops. "Have you reached Presider Hek, Ensign?" he asked her.

"No, sir," she replied. "Not yet."

"Keep at it."

Worf's prime backup, Lieutenant Gomez, was handling the Security station in the Klingon's absence. Picard addressed him. "Mr. Gomez, tell me about the war."

"Captain, the Lethanta are under substantial attack by heavily armed units of the Krann fleet," Gomez said. "Virtually all orbital facilities surrounding Nem Ma'ak Bratuna have been destroyed, with large loss of life. So far, Lethantan defense forces have prevented any significant additional damage to ground-based facilities, but there have been several new medium-yield nuclear missile strikes within the larger cities, and Lethantan ground defenses are beginning to collapse. A large Lethantan space force is heading for the midst of the main Krann fleet, apparently to conduct reprisal attacks against the Krann civilian population."

"Very well. Ensign Harkey, send the following message to Presider Hek and the First Among Equals. 'As the representative of the United Federation of Planets, I am proposing that both sides establish and observe a ceasefire in place before this war grows any wider.'" Picard chose his next words carefully. "'There is no point in fighting. There is no issue here worth fighting about. We must put the past behind us and build a future, but we are fast losing any hope of doing it. I look forward to your affirmative response to this message.' End it there."

"Captain?" Gomez reported. "The Lethanta are now engaging elements of the main Krann fleet. Three large Krann ships have been destroyed. They were city ships, sir." He paused. "Estimated combined population, one point four million."

Picard sighed. Any chance of peace seemed gone.

"The First Among Equals is calling, Captain," Harkey reported.

"On screen." Picard began to speak and then stopped, shocked. He had never seen a man seem to grow so old overnight.

"Kerajem," Picard began almost gently, "please stop this madness. This war can only lead to the destruction of both races. You must realize that."

"I know that better than anyone, Captain Picard— but we lost three cities full of people in the first six minutes of this renewal of the war, not to mention the thousands of our people who were killed in the orbiting factories and other facilities. There must be an accounting."

"We've watched as your ships destroyed three large Krann vessels just minutes ago. The Krann craft were city ships, populated by nearly a million and a half civilians."

"Those ships were destroyed in reprisal for the loss of our cities. We are the ones who were attacked, Captain. Not they."

"Then your dead are revenged, First, for what that is worth. Can we not stop there?"

Kerajem bowed his head wearily. *"We will stop if they will stop, and not otherwise,"* he said. *"We did not want this war, Captain Picard, but we will not run from it."*

"If I can arrange a ceasefire in place, will you observe it?"

"Yes—if you can arrange it. Meanwhile, we fight."

"I will do my best. Picard out. Get me Hek," he said to Harkey through clenched teeth.

Harkey looked up. "Presider Hek is calling *you*, Captain."

"Put him on screen." Picard took a deep, calming breath. "Presider Hek," he said, "I want to offer a proposal for a ceasefire—"

"Forget it," the Krann leader said. His eyes seemed afire. *"This is not the time for a ceasefire. My people have waited for millennia for this day. Today we destroy those who nearly destroyed us. You won't stop us. Nothing can. Our third wave is about to begin its attack on Nem Ma'ak Bratuna."* He laughed. *"There won't be much left for the fourth wave to mop up, not after that. Then will come the planet-wide radioactive dusting, and that will be that."* There was suddenly an expression of sheerest joy on Hek's face. *"Finally, finally, we have arrived at the day of the death of the hated Lethanta,"* he crowed. *"My ancestors will be able to rest at long last."*

"The Lethanta are destroying your ships," Picard said. "Can't you see?"

"They've blown up three city ships," Hek responded. *"That leaves us with a paltry fifty-two thousand and some odd. By the way, Captain, how are you feeling?"*

Picard frowned. "We immediately detected your attempt to infect the ship, Hek. It wasn't even close to successful."

Hek grinned. *"I confess I'm disappointed, Picard. Despite your self-proclaimed neutral status, your continued presence in this system makes me nervous. I simply don't trust you, Captain. My people informed me that the virus they used was undetectable."*

"Perhaps it was—for you. Not for us."

"My," Hek said. *"You are advanced."*

"And the superweapon in Bay Fourteen was—?"

"A telescope, tarted up to look like it could blow a hole in your precious Enterprise. You were supposed to see right through it, of course, and you did—just as you were supposed to detect that young Wiggin was planted at the party by our intelligence people. Captain, we knew where your people were on our flagship the instant they arrived. We've had centuries to install sensors in every nook and cranny of this vessel. Nothing here escapes notice. Nothing. When your Riker and Troi suddenly appeared, we deduced that your civilization possessed some form of matter transmission— and so you do; now that's a secret I'd like for us. In any case, when Riker and Troi arrived, we integrated them into our strategic planning."

"All of this nonsense with Wiggin was to distract us from the real plot against us," Picard said. "All the while, you were infecting Counselor Troi with the virus."

"Correct," Hek replied. *"It's spread quite easily by skin-to-skin contact, and Wiggin kept patting Troi on the hand. Troi then unwittingly passed it to Commander Riker. It's a wonderful little virus, Captain. All it does in the first few hours is make you drowsy and take the edge off your appetite. Then, sometime during the second day, your heart and lungs suddenly become*

inflamed and septic, and out you go. Of course, we've all been immunized."

"How convenient for you."

Hek stifled a yawn. *"Is there more, Captain? Because if there isn't—"*

"I suppose there is nothing more to say at this time."

"Then good-bye."

"Sir?" Gomez said. "Shuttlebay Three reports the shuttlecraft has returned with all hands aboard. One wounded, sir. Ensign Ro. Dr. Crusher is on her way there now."

Picard sighed. "Very well."

The top officers of the *Enterprise,* except for Riker and Troi, had gathered in the conference lounge for a briefing on the Lethantan-Krann war. The first officer and the counselor had been placed in isolation by Dr. Crusher, but they were attending the meeting through the ship's communications system.

"The third attack wave is now in progress," Worf reported. "Presider Hek's expectations of a quick victory seem now to have been without any basis in fact. The Lethanta have been holding their own, but their resources are not unlimited. When their stores are exhausted, they will fall quickly."

"When will they run out of supplies, Worf?" Riker asked.

"In two or three hours, Commander. The end is close. The Lethanta prepared themselves well for this battle, but the Krann attack has been unrelenting. The Lethanta have been forced to throw their reserves into the fighting earlier than they anticipated. They are now fighting a holding action. This cannot succeed."

"How quickly do you think they will fall after their supplies run out, Mr. Worf?" Picard asked.

"I would say immediately, Captain, for all practical purposes," the security chief replied. "The Krann do not intend to occupy Nem Ma'ak Bratuna, but to sterilize it with highly radioactive dust. Most life-forms on the planet will die within hours or days, depending on the strength of the dust and its distribution by the planetary winds. This distribution cannot be uniform, since it is determined by natural forces. As a result, some life-forms may hold out in isolated areas of the planet for weeks or even months, but eventually the poisoned ecosystem will find and destroy them all. Nem Ma'ak Bratuna will be dead."

"How do we prevent that?" asked Picard.

"We can't negotiate a ceasefire," Troi reminded them from her sickbed. *"It takes two to make a peace but only one to conduct a war, and the Krann won't talk peace."*

"Can we stop the Krann?" Geordi asked. "Rather, could we prevent those Krann ships from attempting to sterilize the planet with that dust?"

Picard slowly shook his head. "No. No, we can't do that. Despite everything, we can't take part in this war. The permission we received from both sides to negotiate a settlement, however vain any hope for a settlement has now become, does not permit us to enter the fray. The Prime Directive remains in effect."

"Harkey to Captain," came a voice.

"Yes, Ensign. What is it?"

"Sir, the First Among Equals is calling you."

"Patch the audio through, please. Kerajem?"

"Captain Picard, I must ask you to leave our planetary system at once. I know you are capable of doing so at considerable speed."

Everyone around the conference table stirred. Picard held up a hand. "Why, Kerajem?"

"I don't believe I need to tell you why, Captain. My

understanding of your Prime Directive is that you can stay here only as long as we desire it. We no longer desire it."

"That *is* an aspect of the Prime Directive," Picard said slowly. "Yes."

"And you are bound to observe it?"

"We are sworn to do so. Scrupulously. All of us are."

"Then please do observe it, and go. Leave our system at once." The First Among Equals paused. *"I would be remiss if I did not thank you for your help, Captain. It was not your fault that peace between us and the Krann was not possible. Go now, with our most heartfelt thanks."*

"The Lethanta have shut down the comm link, Captain," Harkey reported.

"I have a bad feeling about this," Riker said. *"It's too sudden. It doesn't fit with Kerajem's past actions."*

"I agree, Number One," Picard said. "There's no clear reason for this. Picard to Harkey."

"Harkey here, sir."

"Ensign, where was Kerajem calling from?"

"He was in his office at Government House, sir."

"Very good. Picard out." He rose from the table. "I'm going there now for a one-on-one with Kerajem. We'll get to the bottom of this. Mr. Data, go to the bridge and take the conn."

"Permission to accompany you, Captain," Worf said immediately.

"Denied. I have to do this by myself."

"Sir, you intend to beam into the middle of a war zone, and I cannot—"

"You've done your sworn duty in warning me about it, Lieutenant. Now desist."

Worf looked resigned. "Aye, sir."

"Excuse me, Captain," Geordi asked. "But didn't

Kerajem just withdraw his people's permission for us to be here?"

"Yes, he did."

"Well, then, aren't we violating the Prime Directive in pursuing further efforts at mediation?"

"Not at all," Picard said. "The Krann have not yet withdrawn *their* permission for us to intercede in this war, and that is exactly what I intend to do when I go to visit Kerajem."

Chapter Eighteen

PICARD MATERIALIZED right in front of Kerajem's desk. The First Among Equals looked up.

"I knew you'd show up anyway, Picard," the First said, utterly weary. "I figured a little thing like a sacred oath wouldn't stop you."

"I haven't violated my oath, Kerajem," Picard said. "I'm simply taking advantage of a loophole. Please tell me what's happening."

"We're losing the war for our survival, that's what's happening. The other ministers went home or wherever it is they find the most comfort. The vote was taken and the agreement was made, and now there's nothing left for anyone to do—except me, of course." Kerajem rose from his desk and, walking over to the window, looked out over the ruins of the capital city. There was dense smoke on the horizon. "The mountains are on fire," Kerajem said almost absently. "I'm from there, you know."

"You'd mentioned it to me."

"Oh. Yes. Yes, I had. I suppose my hometown is

gone now. It would be right in the middle of that main column of smoke, right there past the peak. See it?"

"Yes."

Kerajem gazed up into the clear green sky. "They tell me there's quite a battle going on up there, about two hundred kilometers above our heads."

"We've been keeping tabs on it."

"So have we, as I think you'll understand. I heard one of your people was badly wounded after the initial attack. Will she make it?"

"Our doctor says that she will."

"I'm glad. Captain Picard, do you know why we've called this world The Last Stand?"

"No. Please tell me."

"Because it is exactly that." Kerajem turned away from the window. "It is our world, our refuge, the last hope for our survival. It is the place where we determined in our prehistory that if the Krann ever came our way, the millennia of madness would finally end. Even when we forgot our origins and descended into barbarism, our purpose remained intact. When we rediscovered the truth decades ago, we also rediscovered our resolve to see this whole mad business end. We have made a stand here, our last stand. The madness will end today—and that is why you and your people must leave our system immediately."

"What are you talking about, Kerajem? Please tell me."

"*Listen* to me! If you stay here, you'll die with the rest of us!"

"Tell me what you're talking about!" demanded Picard. "There is *always* hope, Kerajem. If I believe in anything, I believe in *that.*"

Kerajem turned away. "We developed a project. It was a defense project. We called it Plan Blue Ultimate. It's a weapons system. We performed the final tests on it shortly before you showed up."

"Shortly before—?"

"The tests were successful and we put Blue Ultimate into effect, hoping we would never have to activate it." Kerajem walked over to his desk. "We hoped against hope that it wouldn't come to this, but we have just about run out of time. The madness must stop now, and it falls to me to make sure that it does." He opened a drawer. There was a black box inside. Kerajem opened it and pressed a button and threw a switch.

"What did you do, Kerajem?" Picard asked.

"I've just made sure."

"Wait a minute," Picard said. "We came here because we detected three brief warp-field signatures—oh, *no.*" The captain went utterly pale. "You can't possibly mean what I think you mean."

"I see you finally understand," Kerajem said, shaking his head. "Forgive me, my friend, but it wasn't until this morning that I realized our Blue Ultimate technology and what you call warp drive must be one and the same thing. At least know that I wasn't lying to you about our not possessing warp technology when you asked me about it. I didn't realize we'd invented it."

Picard paled. "And you've also discovered that activating a warp field within the Cochrane radius of a main-sequence star will explode that star into a nova."

"Yes. Yes, we have. Three of our warp-field generators are orbiting the sun at a certain critical distance. I've activated one of those generators with this radio relay. The Krann will be gone—and so will we. You'd better leave now, Captain."

Picard slapped his communicator. "Transporter Room Two, this is Picard. Put me on the bridge *right now.*"

As his friend disappeared into thin air, Kerajem felt

no regret. He would have left just as quickly, given the chance.

Heads turned as Picard materialized on the bridge. "Mr. La Forge," he called, "I want our best speed to the local star."

"Aye, sir," came Geordi's somewhat puzzled voice. *"You'll get our best."*

"Ensign Ro, lay in a course. Lock it in. Maximum warp. Engage. Picard to Dr. Crusher."

"Yes, Captain?"

"When can I have my first officer back?"

It was just then that the turbolift doors slid open and out walked Riker and Troi. "Reporting for duty, Captain," Riker said as the counselor took her seat.

"Never mind, Doctor," the captain said. "Thank you. Listen, all of you. I've just talked to the First Among Equals. Some forty seconds ago, he sent a radio signal to activate a warp-field generator that is orbiting the local star well within the Cochrane radius."

"The Lethanta are blowing up their own sun?" Troi gasped. *"Why?"*

"To take the Krann with them," Picard said. "No Krann ship could hope to outrace a nova wave front. Everyone in this star system would die—except for us. We could escape."

"What would you like us to do, Captain?" Worf asked for them all.

"There is a light-speed radio wave heading for one of three primitive warp-field generators orbiting closely around the local star. We are presently outracing that radio wave. I intend to find the targeted generator and destroy it before it can be activated." There was iron in his voice now. "I intend to prevent this nova from occurring."

Data spoke up. "Of course, Captain, if we do not

locate the correct generator in time, we will ourselves be caught in the formation of the nova."

"Better find it quickly, then," said Picard. The captain seated himself in his chair and, outwardly, appeared calm. Counselor Troi, sitting next to him, knew better. In the years she had known the captain, she had never detected such agitation within him.

Chapter Nineteen

THE RADIO WAVE would take just under eight minutes to reach the warp-field generator from Nem Ma'ak Bratuna. It had been sent six minutes ago. Every sensor aboard the *Enterprise* was strained to the limit and beyond in an attempt to find the generator before the radio wave could activate it.

It was worse than finding a needle in a haystack. They were trying to find the barest speck of matter against the biggest sea of electromagnetic radiation in that part of space.

Troi was beginning to read something new in Captain Picard, something she had never before felt from him.

Despair.

"Captain," Data suddenly said, "I am picking up what I believe to be the radio wave sent by Kerajem to activate the generator."

"Are you sure, Data?" Picard asked. Troi blinked with the suddenness of his change of mood.

"Reasonably so, sir. It has every indication of

having been generated artificially, and it is heading in the proper general direction." He paused. "I have extrapolated the path the wave will take to its target. May I suggest, sir, that we concentrate our efforts to locate the generator along that path?"

"Make it so. Mr. Worf, I want photon torpedoes ready to go on my order. We will not have much time."

"Aye, sir."

"Captain!" Harkey cried. "I have a blip at three twenty-two mark seventeen! Range forty-three thousand kilometers."

"Let's see it." The image on the screen swam for a second. There was some interference in the image because of the proximity of the *Enterprise* to the local star, but—wasn't that it? *Could* that be it?

"Torpedoes ready, Captain," Worf reported. "I am having difficulty locking onto the target. We are quite close to the local star."

"Do what you can, Lieutenant. Time to generator reception of destruct code, Mr. Data?"

"Twenty seconds to zero, sir."

"Mr. Worf," Picard said tightly, "target that damned thing and *fire!*"

"No lock, Captain," Worf said. "Firing in manual mode. Torpedoes away."

Picard and everyone else watched the screen as the flight of four glowing red torpedoes coursed quickly away from the ship. The captain could almost feel Worf's concentration as a physical force as the Klingon worked quickly and efficiently behind him.

"Ten seconds to zero," said Data.

"Second volley ready, Captain," Worf reported.

"One way or the other, Mr. Worf, a second volley will not be necessary."

"Five seconds, sir," Data said.

There was a flash of blinding white light from about forty-three thousand kilometers away, and then there was another.

"Target destroyed, Captain," Worf reported.

"The count is zero, sir," said Data.

They all paused for a moment.

"Well," Troi said brightly, breaking the silence, "we're all still here."

"Indeed," said Picard. "I suppose we got the right one, after all. Good shooting, Lieutenant. Harkey, get us back to Nem Ma'ak Bratuna. Maximum warp. I want to talk to Kerajem again before he decides to do something else insane."

"Course laid in, sir."

"Engage."

It would not be long now. Kerajem wondered if he would have time to see the sky light up in amazing fashion just before the end. Probably not, he decided. Some of the scientists on Plan Blue Ultimate had gotten together to write a classified piece on what the nova would do to Nem Ma'ak Bratuna—blow off the atmosphere, boil off the seas, maybe even blow off the crust of the planet. At the core of the piece was the notion that no one would feel anything as the wave front engulfed the world.

That was good. Kerajem was tired of feeling.

With ten seconds left in his life, Kerajem suddenly heard a voice behind him. "Hello again, my friend."

He whirled. *"Picard?!?* What are *you* doing here?"

"I'm here to try to talk some sense into you. No, your sun hasn't gone nova. We stopped it."

Kerajem went pale. *"How?"*

"Never mind. Killing everyone is an act of despair. There is still hope of peace. Is that understood?"

Kerajem nodded slowly.

"Good. Now please come with me. We're returning to the *Enterprise*. Picard to Transporter Room Three. Two to beam up."

Picard was again standing on the bridge, this time with Kerajem at his side.

"Let me make myself clear," Picard told the Krann bureaucratic functionary who was on screen. "The First Among Equals and I *will* talk to Presider Hek within three minutes."

"The Presider will speak to no one at this time," the functionary said. "The Fleet is in a state of emergency."

"The Presider will speak to me," Picard said, "or the entire Krann fleet will be destroyed—not by us, but by the Lethanta. I promise you that they have the means. He had *better* talk to me."

The bureaucrat looked doubtful. "The Presider has left orders—"

The transmission was interrupted. "Never mind," came a familiar voice. The image of the functionary was replaced by that of Presider Hek. "I monitor all this claptrap, Picard, even during Fleet Congress meetings." The Krann leader was standing at the lectern in the Great Hall. "You're talking to the entire Congress this time," Hek told Picard, and there was a chorus of cheers. "What do you want now?"

"I want you to listen to me, Hek," Picard said. "I want you to listen to me very carefully. Unbeknownst to us, the Lethanta have developed a device that can explode their star. It is a doomsday weapon, and it is intended to destroy your entire Krann fleet, should you destroy the Lethanta, by exploding this star and catching you all in the wave front. Both races will perish, not just one."

There was some muttering in the background from the members of the Congress, but Hek only laughed.

"Why should I believe this nonsense?" he said derisively. "This isn't even very entertaining."

"Look at me, Hek," demanded Picard. *"Look at me.* You are the supreme leader of a race of three billion people. You have *some* skill at reading people. Tell me: *Am I lying?"*

Hek looked at Picard for a long, long moment. "All right, Picard," Hek said finally. "Either you're telling the truth, or you're the greatest liar I've ever met—and I don't think you're anywhere near that good." That drew a laugh from some of the Congress members. "A doomsday weapon, you say? The Lethanta can actually blow up a G_0-type star? From what I understand of stars, that can't be done."

"Yes, it can."

Hek waved a hand. "All right. Let's assume for the sake of argument that the Lethanta can do this. What are we supposed to do about it?"

Picard began ticking off Kerajem's demands on his fingers. "The Krann fleet must cease all hostilities against the Lethanta at once. All Krann vessels are to remain at station-keeping. The Krann and the Lethanta will immediately commence meaningful, Federation-mediated negotiations to resolve their differences."

Many members of the Fleet Congress began to boo, and Hek almost smirked. "You actually want us to have 'meaningful negotiations' with the people who destroyed our world," he said. "Picard, I'm astonished. Perhaps we'll let them live, if what you say about the doomsday weapon is true—but come to an *agreement* with them? You're hallucinating."

"Nonsense," Picard said, and he allowed his annoyance to show. "Your war against the Lethanta isn't any noble crusade, Hek. It's nothing more than an elitist ploy to spread wealth and power among the civilian and military leadership of the Krann. Most of your people have never even *heard* of the Lethanta, much less want to go to war with them."

The turbolift door slid open, and Beverly Crusher stepped onto the bridge. Picard turned and saw her. "Ah, Doctor. Have you completed your work?"

"Yes, Captain, and so has Mr. La Forge. I have the results you asked for—and the proof." She looked at the screen and held up an isolinear chip.

"What's this about, Picard?" Hek demanded.

Picard clasped his hands behind his back and began. "As you know, Presider Hek, we recently visited your ancestral homeworld and took a large number of biological samples. Necessarily, we also took some samples of the biological agent that ran rampant on your original world and killed all higher orders of life. Dr. Crusher has spent a great deal of time since then trying to figure out just what this biological entity was. Would you like to continue, Doctor?"

"I'd be pleased to, Captain. Presider Hek, I have done a thorough analysis of that biological agent, and I have the findings here. I regret to inform you that the agent is not Lethantan. It is entirely of Krann origin, and it is entirely natural."

"Eh?" Hek said, looking confused. "What's that you say?"

"The virus that destroyed most life on your world arose naturally. It happens, Presider Hek. The catastrophe that befell your world was a natural occurrence. The Lethanta did not attack you. When you bombed their world, the few survivors left that star system as quickly as they could. They never attacked your planet in retaliation for your attack on them."

"I don't believe it!" Hek exploded. "The Lethanta killed our world! *The virus was not an accident!*" The members of the Fleet Congress began shouting.

Kerajem nearly collapsed, and Beverly rushed over

to steady him. "I'm sorry," she told him. "I didn't realize this would be quite such a shock to you."

"This is beyond belief," said the First Among Equals. "Dr. Crusher, Captain, all our people have been brought up with the terrible guilt of knowing that we destroyed the world of the Krann for no reason other than spite. Now it turns out not to be true. It never was." There was a touch of wonder in his voice as he said it.

Picard addressed the Krann leader. "Presider Hek, Dr. Crusher's findings are being broadcast throughout your Fleet even as we speak. Every device you have that is capable of storing and printing out information is receiving a copy of Dr. Crusher's report. Your scientists are free to check it—in fact, knowing scientists as I do, they are certain to check it whether you approve of it or not. There is also a summary of the report that has been phrased in layman's language, and it is being distributed over your information networks to as many of your three billion as we can reach. There is also a brief but interesting account of your government's role in prosecuting this unnecessary war against the Lethanta. This report has been included as part of the mission you assigned us under our Prime Directive to preserve the interests of the members of the Krann Fleet."

"How *dare* you!" Hek blustered.

Picard was placid. "There are a number of things our people are very good at, Presider Hek, and one of them is getting information into the right hands. Our people have a saying, Hek: 'Ye shall know the truth, and the truth shall make you free.'"

Epilogue

IT HAD TAKEN TWO WEEKS to have a Federation negotiating team formally assigned and dispatched to the Lethanta-Krann negotiations, and another week to get the team properly briefed, but it was finally done. The professional diplomats were on the job, and the *Enterprise* was free to move on.

Captain Picard was in Ten-Forward, looking out the window at Nem Ma'ak Bratuna. Riker was standing next to him. "They'll be fine, I think," Picard said. "With Hek out of office, slightly more moderate people have come into power in the Fleet Congress. The emphasis here is on 'slightly,' of course."

"Yes, sir," Riker agreed. "They'll have a lot to talk about. Many of the Krann, especially the younger people, want to settle in this star system."

"And many do not," Picard pointed out. "That puts a large part of a vast fleet on our doorstep, and the Lethanta are on the edge of developing warp drive for use in starships instead of doomsday weaponry. What if they should get together?"

"Let's hope they stay friendly if they do."

"Indeed. You know, there's one thing—"

"What's that, sir?"

"Ro Laren mentioned it to me during her convalescence, and I must confess I hadn't realized it myself. She said she'd seen parked ground vehicles all over the capital city while she and Data were there. It bothered her for some reason, but it didn't hit her until later what that reason was. There was something we had *not* seen parked, not anywhere. Something important."

"And what was that, Captain?"

"The asteroids, Will—the asteroids the Lethantans arrived in. They're not in orbit anywhere in this system, and if they'd impacted on the planet following orbital decay, we'd have seen traces of those impacts; those rocks were *big*. So where did they go?"

Riker thought about it for a moment. "I have an idea about that, sir."

"So do I, but it staggers me to think about it."

"Have you asked Kerajem about it?"

"No," Picard said. "I won't do that, Will. I won't make him tell me his people's most important secret."

"Yes," Riker said. "If all else fails—"

"Exactly," Picard agreed, looking out at all those millions of stars. "I wonder if we'd have the courage to do the same?"

The cell was cold and uncomfortable, but Hek Portside Hull Patcher had grown used to discomfort since his unseemly departure from office. He had started out cold, broke and hopeless; if he finished up that way, well, it was all right by him. There was a bunk and a toilet and some insects, and that was it.

As a matter of fact, Hek was bored. They had given him nothing to read or write with for the nearly three weeks he'd been held here, and there had been no one to talk to or yell at. His was the only occupied cell in the entire block. If he was going to be executed, he wished they'd get on with it. They'd thrown him out of office for starting the war for no reason, and then they sentenced him to death *in absentia* for all sorts of crimes, not the least of which involved making a lot of his peers fearful of him while he was Presider.

Hek wondered if they'd make him take a walk into Hek's Closet. That would be appropriate. Whatever they did to him, it would probably be kinder and quicker than what had happened to Graff, the poor wretch.

There was suddenly a *clang!* from somewhere down the row, and then there came the hollow sound of footsteps. Someone was coming. Although he had no timepiece, Hek knew it was too early for the next meal. Someone was actually coming to see him—or space him.

It was Drappa Fuel Filter Examiner, Leader of the North Nation and the new Presider. "Hello, Hek," he said in that dull, grating voice of his.

"Greetings, Drappa. Congratulations, I think."

"You're in no position to make jokes." Drappa thumbed open the door of the cell and entered. "Mind if I sit down?" he asked, throwing himself onto Hek's bunk. "I have a proposition for you."

"I'm listening."

"The Fleet Congress has tentatively decided that our people will settle on the fourth planet of this system and that we'll dismantle the Fleet. We're going to make that proposal at the next round of the Federation talks, and we're sure it will be accepted. It'll certainly make the Federation happy."

271

Hek was shocked. "Why? It flies in the face of all that we are!"

"Because the population wants it that way," Drappa told him. "Many of our people believe the days of the Fleet are over because we'll soon get warp drive for ourselves, now that we've been given the hint that it exists. Faster-than-light travel will make our present ships obsolete, certainly, but that hardly matters."

"It doesn't?"

"Not to most of our people. We're being granted a pristine world of our own, a new Ma'ak Krannag, and they want to live there. Only a few of our people want to remain spaceside and live the way we've been living all these centuries, always free, but those few represent enough people to fill perhaps fifty of our larger ships. And there's something else, too."

"What is it?"

"These peace talks may not succeed, Hek. Everything seems fine now, but war could still break out between us and the Lethanta. Millennia of hatred and suspicion do not evaporate away into vacuum just because a doctor sees something odd through her microscope. And there's another thing, too. Even if the talks *are* successful, war could still come a century or two from now. It happened just that way once, long ago, back in our native star system. It could happen here as well."

"I can certainly see that. And if it does—?"

"If it does," Drappa said, "I don't want *any* of the Lethanta to escape our vengeance, to mock us by their continued existence, should *we* become extinct. Hek, I've learned something. Something vital. When our Fleet was first detected coming in, the Lethanta went back into space, back to where they'd left their asteroid ships thousands of years before, and they recovered and refurbished them. They packed the asteroid ships full of volunteers and supplies, and they sent them on their way again. That's why they called this star The Last Stand, Hek. This is where they were going to sacrifice themselves and destroy us in order to protect the small group of their own people they'd sent farther on."

"Which way did they go?"

"I don't know," said Drappa. "The asteroids are shielded against our sensor probes—and the Federation's, too, for that matter. The asteroids could have gone off in any direction and at any acceleration. For security reasons, their destination wasn't to be selected until they were out of this star system. The asteroid ships could have remained together or split into several flights headed in different directions, and they have been on their way for decades. They'll never be found except by the sheerest accident while in flight. Now, Hek. How would you like to be the commander of a Seventh Fleet, a new Fleet, dedicated to finding and dealing with these escaped Lethanta when they finally *do* arrive at their destination?"

"A Seventh Fleet?"

"Yes. Your mission would be the same as that of our beloved forefathers of the First Fleet—find the Lethanta. The job won't be completed within your lifetime, no—but it would be a job that would last for the rest of your life. If war comes and there are to be survivors, we want them to be Krann and not Lethanta."

"And you want *me* for this duty?" Hek asked. "Why?"

"I can think of no one better suited for this life. I need your single-mindedness and your fanaticism." He smiled, but it was a dangerous smile. "Executing you would be a waste of material."

Hek thought for a moment. "Won't this Seventh Fleet be detected on the way out?"

"We've altered the cloaking systems aboard the selected ships," Drappa said. "They are again undetectable. The Federation knows that the ship census is inexact. Fifty ships among a hundred sixty thousand will never be missed. You'd be free to go out there, go anywhere, all on your own. You and your descendants will go to other star systems and build new ships as you need them." He paused. "Things would be the way they were meant to be."

"Yes," Hek said softly. "Things would be the way they were meant to be." His aquamarine eyes shone in the gloom of the cell.

"You can think about this for a while, if you want," Drappa said, rising from the bunk.

"I don't need to think about it at all," Hek replied.